Praise for *Som*

"*Some Things Aren't Meant to Be* is a lovely, bittersweet romance, grounded in sharply accurate depictions of a hardscrabble Vermont dairy farm and a rural Catholic diocese. It is well-written, believable, and compelling."

—Tom Slayton, editor-in-chief of Vermont Life (1986-2007) and author of *Searching for Thoreau: On the Trails and Shores of Wild New England* and other books

"Emotional honesty and a keen understanding of people and relationships are combined in this moving and deeply satisfying new novel by Peter Cobb. Beautifully written, *Some Things Aren't Meant to Be* tells the story of John Gauthier…from his early days in 1929 working on a Vermont dairy farm and in love with the owner's wife to his later life as a Catholic priest in the early 1960s. With themes of buried love and striving to do the right thing, the story skillfully spirals outward from the farm and back again."

—Catherine Drake, author of *The Treehouse on Dog River Road*

"An impressive blend of a coming-of-age tale and a later-life examination of what one has become. Cobb surprises with his knowledge of farm life, his store of childish pranks played on priests and teachers, and his ability to mold his main character. The writing is polished, engaging, and entertaining in the best sense of fiction—appealing characters and interesting stories. It's a fine effort."

—Allen Gilbert, journalist, teacher, ACLU-VT executive director, and author of *Equal is Equal, Fair is Fair: Vermont's Quest for Equity in Education Funding, Same-Sex Marriage, and Health Care*

SOME THINGS AREN'T MEANT TO BE

SOME THINGS AREN'T MEANT TO BE

A Novel

J. Peter Cobb

Montpelier, VT

Some Things Aren't Meant to Be: A Novel ©2023 J. Peter Cobb

This is a work of fiction. Unless otherwise indicated, all the names, characters, businesses, places, events and incidents in this book are either the product of the author's imagination or used in a fictitious manner.

Release Date: August 27, 2024

All Rights Reserved.

Printed in the USA.

Published by Rootstock Publishing
an imprint of Ziggy Media LLC
info@rootstockpublishing.com
www.rootstockpublishing.com

Softcover ISBN: 978-1-57869-175-3
eBook ISBN: 978-1-57869-176-0
Library of Congress Control Number: 2024909937

Cover and book design by Eddie Vincent, ENC Graphic Services. Author photo courtesy of the author.

For permissions or to schedule a reading, contact the author at jpetercobb@gmail.com.

To my late sister Anne Marie Balk, one of my first readers, who died too young, and to my wife Cindy, whose support means everything to me.

Chapter 1

April 1962

Sacred Heart Parish, Providence, Vermont

Father Amand Symanski stands in the main hallway pinning a message onto the bulletin board next to the principal's office. The message says, ALTAR BOYS' PRACTICE TODAY - 3:30. Yesterday, he told the boys there would not be practice but he has changed his mind. He will announce the same message on the school's PA system later this morning.

Father Symanski wears a black shirt with a white clerical collar, neatly-pressed black pants with a black belt, and black shoes that are so shiny the leather looks plastic. The shoes cost more than most parishioners at Sacred Heart Church earn in a week. He checks his watch. The late bell rang five minutes ago. "Where is that boy?" he mumbles to himself.

The front door to the school bangs open and Patrick Colman bolts through. He trots by Father Symanski without seeing him. His eyes are still getting used to the darker inside of the building compared to the bright sunshine outside. He walks halfway to his locker, about twenty yards from the main door, and stops to scuff his right sneaker against the tile floor. The hard scuff produces a loud squeak. He repeats the squeak with every step from there to his locker.

Father Symanski follows Patrick. When he catches up to him, he grabs Patrick's right shoulder. Patrick is startled and drops his books to the floor with an echoing clatter.

"Mr. Colman, you're late," Father Symanski says.

"Yes, Father," Patrick says, as he bends down to gather his books.

"Don't be late again."

"I won't."

"Patrick?"

"Yes, Father."

"Do you love Jesus?"

"Yes, Father."

"Mr. Colman, don't lie to me. Do you love Jesus?"

"Yes, Father, I've already told you I love Jesus."

"Where were you yesterday?"

"Um . . ."

"You missed Latin. Boys who love Jesus don't skip Latin practice. Where were you?"

"I was . . ."

"I know where you were, Mr. Colman. You were playing baseball with the boys from Providence Junior High."

"No, I wasn't, Father." He looks at the immaculate floor and shuffles his feet.

"Don't lie to me, Mr. Colman. I saw you. You still have mud on your sneakers." Father Symanski's eyes travel down to and back up from Patrick's feet.

"I'm not lying, Father." His voice cracks.

"Why did you miss Latin yesterday? All the other altar boys were there, all of them. Why weren't you there?" His voice booms down to the far end of the hallway.

"Um . . . ." Patrick mumbles.

Father Symanski can barely hear him. "Because you were playing baseball, that's why, Mr. Colman. Do you love baseball more than Jesus?"

"No, Father."

Two boys walking toward them stop to listen. Father Symanski waves them away. "Not your business, boys. Go back to class."

"Father Symanski," Monsignor John Gauthier yells from down the hall. He walks briskly toward Father Symanski and Patrick. His robe sways as he walks. "Patrick, I understand you missed Latin practice yesterday."

Patrick's eyes fill with tears.

"It was the first warm day of spring. I would have missed it too. It's snowing now, snowing hard. You picked the perfect day," Monsignor Gauthier says.

Father Symanski exhales deeply. "The Mass is sacred. The boys need to know their responses. They must pronounce the Latin words correctly. All of them should attend; no exceptions for baseball or for a warm spring day," he says.

"Cut the boy some slack. He's thirteen, I barely knew who Jesus was when I was thirteen." Monsignor Gauthier coughs to clear his throat. "Patrick, do you love Jesus?"

"Yes, Father."

"Good for you. I do too. Come with me, boy." He places his right hand on Patrick's left shoulder. "Father Symanski, tell Sister Ryan that Patrick is with me—he'll be late for class."

"How late?"

"I don't know, just say *late*."

Father Symanski leans toward Patrick. "Make sure you go to confession Saturday. Lying is a sin." He lightly pokes Patrick's shoulder, turns his back to Monsignor Gauthier, grimaces and shakes his head.

Monsignor gently pushes Patrick toward the main entrance to the school. "Come. I've got a job for you, Mr. Colman. One I've been meaning to do for months." He walks Patrick to the rectory and up to his second-floor apartment, which smells like pipe tobacco. A black-and-white photo of the Taj Mahal in a walnut frame is mounted on the wall to the left of the door.

"Is that in India?" Patrick asks.

"Yes, it is. I took that picture when I was twenty-two years old, just out of college, 1924—thirty-eight years ago this summer. Seems like it was just yesterday. Best two years of my life. I thought I was going to be the next Theodore Dreiser. I went to India to create an adventure and then write a novel. I found my story and wrote my novel, but I learned I couldn't write worth beans. I've written three novels and at least a hundred short stories, all of them pretty terrible. I've tried hard, Mr. Colman, but I failed. Ever heard of Theodore Dreiser?"

Patrick shakes his head.

"You're too young. When you're older, promise me you'll read *Sister Carrie*."

Patrick mumbles, "Yes, sir."

Monsignor Gauthier guides Patrick through the living room to the den. Bookshelves are mounted along each side wall from one end of the room to the other, from the floor to the ceiling. Two maple bookcases, each five foot tall, are flush against the back wall, jammed with record albums. Half a dozen albums are scattered on top of a large, maple desk. A pipe rack with four pipes, a green desk lamp, a notepad, a dictionary, a pocket watch, a set of keys, and a thesaurus are also on the desktop.

"I want you to make sure all the albums are in alphabetical order. You do know the alphabet?" Monsignor smiles.

"Yes, Father." Patrick's words tremble.

"Patrick, relax, that was a joke. You're in seventh grade. If you don't know the alphabet by now, we're doing something terribly wrong here at good old Sacred Heart School." He points to the record albums. "Start with the *B*s—I don't have any *A*s—on the left bookcase, top shelf, left side, and work your way down the bookcase. Sort by composer, not by the title of the album. Pull out any album that's out of order and stack it on the desk. Can you do that?"

"Composer?" Patrick asks.

"Bach, Beethoven, Mozart. Have you heard of them?"

Patrick nods.

"Good. Most of the albums will say music by whomever. If you're not sure, leave it where it is."

"Yes, Father."

"Patrick, this is an easy task and it gets you out of class. What could be better?"

Patrick smiles. "What if there's more than one composer on the album?"

"That always screws me up." He thinks for a second. "If there is more than one, leave it where it is."

"Yes, sir."

"It should take you about two hours, maybe less. I'm going downtown, so I'll leave you here on your own." He grabs a piece of paper from the notepad on the desk and writes a note. "When you get back to class, give this to Sister Ryan." He folds the paper and hands the note to Patrick. "If you get hungry, there's food in the refrigerator and cookies in the breadbox. Just don't drink the beer." He chuckles.

Patrick starts where he was told, at the top shelf, left side. *Bach, Beethoven, I've heard of them. Irving Berlin, no clue. Georges Bizet, nope. Brahms, "Lullaby and Goodnight," I know that song. Chopin, I know him, I saw the movie. He dies.* He pulls the Chopin record from the sleeve. It slips from his hand, bounces off the desk, hits the floor, and cracks. "Fuck. Oh fuck, oh fuck. Oh no, no, no, no, no," he says.

He picks the record off the floor. The crack is three inches long. He searches the desk. He finds a bottle of Elmer's glue and spreads the glue on the crack, presses the vinyl together, wipes away the excess glue with his finger, shoves the record into the paper sleeve, the sleeve into the cardboard cover, and places the record on the last shelf after Wagner.

"How are you doing, Patrick?" Monsignor Gauthier says, startling Patrick.

"Fine, Father." He can barely speak. His pulse is so strong he is sure Gauthier can see the veins on his neck throb.

"Good. Forgot my car keys, always forgetting my keys." He walks to the desk and spots the open drawer and the bottle of glue. "Did you glue something, Patrick?"

"No, Father."

"I must have left it out. My memory is slipping. Next thing you know, I'll be in a home for forgetful old priests." He smiles and tosses the glue bottle into the drawer and closes it with his right knee. "What time is it?"

"I don't know, Father. There's a watch right there." He points to the pocket watch on the desk.

"That old thing? Hasn't worked in years."

"Why do you keep it?"

"Just do." He grabs the car keys and pocket watch from the desktop, steps to the bookshelf, searches for a few seconds, and pulls a paperback book from the third shelf. "I want you to read this book, *A Separate Peace*. Wonderful book. High school level, but you can handle it."

"I don't know, Father, I got a C in English. Maybe it would be a better book for somebody else."

"You can do it, I'm sure. I've seen your essays, you're the best writer in this school, the best since I've been here. No one else is even a close second."

Monsignor Gauthier reads the first paragraph. "*I went back to Devon School not long ago, and found it looking oddly newer than when I was a student there fifteen years before. It seemed more sedate than I remembered it, more perpendicular and straight-laced, with narrower windows and shinier woodwork, as though a coat of varnish had been put over everything for better preservation."*

He closes the book and hands it to Patrick. "Make sure you remember this scene. Can you do that?"

"Yes, Father."

"I'm going to test you, so pay attention to what you read."

"Yes, sir."

"Three weeks, I'll test you in three weeks." He jingles his car keys as he walks toward the door. "Three weeks, Mr. Colman."

"Yes, sir."

Gauthier exits the building. Patrick's heart is still beating hard. He considers removing the Chopin record and taking it with him, but he leaves it on the shelf.

Chapter 2

August 1928
Doty Farm, East Providence, Vermont

"Gauthier, what the hell are you doing?" dairy farmer Charles Doty says. He hacks a wad of mucus from the back of his throat and spits it to the ground. He wears denim pants, brown leather work boots, and a red-and-black flannel shirt and is holding a lighted kerosene lantern in his left hand. He is tall, six-foot-four. His shoulders are broad and his arms are strong. His blond hair is a rumpled mess. A golden retriever leans against his legs, growling at his farmhand, John Gauthier. Charles swats the dog's nose. "Butch, stop it."

John is standing at the hind end of a Holstein cow, trying to push it to the middle of the barn. His right side, from his head to his shoes, is covered with cow manure. He digs manure out of his ear. "I'm trying to get this cow out of her stall so I can milk her. She won't budge," he says.

Charles shakes his head and grins. "First off, Gauthier, it ain't a stall, it's a stanchion. Stalls are for horses. And second, we milk the cows in the stanchions, not in the middle of the goddamn barn. If we did that, it would take all day. We'd never get nothing done."

"There's not enough room in here," John says. He pounds the side walls to prove what he just said.

"There's plenty of room. Plus, that's Cow Fifty, she gets milked last." He grabs a towel hanging from a nail on the right wall and tosses it to John. "Clean yourself up."

John wipes his hair, shoulder, side, and pant leg. "That's not Cow Fifty. You've got only thirty-one cows, I counted."

"I didn't say she were the fiftieth cow, I said she were Cow Fifty. She lives in stanchion fifty."

"How do you know which stanchion is which? They're not marked."

"Gauthier, use your head. There are fifty stanchions in the barn, twenty-five along the left wall and twenty-five on the right wall. Stanchion one is over there." He points to the left wall. He walks through the barn and hangs the lantern on a wire hook dangling from the ceiling. "We milk 'em in two shifts. We milk the first sixteen cows, Cow One through Cow Thirty-four, then we take a break and stretch our arms and legs and backs, and then we milk the next eight cows."

"That's only twenty-four. What about the other seven cows?"

"We got seven dry cows, Gauthier, I told you that yesterday. Didn't you hear a good goddamn thing I said?"

"How do you know which cow is which? They all look alike to me?"

"They're all different. You'll figure that out soon enough. Don't matter if you do or don't, cause cows are creatures of habit, they'll go in the same stanchion every time, whether you guide them there or not. Most cows are pretty docile, sweet creatures who can be encouraged to go where they're used ta goin'. *Encouraged*, Gauthier, not forced. Cow Fifty, she's different, she's as stubborn as a mule."

He pulls a cigarette from the top of his left ear, lights it, and blows the smoke toward John. He spits into the dirt and rubs the spit with the toe of his left boot, walks to the sink at the back wall, fills a five-gallon wooden bucket with soapy water and iodine and another bucket with water, wets two rags, and grabs two empty milk buckets from under the sink. He hands John a milk bucket, the damp cloths, and the two cleaning buckets. "You start here with Cow Thirty-two and I'll start with Cow One. The stools are over there." He points to the back wall, where several stools are hanging from long nails.

John tosses the damp cloths onto his right shoulder, retrieves a stool, walks to stanchion thirty-two, places the stool next to the cow, sets the milk bucket under the udder, and grabs the front two teats.

"Gauthier, wash your goddamn hands and cover them with Vaseline," Charles says.

"Sorry, forgot."

John washes and lubricates his hands. He returns to the cow, sits on the stool, and tugs on the teats.

"You didn't hear a damn thing I said yesterday, did ya? Use the damp cloth with the soap and iodine and wipe the mud and manure off the udder before ya start milkin'. We don't want no cow shit in our milk. Then wipe with the wet cloth with no soap. It ain't that hard. Use the soapy cloth to get the shit off and the wet cloth to get the soap off. When your milk bucket's full, dump the milk into one of them milk cans." He points to the cans at the far end of the barn. "And make sure you use a goddamn filter. Once the milk can is filled, secure the top and place it in the concrete tub in the milk room. There's cold spring water running through the tub. Gotta keep the milk cold.

"After we finish milkin', we guide the cows to the field, feed the horses, and eat breakfast. After breakfast, I'll hitch the horses and we'll load the cans. I'll take the milk to the creamery in Providence, seven miles from here. Takes about two hours and a half to get there. You'll clean the barn and put down new wood shavings and feed the calves and the heifers. After that, if you're smart, you'll take a nap, an hour or so, so you can be ready for the next round of chores. If you don't take a nap, Gauthier, you ain't gonna make it long, that's for sure."

John cleans the udder, grabs a teat with his right hand, and tugs on it. Charles shakes his head, grabs John's shoulders, easily lifts him off the stool, and places him next to the cow. Charles is a much bigger man than John—taller, wider, and stronger. John is five eight, thin but not skinny, one hundred sixty solid pounds. He has ink-black hair, thick eyebrows, large brown eyes, and long eyelashes. He could pass for a teenager.

"Stop. Don't do anything till I get back," Charles says. He walks to the sink and washes and lubricates his hands. "You went to college, right?"

"Yup—got a BA in American literature. Graduated third in my class."

"Sure as hell didn't get no degree in common sense."

"Nope. I did not."

Charles sits on the stool and pulls the bucket out from under the cow.

"Here's what you do. Can you remember this?"

"Yes, sir." John nods and salutes him as if Charles were his drill sergeant.

"Don't call me sir, I'm just two years older than you. I'm Charles, not Mr. Doty."

"Yes, sir, Mr. Charles, sir." he says and grins.

"You gotta massage the udder when you clean it. That relaxes the muscles. You wiped it like you was wipin' snot off your nose. Then grab the teat like this." He places his right thumb and forefinger at the base of one of the teats. "Curl your fingers around the teat and squeeze it downward against the palm of your hand." He squeezes the teat twice. A splat of milk squirts to the ground with each squeeze. "Always squirt the first few ounces to the ground to make sure there ain't no dirt or shit still on the teat." He replaces the bucket under the udder and squirts several ounces of milk into the bucket. "Got it?"

"Got it." John nods.

"Start with the front teats and alternate from teat to teat. Squeeze until each teat is empty. The milk should stream into the bucket. Use both your hands, otherwise your fingers and wrist will get too sore."

"I've got it."

"You got it all right, and Calvin Coolidge is gonna start babbling like a teenage girl. Gabby Cal." He scratches his nose. "One more thing, Gauthier, you're likely ta get swatted in the face with the cow's tail, a wet, urine-, and shit-soaked tail. Just be ready, happens every day."

"Can't wait."

The two men milk for an hour. John stands up, rubs his hands together, and stretches his back. Charles stands up from his stool, stretches his back, and walks toward John.

"Gauthier, you've only milked three cows. Yesterday, the wife milked twice as fast and she's seven months pregnant. At this rate, we'll be here milkin' till it's time for the second milkin' tonight."

"A second milking?"

"I told you that yesterday. You didn't listen much, did ya? Two milkin's a day, five thirty in the mornin' and five thirty at night, seven days a week, three hundred sixty-five days a year, three hundred sixty-six on leap year. These ain't no bankers' hours."

The men finish milking at ten. Charles looks at his watch. "Not too bad.

Coulda been a hell of a lot worse." He tosses the wiping cloths into a bucket next to the sink, washes his hands, and kicks cow manure off his boots. "Let's go get sumthin' to eat, I'm starved."

John starts to walk out of the barn. "Gauthier, never, never, never leave lanterns on in the barn, you could burn the whole goddamn place down. Thirty-one burnt cows would really stink." When Charles says "cows" the word sounds like "kayows." He extinguishes the flames from all three lanterns and points toward the house. "Time to eat."

The Doty farmhouse is two separate buildings connected by a common wall. The front section, built in 1853, is a one-story brick house with six rooms. All the windows rattle in the wind and the roof leaks during a heavy rain. The back, a two-story wood building, has seven rooms, including a kitchen no one has used since Charles's mother died twenty years ago and a bathroom. It is very cold when the temperature dips below zero. John's bedroom is in the back section.

The house smells like bacon, coffee, and fried onions, which Charles's wife, Audrey, has cooked, along with eggs, oatmeal, hash brown potatoes, and toast. Sliced apples and pears round out the spread. She grabs three plates from the cupboard next to the sink and waddles to the kitchen table, her left hand pushing against her back. She is nearly as wide as she is tall. "You're a total mess, looks like somebody dipped you in manure," she says to John. She laughs so hard she has to sit down. "I hope I don't pee my pants." She smiles and composes herself. "How's day one going?" She chuckles as she speaks.

"I don't know, I'm still half asleep. Charles got me up at four thirty. That's crazy. I've never gotten up that early in my entire life." He tries to make a fist with both hands, but he can't close his fingers on either hand. "I can barely move my fingers." The two men wash their hands at the kitchen sink.

Charles grabs a washcloth from under the sink and wipes cow manure off the back of John's shirt. "You missed a spot." He bends down and wipes John's pants. "It gets easier. Either that or you'll quit."

"I'm not a quitter," John says.

"That's what the last guy said. Quit after three days. Didn't show up for the mornin' milkin'. I went to his room to get him, and he was gone. Slipped out sometime in the middle of the night. Didn't even hear him leave. Never came back, not even for his pay. Are you gonna slip out in the middle of the night, Gauthier?"

"Don't plan to."

"Good."

Charles and John sit at the kitchen table. "John, just so you know, nobody covered with manure sits at this kitchen table to eat," Audrey says.

"Sorry," he says, as he stands and starts toward his room.

"He's fine, I wiped him clean," Charles says.

"You did not." She points to the door to the back building. "Go to your room and change." She sounds like a teacher scolding a naughty child.

"Yes, Mom," Charles says and laughs.

. . .

Charles and Audrey eat so fast, it surprises John. "Eat up," Audrey says to John.

"Want to hear sumthin' funny?" Charles says to Audrey. "Gauthier, how much you weigh?"

"I don't know, one hundred thirty pounds, maybe one forty, not sure."

"And you got a college degree, right?"

John nods.

Charles chortles as if he were telling a funny joke and he can't wait to get to the punchline. "So this one-hundred-forty-pound, skinny college man, flatlander, city boy, tries to push a thirteen-hundred-pound cow to the middle of the barn. Can you believe that?"

"Cow Fifty?" Audrey says.

"Yup, Cow Fifty." He smiles and shakes his head. "So, Gauthier, what made you think you could push a thirteen-hundred-pound cow across the barn?" Both he and Audrey smile.

"I don't know, seemed like the right thing to do at the time."

Audrey stands up and grabs her belly. She is John's age, possibly a year or two younger. She has shoulder-length red hair, piercing blue eyes, a face full of freckles, a dimple on her right cheek, and a warm smile. "She's kicking really hard this morning. I don't think I'm gonna make it nine months." The baby kicks her. She grabs John's right hand and places it on her bulging stomach. "Can you feel that?"

"Yes, I can. I've never felt anything like that before. How do you know it's a girl?"

"I was sick early in the pregnancy. That means she's a girl."

"I don't think that's true," John says.

"It's true all right," Charles says. He gathers the dishes and places them in the sink. He wipes his face dry with his shirtsleeve. "Gauthier, why the hell are you here?"

"I'm eating breakfast."

"Not here in the kitchen, dumbass, here in Vermont?"

"I answered your ad. I'm here to work for you, to work on your farm."

"I know that, but why are you *here*, in East Providence, in the middle of frickin' nowhere? You got a college degree. You're gonna work fifty hours a week for what, twenty-five bucks? I'm paying you next to nothin'. You could do a hell of a lot better. You're not hidin' out from the law are ya, Gauthier?"

"Nope, I'm hiding from my father, not the law."

"Why you hidin' from him?"

"He wants me to join his business. He runs a construction company in Connecticut, and he builds skyscrapers in New York City and Boston. He says I've got to stop wasting my life and join his company."

"Gauthier, use your head for something besides a hat rack. He's right. Why work here, fifty hours a week, when you could be making ten times what you're making for half the work?"

"My father works plenty hard. He's never home."

"Maybe so, but I bet at the end of the day he can open and shut his hands without pain. This ain't no life for you Gauthier. You can do better."

"Maybe I don't want to do better."

"Suit yourself."

Audrey lumbers to the sink, swatting flies as she walks. She fills a glass with water and hands it to John. "If you're going to work here and last more than three days, you need to drink lots of water."

He takes the glass from her and empties it in three loud gulps.

"Time to get the girls to the field," Charles says. He points to the front door.

John rises from his seat and rubs his sore hands against his thighs.

"It'll get easier, it really will," Audrey says.

"I hope so. I've worked only five hours and I can hardly move. I don't know what's more sore, my hands or my back."

"Farming ain't for sissies, that's for sure," Charles says. He gently tugs on

John's right arm and then exits the house.

"Thanks for making me laugh. Haven't laughed that hard in years." Audrey gives him a broad smile. "Used to the smell of cow manure yet?"

"Not yet."

"You'll get used to it, I did."

"Maybe, but I don't think I'll ever get used to the flies."

She swats a fly away from her face. "What flies?"

They both laugh.

"Don't worry, they'll be gone by November."

"Looking forward to it. Hard to sleep with the constant buzzing."

"You'll get used to that too."

"I hope so."

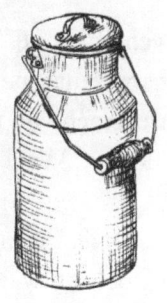

Chapter 3

October 1928
Doty Farm, East Providence, Vermont

Charles Doty is swatting a heifer's nose with a twig and leading it toward the grazing field. Snow is spitting in his face. "Gauthier, you been here eight weeks, what do ya think?"

"Actually, I've been here ten weeks."

They guide the cows to the field across the road from the barn. By the time the last cow is near the field gate, the falling snow is so heavy it's hard for them to see. Snowflakes sting their eyes. Cow Fifty doesn't want to go into the pasture. She turns and walks back toward the barn. Charles lightly swats her face with a stick. The cow stops. "Move, you fat blob," he says. He taps the cow and guides her head toward the field. The cow looks at him but refuses to move. He swats her a second time. The cow turns and joins the herd. Charles shuts and latches the gate. "So, Gauthier, whatcha think?"

"I'm getting used to it, but it sure is hard work, especially the hours. My hands are always sore. Sitting on that milking stool is a real backbreaker."

"My back's been sore since I were twelve. And the hours are a bitch. Farmin's a life, Gauthier, not a job." Cow Fifty butts the gate with her head.

Charles swats her. "Stop it. If that cow were a person, I'd fire her fat, sorry ass."

"I'd shoot her," John jokes. Both men smile.

"Ever hunted?" Charles says.

"Never fired a gun. Never even held one."

"I figured as much. We'll change that, next month's deer season. I'll get you a gun and a hunting license, teach you to shoot. You can kill some tin cans behind the garage. You'll love it. We'll get you an eight-point buck. I know where he lives."

"I'm not so sure. Sounds gruesome." John pulls his hat over his ears and blows hot air onto his hands. "Does it always snow in October?"

"Some years yes, some no. Probably the last day we'll get the cows in the field till spring." Charles wipes his nose with his sleeve. "We gotta get you to town today and get you a real winter jacket, better boots, and hat and gloves. Vermont gets pretty damn cold in January and February—some days twenty-five below frickin' zero. When I bring the milk to the dairy, you should come with me."

"I've already got a winter coat, gloves, and a hat, as you can see." He points to his jacket.

"No, you don't. What you got on might cut it in Connecticut, but not here. And those boots of yours, whatever you paid for them were too much. You'll slip on the ice and crack yer tailbone. We'll go to Providence today after we shovel the manure."

"I don't have enough money."

"Give me a break. You're rich, a regular John D. Gauthier."

"My parents are rich."

"Relax, I'll pay."

"I can't do that."

"Okay, Mr. Stubborn, I'll take it out of your pay. Either way, you need warmer clothes."

"Ever thought of getting a truck?" John says.

"On these roads? Are you kidding me? The wagon works just fine. Wait till spring, the mud will be up to your ass. A horse can walk through mud, a truck gets stuck."

"Charles, I need you," Audrey yells from the porch. She waves her arms as if sending a message by semaphore. "My water broke. She's gonna come quick."

The wind is too strong for either man to hear her clearly. "What she say?" Charles says.

"Something about water," John says.

"Jesus H. fucking Christ, I hope the goddamn pipes ain't froze again, it ain't that cold." He spits into the dirt and slaps his right thigh with his work gloves. The men walk to the house.

"I'm in labor, Charles. Get the midwife."

"You can't be. You ain't due till the end of November, four weeks from now."

"I don't think I've got four more hours. You need to get the midwife."

"What about the hospital?" John says.

"I'm not going to the hospital," Audrey says.

"Gauthier, I'd send you, but you'd get lost." He kisses and hugs Audrey, walks to the barn, and readies the horse and carriage. "I'll be back in about five hours, maybe a bit longer with the snow."

Audrey grabs John's arm. "Help me to the kitchen." She leans all her weight on his shoulder. He almost tumbles to the ground. She sits at the kitchen table and drinks a glass of water. She grimaces and rubs her stomach. Her forehead, hair, and arms are covered with sweat.

"What if you have the baby before the midwife gets here, what do I do? I'm not ready for this," John says. His voice stammers.

"John, stay calm. I'm the one having the baby, not you. Time my contractions, can you do that?"

"I don't have a watch."

"There's a clock on the wall."

She stumbles across the kitchen, waddles to the bedroom, and lies on the bed. John walks with her. He holds her shoulders to make sure she doesn't fall to the floor. She gets a hard, deep contraction. "Damn, that hurts. Feels like somebody dropped an anvil on my spine." She grabs John's left arm and bites it. Her teeth don't break his skin but the bite leaves marks on his arm.

"Why'd you do that?" John says.

"I don't know why, I just did." She wipes her forehead with her sleeve. "Take off my pants and underwear."

"I can't do that." His voice cracks.

"Take off my damn pants and underwear. This isn't going to last long."

He looks away from her as he removes her shoes, socks, pants, and underwear. He tosses the clothes toward the dresser across the room and clasps his hands together to keep his arms from shaking.

"Now go to the bathroom, wash your hands, get some clean towels. Can you do that?"

"Yes," he says but he doesn't move.

"John!" She snaps her fingers. "Go."

He sprints to the bathroom, washes his hands, and grabs a dozen towels from the closet.

"There's a pair of scissors in the second drawer and some kite string. Bring them here."

When he reaches to open the drawer, the towels in his arms fall to the floor. "Dammit all to hell," he says.

"You've been here since August. I've never heard you swear before."

"First time for everything." He grabs the towels, scissors, and string and returns to the bedroom. His heart is beating so hard he wonders if Audrey can hear it throb.

"This is it, John, I'm having my baby." She grimaces and pushes hard. "Do you see the head?"

"No." He is looking at the back wall.

"When you see the head, you'll need to grab it and support it. Can you do that?"

"No."

"Yes, you can. You can and you will. When you grab the baby's head, don't pull. Once the shoulders are out, lift her toward my stomach. You can do it."

"No, I can't."

"You can and you will." She grabs his arm and yanks him to her as she speaks.

The next contraction is even more painful. She bites John's arm again, harder than before. His arm bleeds. He wipes the blood with a towel.

She gets another contraction fifteen minutes later.

"When she comes, she'll be slippery, so be careful. How long since the last contraction?"

"I don't know."

"You're keeping track, remember."

"I forgot."

The contractions repeat about every fifteen minutes for several hours.

Both Audrey and John lose track of the time. "Get me ice," Audrey says. She crunches the ice and swallows the chips. "Oh fuck," she says with the next contraction. "When is this going to end?"

"Three minutes since the last one," John says.

"Good, we're close, real close."

John checks the time on the clock on the clothes dresser. It is three twenty-six. Six hours since Charles left. *I can't do this,* he thinks.

"I'm going to die," Audrey says with the next contraction. The baby's head appears.

"I see the baby's head. What do I do?"

She grabs his right arm and pushes it toward her crotch. "Grab her." John grabs the baby's head. Its shoulders appear. He supports its back with his left hand and guides the baby to Audrey's stomach. Audrey sighs.

"It's a boy."

"No, it can't be."

"It is."

"Clean his mouth."

John wipes the boy's mouth clean with his finger. The baby cries hard. The cry startles John. Audrey grabs his right hand and pushes it toward the baby's face. "Wipe his face clean with a cloth."

He wipes the baby's face. "What do I do next?"

"You need to cut the umbilical cord."

"How?"

"Use the string like a clamp, one clamp on each side of the cord. Then cut the middle with the scissors."

"Will it hurt you?"

"No."

He ties two pieces of string tightly around the cord and cuts between the strings. The cord is harder and more difficult to cut than he expected. Audrey pulls the baby up to her chin and sniffs the top of his head. "Put a blanket over him," she says. John covers the boy. Audrey rubs the baby's head and weeps.

"Don't cry. I'm so sorry," John says.

"Don't be sorry, you did good." She pats her heart. "Put your head on my shoulder." She strokes John's sweaty hair and fiddles with his ears. "You're a good man, John , thank you." He cries with her.

The front door opens. Charles and the midwife enter the house.

"It's a boy, Charles, it's a boy," Audrey says.

"No, it can't be."

"It is." She holds the boy up for him. "Hold him, he's your son."

"I'll drop him." He walks away from her to the door, turns around, and steps back to the bed.

"We should name him John. John delivered him," Audrey says.

"Okay, John Charles Doty. I like that," Charles says.

"Has the placenta come yet?" the midwife asks.

"No, not yet," Audrey says.

"Why don't you two boys go into the living room? I'll let you know when to come back," the midwife says. She points to the door. Neither man moves. She walks to the kitchen, washes and dries her hands, and returns to the bedside. "Go. Now."

"I'm not going nowhere. That's my son," Charles insists.

"Charles, just go," Audrey says. She waves him away.

The men step into the living room. John sits on the couch. Charles paces the room like a nervous dog.

"I've got a son, Gauthier. I've got a son."

"Yes, you do. John Charles Doty. I like the sound of that."

"Do you want a cigar? I bought some for the birth."

"Not really."

"Me neither."

Charles checks the wall clock. It is four thirty. "I guess we gotta get the girls back in the barn and milk 'em."

"I guess we do."

The men walk toward the pasture. Charles grabs John's left shoulder and stops him. "Gauthier, you look like shit."

"I feel like I've been trampled by a horse."

"You look like you've been trampled by a bull."

"I think I was."

Charles spits into the snow. "It weren't that bad, were it? Audrey did all the work. I bet you just sat there like a dumbass."

"I didn't do much, that's for sure. I was useless."

"You did enough."

"I guess I did. That was the greatest experience of my life."

"Mine too," Charles says. He gently pushes John toward the grazing field. The cows are waiting at the gate, mooing loudly.
"Looks like the girls are restless," John says.
"We're fifteen minutes late. They hate that," Doty says.

Chapter 4

November 1928
Doty Farm, East Providence, Vermont

John Gauthier is asleep in his bed. In his dream he is lying on the bed, drenched with sweat, staring at the ceiling. Still asleep, he pulls off his T-shirt and underwear, throws them against the wall, and kicks the blankets and sheets to the floor. There is a light tap on the bedroom door. "John, it's me, Audrey. Are you okay? I heard you moaning. I'm worried about you."

"I'm fine, leave me alone."

She ignores him, walks into the room, sits on the edge of the mattress, and pushes his naked body to the center of the bed. She unbuttons her milk-soaked shirt, grabs his right hand, and places it on her moist breast. "How does that feel?" He jolts awake at the feel of her breast.

"Gauthier, wake up," Charles says. He's sitting on the edge of the bed, rattling the headboard. He removes John's hand from his shirt, stands up, and shakes the bed. "Time to get up, city boy."

"What time is it?" John mumbles.

"Three thirty."

"Three thirty? Come back in two hours. It's too damn early."

"You sure are swearing like a drunken sailor, Gauthier. You sound like me."

"Could be worse. Why are you getting me up so early?"

"We're milkin' the cows early cause we're going huntin'. You forget? There's a eight-point buck in the woods out there with your name on it."

"I forgot. I was dreaming."

"I seen that. Looks like it were a real good dream."

"Not so good," John says. He closes his eyes, shakes his head, grabs the blanket from the floor, and pulls it up to his waist. *If Charles knew my dream, he'd throw me out the door,* he thinks.

"You grabbed my breast," Charles says. He laughs.

"I was afraid of that."

"Get dressed. The sooner we finish milkin', the sooner you'll get that big, bad buck," Charles says.

"Great, can't wait."

"I'll be on the porch." Charles leaves the room.

. . .

The air is crisp and cold. John blows hot air on his hands. The Milky Way is clearly visible and the Big Dipper is resting on the top of the barn. Six inches of new snow covers the ground with bobcat tracks visible next to the chicken coop. Charles is sitting on the edge of the porch smoking a cigarette. He points to the bobcat tracks. "That son of a bitch wants my chickens. He ain't gonna get 'em. He ain't gonna live till Christmas." He shakes his fist at the tracks, then flattens his right nostril with his index finger and blows a snot wad to the ground from his left nostril. "Perfect day for huntin' deer."

"I'm not so sure I can shoot a deer."

"Yes, you can. Just aim for his shoulder and pull the trigger. Bam—easy as pie."

"Easy for you," says John and follows Charles off the porch toward the barn.

At the barn, Charles lights three kerosene lanterns and sets them on the wires hanging from the ceiling. The two men milk twelve cows. "Gauthier, I didn't think you'd amount to a piss hole in the snow, but you're okay, could be worse."

"Thanks, I think, not sure if that was a compliment or not," John says.

"Were."

"Thanks," John says. "Charles, how did you get this farm? You're pretty young to own a farm."

"It's not mine, not yet anyway. My parents are both dead. It was their farm. I got two brothers and a sister who want me to buy them out, But I ain't got the money, not even close. Everything's in probate court."

"What's the will say?" John says.

"No will."

"How much do you need?"

"Twenty-seven thousand dollars. Twenty-seven thousand I ain't got."

"I've got twenty-seven thousand dollars."

"Don't be stupid."

"I'm not being stupid. I've got a trust fund. Twenty-seven thousand is just a drop in the bucket."

"Are you kidding me?"

"My father's a big-shot builder, I told you that already. He spends more on Scotch and cigars than most people spend on their mortgage."

"You got money in the bank and you're out here freezing your ass off, milkin' cows at three thirty in the frickin' morning? What are you, nuts?"

"Probably."

"I don't want your damn money. I don't want no charity."

"It wouldn't be charity. It would be a loan."

"I don't want no damn loan. Wouldn't be able to pay it back."

"Sure you would."

"No, Gauthier, I wouldn't. Ever heard the joke 'How do you make a million dollars in dairy farming'?"

"No, how do you make a million dollars in dairy farming?"

"You spend two million." Both men smile. "There ain't no money in dairy farming, Gauthier, never was, never will be."

"I don't give a damn if you pay me back or not. I didn't earn the money."

"I don't want your stupid money."

"Do you want to fight in court for the next three years?"

"No," Charles grumbles.

"Then think about it." John walks to the sink, washes and lubricates his hands, and grabs a stool, a milk bucket, and several towels. "Let's break up the routine today. I'll milk Cow Thirty-two, you milk Cow Fifty."

"Sounds like a plan. Not sure if the cows will go along," Charles says.

"Probably not."

Charles walks to the sink, washes, and lubricates his hands. "Get your ass in gear, Gauthier, you got a deer to kill."

"What happened to your parents?"

"What do you care?"

"Just curious."

Charles answers John as he carries his stool to Cow Thirty-two. "My father died last March," he says, loudly enough that John can hear him from across the barn.

"I'm so sorry," John says, just as loud.

"Don't be, he were a miserable son of a bitch."

"How'd he die?"

"Had a heart attack. We were takin' milk to Providence and the wagon got stuck in the mud. I said, 'Dad, let's take the milk off the wagon. Too much mud, too much weight on the wheels. He were too stubborn to listen. He grabbed the stuck wheel and pushed hard, and he kept pushing even when it was clear the wagon weren't going nowhere.

"Then he collapsed, face-first in the mud. I think he were dead before his head hit the ground. Took me an hour to get the wagon emptied and free from the mud. I left the milk cans on the side of the road and took him to Providence. By the time I got to the funeral home, it were six o'clock, too late to go back to the farm. I stayed with my cousins.

"Audrey had to milk the cows by herself—took her almost five hours. Only eighteen people came to his funeral. I counted. My sister and brothers didn't come—said they were too busy. Too busy, my ass. Theresa lives in Franconia, New Hampshire. She married a Canuck from Canada. He barely speaks English. He's 'bout five foot nothing, skinny as a barn cat. My brothers both live in Burlington. I see them once or twice a year. I called them from the post office and told 'em Dad was dead. That were the first time I'd ever used a telephone. Maybe I'll get one someday."

"Get electricity first. They do have it out here, right?"

"Sure do, Gauthier, put the lines up out here last year. How'd you not see them? It were a big deal. The governor came to town and shook everybody's hand, even mine. 'Bet you can't wait,' he said to me. 'I can,' I said."

"So when are you going to get it?" John says.

"Don't know, maybe never. Don't need it."

Charles carries a full bucket to the milk room and dumps the milk into a milk can. "If Dad hadn't died, not sure how much longer Audrey woulda stayed with me. She were at her wit's end. Dad kept walking in on her when she were changing her clothes or taking a bath. He always had some lame-ass excuse why he was in our section of the house and why he had to go into our bedroom. 'Sorry,' he'd say every time, 'didn't mean to.' I told him to stop it, but he never did. Gave the wife the creeps. And yes, Gauthier, I know you walked in on Audrey last week when she were changing. It weren't the same."

"I didn't mean to, really, I was looking for you." His voice cracks. "I begged her not to tell you."

"She thought it were funny. She said your face turned so red you looked like the inside of a watermelon."

"It won't happen again."

"Relax, Gauthier, you're a nervous little bugger."

"What about your mother?"

"She hanged herself when I was twelve years old, from that lantern wire right there." He points to the lantern at the far end of the barn. "She stood on a milkin' stool, wrapped the wire around her neck, and jumped off the stool. I found her myself. Our dog Rex was agitated and he led me to her body. The wire cut deep into her skin. There was a line of blood around her neck. Looked like she were wearing a red necklace."

"How terrible. I don't know what to say."

"Ain't nothing to say. It were terrible. I cried every night for years. When my father heard me cry, he'd say, 'Don't be a crybaby, you gotta move on.' Most nights I'd put a pillow over my head so he wouldn't hear me. He talked a good game but never moved on. He never said much to me before Mom died, but after she hanged herself, he basically said nothing to me for the next twenty years except to tell me when I'd fucked up. I don't miss him for one good, goddamn second."

"Your mother hanging herself, that must have been a shock to a twelve-year-old?"

"Not really. She'd tried twice before, when I was eight, and again when I'd just turned twelve. We knew it were gonna happen—we just didn't know when. She spent most of my twelfth year in a sanitorium in Brattleboro.

That's the year I started milkin', and I been milkin' ever since. We had a farmhand like you. He found her twice trying to kill herself and saved her both times. After the second time, he just upped and left. 'I can't do this anymore. She's crazier than a bedbug,' he said to my father. I took his place. I was the new farmhand—a twelve-year-old farmhand. I had to leave school, so I never did get to high school. You probably guessed." He laughs.

"One day that summer, my uncle Howard took me to Brattleboro to visit her. We rode the train from Providence. My sister and brothers were too young to go. Mom was so skinny and pale, she scared me. When she talked she looked right through me like I weren't even there, almost like she were talkin' to someone behind me. I didn't cry. I wanted to, but I didn't. She hugged me and said, 'Don't cry, Charles. I'll be home soon, before Thanksgiving.' She didn't make it home by Thanksgiving, but she did come home for Christmas. When she came back, Dad acted like nothin'd happened, like she'd just went to town for the day to buy groceries and were back five hours later. It were a strange Christmas.

"I followed her around like a puppy dog at her heels, watching to make sure she didn't kill herself. 'Stop worrying, I'm fine. You're a worrywart,' she'd say every time I got too close. She hanged herself two months later, February 15, 1912, on Dad's birthday. I think she planned the day to spite him." He walks to the sink, throws the wiping cloth into a basket on the floor next to the sink, and returns with two clean cloths.

"My sister, Theresa, and brother Harold barely remember her. Theresa were six and Harold four when Mom did it. My brother Bob and me—we remember the bad days. Dad never hit Mom, but he sure wanted to. He'd bring his fist up to her face and tap her chin. 'Lucky I don't fucking kill you,' he'd say. After they'd fight, she'd hide in the cellar for hours, sometimes for the whole day. Dad would go to the barn with a bottle of whiskey and sleep in the hayloft, even in the middle of winter. The first time she hid in the cellar, I was only nine years old. I cooked dinner for us. I didn't really know how to cook nothin', so I fried bacon and eggs. I gave Harold milk from his bottle and fed him oatmeal with a spoon. I changed his diaper. I had no idea what I was doing. I cut his skin with the pin and he cried. I felt terrible. No nine-year-old should have ta do that."

Both men carry a full bucket of milk to the milk room. "Not too bad, Gauthier. You're getting pretty good at milkin'."

"Better than a piss hole in the snow?"

"A little better, not much." Charles shakes his arms and fingers and stretches his back. "Gauthier, you been all over the world. You been to India and Japan and Hawaii. Not me, I never been no place. I've left Vermont only once. When I was eleven my mom took me to Boston for two days. It was wonderful. I went to Fenway Park and watched the Red Sox play the New York Yankees. The Red Sox won eight to one. I'm a Yankees fan now, but back then I didn't care one way or the other. My mother bought me a baseball glove and I almost caught a foul ball. I put my glove up to catch it, but it were a few inches too high. The man behind me caught it and said, 'Too bad, kid.' Then he laughed and handed me the ball. Best day of my life."

He moves his stool and bucket to the fortieth stanchion. "Enough of this garbage. Let's talk about the deer you're gonna shoot."

"I'm not going to kill a deer."

"Yes, you are, Gauthier, either that or I'll shoot you." Charles laughs. "Just aim and shoot, that's all you gotta do. Bam, he's dead."

John walks toward the far end of the barn, turns, and says, "I challenge you to a milking contest. Let's see who can milk the most cows in the next hour."

"What are the stakes?"

"One dollar if you win. But if I win, you accept my loan."

"I'll take your bet. You got no chance, you're too damn skinny to beat me."

"You ever seen a sled dog? They're skinny but strong," John says.

"All right, the bet's on. No cutting corners—each cow has to be fully milked. A half-milked cow don't count."

"It's a bet."

The two men milk the cows with steely determination.

Charles checks his watch. "Time's up, Gauthier. I got five done. There ain't no way you done more than that."

"I got five too. It's a tie."

"Gauthier, you couldn't milk five in two hours last month."

"That was last month."

"A tie means nobody wins," Charles says.

"No, it doesn't, a tie means we both win and we both pay up." He reaches into his pocket, removes a dollar bill from his wallet, and hands it to Charles. "Here's your buck. Now what you have to do is take my loan. I'm going to write you a check this afternoon."

"I ain't taking your goddamn money."

"A bet's a bet."

"We'll see, Gauthier." He carries a filled bucket to the milk storage room and empties the milk into the milk can. "Two more cows and we're huntin'. It's your lucky day, Gauthier, I can feel it in my bones."

"As I said before, I can't wait."

. . .

"You ready?" Charles says.

"Ready as I'll ever be," John says.

"Good." He hands John a canvas tarp.

"I don't get a gun?"

"Not yet."

"You don't trust me?"

Charles scratches his nose. "We got one rifle. I'll carry it. I don't want you blowin' your damn foot off."

"You own a half dozen rifles."

"We got one today."

"What's the tarp for?"

"If we get a deer, we're gonna have ta drag it back here. That ain't gonna be easy."

"We?"

"Yes, we, Gauthier."

Charles lifts a gray knapsack onto his shoulders. It smells like coffee. The men walk across the grazing field to the woods near the pond.

"Where are we going?" John says.

Charles taps his lips with his right index finger. "Sssshh."

"Where are we going?"

"Will you be quiet? We're going into the woods, where the hell do you think we're going?"

Two hundred yards past the frog pond, a ten-foot wooden ladder is leaning against a tree. Two sheets of plywood are nailed to the branches just above the top of the ladder. "Climb up there," Charles says. He points to the ladder.

"Why?"

"We're gonna hunt from up there."

"Why?"

"You sound like a frickin' five-year-old."

"I do."

Charles clears his right nostril. "The deer run by here every morning. There're ten of them. I been watching them for two weeks."

"So that's why you've been leaving the milking early. I thought something was up."

"Yup, it were."

John climbs the ladder. Charles checks the gun to make sure it is empty. He holds the rifle in his right hand and climbs with his left. Two rungs from the top, he hands John the rifle and the backpack. "Take these and move over."

"What do we do now?"

"We wait."

"How long?"

"I don't know how long, but what I do know is we wait in silence."

John pretends to zip his lips shut.

Charles checks his watch. It's six thirty. He loads the rifle, makes sure the safety is on, and hands it to John. "Don't blow your goddamn foot off." He smiles. He grabs a thermos from the backpack and pours a cup of coffee. "Want one?"

"No thanks, not a coffee drinker."

"Didn't think so."

"So how long do we wait?"

"I already told you, don't know. We wait in silence, remember?"

John zips his lips shut again.

The deer are right on time, almost as if they had an alarm clock. Charles taps John's right shoulder and points to an eight-point buck. John releases the safety, raises the rifle to his shoulder, aims at the buck, hesitates, and hands the gun to Charles.

Charles nods his head, aims, and shoots. The deer freezes for a half second and crumbles to the ground. The other nine deer scatter. "We did it, Gauthier."

"No, you did it. I couldn't do it."

"Why not?"

"I don't know why not, just couldn't."

"Got sumthin''gainst huntin'?"

"Nope."

"It was a team effort, Gauthier."

"Not really."

The men climb down from the tree. Charles hands John a hunting knife. "I shot 'em, you clean 'em, that's our teamwork."

John kneels next to the fallen dear and punctures the skin. Blood spurts onto his face. "I can't do this either."

Charles laughs, grabs the knife from him, and cleans the deer. "Guess the teamwork will be you helping me drag this sucker back to the barn. Probably weighs two hundred pounds, maybe more. You can do that, right?"

"Yup."

"You won't complain the whole time, will ya?"

"Probably not, no guarantees."

"You're a piece of work, Gauthier."

"I am."

Charles spreads the tarp on the ground next to the deer and pulls it onto the canvas. "Grab that corner. No whining."

"Yes, Mr. Dad, sir. No whining."

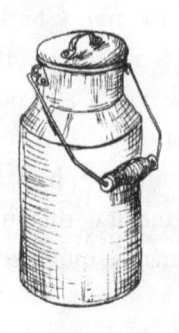

Chapter 5

December 1928
Doty Farm, East Providence, Vermont

The cows are not happy. They want to get out of the barn, but there is too much snow. "Not gonna happen today, girls, not gonna happen till April," Charles says. He and John feed them, which shuts them up. Charles hangs his rake on a nail on the front wall. "Christmas's in three weeks. You a Christian, Gauthier?"

"Not really."

"Well, you are this year. I want you ta take the wife to cut a Christmas tree."

"Why me?"

"Why not you? I'll stay home with the baby."

"I'll stay home with the baby, you cut the tree. It's too damn cold. You're used to it, not me."

"Who's the boss here, Gauthier?"

Charles retrieves a toboggan from the hayloft, two pairs of snowshoes, and a bow saw from the closet in the milk room. He hands John the snowshoes. "You'll need these, snow's a foot deep or more in the woods."

Audrey is standing at the barn door watching the two men. "Not going to go with me today, Charles?" Her words surprise both men.

"Too busy. Would go but can't. Gotta feed and water the cows."

"You just fed them."

"Gotta clean the barn."

"John can clean the barn."

"He doesn't know what he's doing."

"He cleans the barn every day when you take the milk to Providence."

"What's your point?" Charles says.

She shakes her head. "Looks like it's you and me, John." She pulls her dark blue toque over her ears and tightens her scarf. "Mr. Scrooge hates Christmas."

"I don't hate Christmas." He hands John the saw and the toboggan.

Audrey tells Charles the baby is asleep and should stay asleep for the next two hours but no guarantees. "What else is new," he says. Little John has not yet slept through the night. Most nights he wakes up two or three times, sometimes more.

Audrey and John cross the back pasture to the maple grove at the far end of the grazing field, three hundred yards from the pasture gate. "How far is it?" John asks. He is breathing hard. There are ice crystals on his upper lip, eyebrows, and nose hairs.

"Not far. It's a beautiful day. Great day to walk in the woods." They walk toward the sun. The light reflected on the snow makes them squint and shield their eyes.

"It's freezing," John says.

"This is nothing, wait till February."

They walk a quarter mile through the maple trees to a small pond covered with ice and snow. Audrey points to the far side of the pond. "The pine trees are over there."

She examines one tree, then a second tree. She grabs John by his shoulders and pulls him next to a tree. "How tall are you?"

"Five eight, maybe five nine, why?"

"Trying to determine how tall this tree is. We need an eight-foot tree." She compares the top of his head with the top of the tree. "Too short."

"Me or the tree?"

"Both." She laughs and tugs him to a different tree. "Too tall."

"What is this, the three bears?"

"Yes, and I'm Goldilocks."

She finds a perfect tree. "All right, John. Cut that tree down."

"How?"

"What do you mean, how? You kneel in the snow and saw. Charles is right, you have no common sense."

"I'll freeze to death."

"You won't freeze to death."

"If I do, it's on you."

"I'll cry at your funeral."

He removes his snowshoes and clears the snow from the base of the tree with one of the shoes. He kneels down and places the saw blade against the bark and pushes and pulls the saw back and forth against the trunk. "This is really hard."

"Whine, whine, whine, you've been whining since we left the barn."

"Have not."

"Yes, you have." She makes a snowball and tosses it at his head. The snowball knocks his hat off his head.

"Are you kidding me?" He looks up at her.

She makes a second snowball and lightly tosses it toward his face. The snowball hits his nose. He drops the saw and stands up next to the tree. "You better run."

"You can't catch me." She turns about-face and plods three paces away from him. He leaps toward her but sinks deep into the snow. He pulls his legs free, leaps toward her again and plops, face-first, at her feet. He grabs his hat, shakes it clean, and wipes his face with his glove. She grabs a handful of snow and trickles it down his neck.

"You're so dead," he says. He stands up, leaps toward her, catches her legs, pushes her to the snow, and pins her like a wrestler. "What should I do to you?" He grabs a handful of snow and holds it two inches from her face.

"Don't you dare, John Gauthier."

He trickles the snow onto her face.

"Uncle, uncle."

"How about we cut a Christmas tree?" he says. He gets up, brushes the snow off his pants, and walks back toward the tree he was cutting.

"Aren't you going to help me up?" Audrey asks.

He grabs her arms and pulls her off the snow so hard they bump together. He lifts her hat from the snow, shakes it clean, and hands it to her. "Put it on my head, John, my hands are too cold." He removes his gloves, pulls her toque over her hair, and tucks her ears under the wool. "Your hands are as cold as mine," she says.

He finishes cutting the tree and lifts it onto the toboggan.

"Before we go, let's make two snow angels," she says.

"It's too damn cold."

"Stop whining and lay down next to me." She lies in the snow and makes a snow angel. He drops to the ground next to the toboggan. "No, next to me, we want the angels' wings to touch." He lies next to her and carves his angel. Both of them rise from the snow and admire their creation. "Perfect," she says. "That's the one good thing about winter. You can't make a snow angel in the rain."

John pulls the sled forty yards and stops. "This is really hard, harder than raking hay. I don't know if I can make it all the way back to the barn."

"Is hard the only word you know?"

"No. Difficult, demanding, exacting, laborious, and I've got dozens more."

"Are you going to whine all the way home?"

"Yes."

She tosses a snowball. It hits his chest. "Every time you whine, I'm going to hit you with a snowball."

"You wouldn't dare."

"Oh yes, I would." She grabs the toboggan rope. "If we both pull, will you stop complaining?"

"Maybe. No promises."

She stops, bends down, and grabs a fist full of snow. "Next time you whine, bam, right in the kisser." She kisses his cheek. "That's where the snowball will hit you next time you whine." They drag the tree around the pond and through the maple trees. "Tell me about India. It sounds exotic and exciting."

"It's incredible. The cities are loud and crowded and so full of energy. It's nearly impossible to walk through the streets without bumping into someone. I thought New York City was crowded but nothing like Bombay. One time I saw a monkey walking alone in the middle of the street. He looked like he was on his way to work. Nobody seemed to notice him but me. I hiked in the Himalayas for a month. Your mountains here are nothing, not even foothills.

Even the Rockies are nothing compared to the Himalayas. It was the best two years of my life. Sometimes I wish I had never left."

"Why'd you leave?"

"I had no choice."

"Why not?"

"I fell in love with the wrong girl."

"Don't you mean the wrong woman?"

"No, I mean girl. She was way too young for me. I was twenty-two, she was only sixteen. I didn't mean to fall in love with her, but I did. She was the most beautiful woman I had ever seen."

"Even more beautiful than me?" She laughs.

"I hadn't met you yet."

Audrey smiles a timid smile. "What happened?"

"Even though she was only sixteen she was already promised to a forty-two-year-old widower with four children, three of them older than she was. She didn't want to marry him. She told me she would kill herself rather than marry him."

"What was her name?"

"Amara. Amara Khatri."

"Beautiful name."

"It is. Amara means 'eternal.'"

"Did she marry him?"

"No. When he heard she was in love with me, he called off the wedding. He said she was a worthless whore and he spat in her face. Her father and two of her uncles beat her up so badly her face was marred. 'You shamed me,' her father said. He and his brothers threatened me. 'You're lucky you're an American. If you were Indian, I'd cut out your eyeballs and stuff them in your mouth,' her father said. He told me if I didn't leave India, he'd turn me into a eunuch."

"I don't know what that means," Audrey says.

"I wouldn't have a penis."

"Ouch."

"I was too stupid to be afraid, at least at first. 'You can't threaten me, I'll go to the police,' I said. There's no creature on earth more stupid than a young man in love. 'Go right ahead,' he said. 'My cousin Reyansh is the chief of police and my uncle Vishesh is the assistant to the governor-general.' He pulled a long knife out of its sheath and tapped my crotch with it. 'If you don't leave, I'll cut off your tiny penis and shove it up your skinny ass,' he said. One of the men said he was the deputy police chief. 'Would you like to file your complaint now?' her father said, smirking, and pressed his knife against my throat. 'If you have any brains, you'll leave India tomorrow.' He sounded like a hissing snake. I left that weekend."

"What happened to Amara?"

"I don't know. I assume she is living a sad, lonely life. I doubt she will ever get married. I ruined her life."

"No, you didn't, you didn't ruin her life, you fell in love. Her father ruined her life."

John stops and reaches for Audrey. "Audrey, I did ruin her life. I was an arrogant fool. I shouldn't have fallen in love with a girl so young. I should have known better. I should have known more about India. Typical American, I knew nothing. I treated her like she was an American girl. She wasn't. She was a young Indian girl promised to an older man. It wasn't my place to get in the way. I ruined her life forever and almost lost my own life. I will never forgive myself."

"It wasn't your fault, John."

"Yes, it was. Remember when I said I was hiding out from my dad? That was only half true. I'm not hiding just from him; I'm hiding from myself. I don't deserve a good life."

Audrey hugs him hard and grabs his chin with her gloves. "You're a good man, John Gauthier. You did a stupid thing but you're still a good man." She hands him the toboggan rope. "We've got about a half mile to go and it's not getting any warmer." She grabs a handful of snow and holds it up to his face. "Remember, anymore whining and pow, right in the kisser."

"Snow or lips?"

"Snow."

He laughs. "I'll be good."

"You better be.

Chapter 6

April 1962
Sacred Heart Parish, Providence, Vermont

Patrick Colman is at the top of snow-covered Shriver Hill with his best friends Paul Fermonte, twins Mike and Sean O'Riley, and Maurice Nolan. They call themselves the Five Musketeers. Their parents call them the Five Clowns. They have a secret handshake, a secret hideout, a secret stash of *Playboy* magazines, and a secret signal yell they think sounds like a hooting owl but doesn't. "Whoo, whoo, whoo!" yelled as loud as possible means "I'm over here, where are you?" When they don't want anyone to know what they are saying, they speak in what they think is pig Latin. "Etslay, eetmay, at our ecretsay ideouthay" means "Let's meet at our secret hideout." Their parents are never fooled.

They all have Flexible Flyer sleds with metal runners and a steering lever at the front. At the bottom of the hill, twenty yards across flat ground, a two-story apartment building is suspended ten feet above a cement floor on nine cement pillars, three pillars in each of the three rows. There are four staircases under the building to the apartments, six apartments in each section. Everyone in town calls the building the Chicken Coop.

"Here's what we're gonna do, men," Paul says. "We're gonna see who can come closest to that cement post without hitting it." He points to his left, to the front pillar at the far end of the building. "You go first," he says to Maurice.

"I'm not going first, you go first," Maurice says.

"You're goin' first, asshole," Paul says.

Maurice picks up his sled, runs ten feet, and jumps on it, head at the front, belly on the wood, hands on the steering lever. He aims to the left side of the pillar. He misses the post by about three feet.

"You're a weeny," Paul yells.

Sean is next. He slides two feet from the post. His brother Michael is closer, with about a foot of clearance. Paul goes next. He barrels straight down toward the center of the cement post and doesn't steer clear until he is less than three feet from it. He slides by the left side, ten inches from the pillar. He stops his sled, jumps up, and measures the distance from his sled's rudder mark to the post. "Ten inches, bucko, beat that," he yells to Patrick, who is still at the top of the hill. He posts a victory *V* with his arms.

Patrick studies the hill. His knees are shaking. He is determined to win. He jumps on the sled and slides fast, toward the center of the pillar. Two feet from the post he turns the rudder sharp left. But he is too late. The rudders hit ice and the sled doesn't turn. The front of his sled hits the post. His body slithers across the wood, and his face smashes into the pillar.

"Oh shit," Paul says. The boys run to Patrick. His face is covered with blood, and he is unconscious. "I think he's dead."

"What do we do?" Michael says.

"Run," Paul says.

The boys run fifty feet from the building and stop. "What about our sleds?" Sean says. They grab their sleds and run away.

Patrick wakes up in a fog. The metal at the front of his sled is bent and the steering lever is cracked. There is so much blood in the snow it looks like someone butchered a pig. He rubs the blood from his chin. His nose hurts. "Where am I?" he says out loud. He tries to stand but falls down into the snow. He pulls his mitten off his right hand and touches his sore nose with his fingers. He doesn't remember much of what happened. He remembers jumping on his sled, but nothing else. He shakes his head, stands up, grabs the rope, and pulls the sled across the parking lot to his house just beyond the far side of the lot. He stops and throws up. His vision is blurred. When his mother, Tia, sees his bloody face she rushes him to the hospital. The doctor says he was lucky he hadn't broken his neck. Patrick's nose is broken, his chin is bruised, and he has a concussion. Patrick's father, Tom, tells him if he does it again, *he'll* break his neck.

. . .

Sister Ryan checks the bandages on Patrick's face. The skin on his right cheek is purple, his nose is covered with a big, white bandage, and both eyes are black. "What happened, Patrick?"

He tells her about the sliding accident. She calls the other Musketeers to the front of the classroom and asks them what happened. All four say they have no idea. Patrick glares at them. "You liars," he whispers.

"What was that?" asks Sister Ryan.

"Nothing, Sister."

She sends Patrick to the principal's office. Sister Bartholomew, the principal, is very concerned. She doesn't like Patrick's father. Tom complains loudly and often about everything, big or small. Everybody is stupid but him. Even worse, he never attends Mass. Mass is for chumps. She thinks Tia is a saint for living with him.

"Patrick, how are things at home? You can tell me, I'm here to help you. Don't be afraid. I'm your friend," Sister Bartholomew says. She asks him another half dozen questions. He retells the story about sliding into the cement post. "Is that so?" She calls Monsignor Gauthier. He gets called to the school only when the problem is serious. He hates getting called to the school. His idea of a perfect day is to play classical music on his stereo and read one classic novel after another and not deal with the nuns if he can avoid them.

"So, what happened? It looks like you smashed your face into a tree," he says and chuckles.

"I smashed into a cement post," Patrick says. He tells Gauthier about the sliding contest and says his friends saw what happened.

"They saw nothing," Sister Ryan says.

They were there, they left me to die, they're not my friends, I hate them, Patrick thinks.

"Yes, they did," Patrick says. He names them. Monsignor Gauthier tells Sister Ryan to get the boys. They fess up the truth even before he says anything.

"You're lucky you didn't break your foolish neck," Gauthier says. "Boys, next time a friend smashes his head into a tree and knocks himself out, don't run away, get help. Don't be knuckleheads."

"Yes, Father," they say as one. They look ashamed.

The next day Patrick's father brings the mangled sled to Sister Ryan's class. "I understand you think I hit my son." He drops the sled onto the floor. "I didn't hit him, but I sure would like to knock some sense into that boy. Sometimes he's so stupid he scares me." He doesn't say anything else, and he doesn't wait for a reply. He walks out of the room. Sister Ryan tells Patrick to carry the sled to the dumpster.

Chapter 7

April 1962
Sacred Heart Parish, Providence, Vermont

Patrick is standing guard at the door to the church sanctuary. His legs are shaking. The only light in the room is from the two streetlamps on the road behind the church. His friend Paul Fermonte is holding three bottles of communion wine. One bottle is for Monsignor Gauthier, one for Father Symanski, and the third for Father Cantone. Gauthier's wine is a dark Syrah. Symanski's and Cantone's wines are lighter, pinot noir for Symanski, zinfandel for Cantone.

Paul places a piece of Scotch tape even with the top of the wine in Gauthier's bottle. He marks the wine level on the other two bottles with the tape. "All we gotta do, men, is add water and make sure the level in the bottle is the same as it is now, and no one will know," he says. The others nod in agreement. He takes a swig from Gauthier's bottle. He grimaces at the taste and the sting of the alcohol. "Delicious," he says. He hands the bottle to Patrick.

"I love wine," Patrick says.

"You liar. You've never had wine before in your life," Paul says.

"I have too." Patrick drinks a gulp from the bottle and spills several drops on his chin. He wipes his chin dry with his sleeve.

Paul grabs the wine bottle, steps to the sink across from the closet, and carefully refills the bottle to the level of the tape.

Michael O'Riley takes a big, loud gulp from Symanski's bottle. He removes his baseball cap and rubs the sweat from his forehead. "I think I'm drunk."

"You're not drunk, you're just stupid," Paul says and slugs him on his shoulder.

O'Riley hands Paul his bottle. Paul drinks a mouthful and refills the bottle with water to the tape line. He holds the bottle to the outside light to check the level of the wine and water. "Perfecto."

O'Riley's twin brother, Sean, sniffs the cork from the third bottle. "You're supposed to sniff the cork first." He shakes the bottle lightly, sniffs the top, takes a gulp too big for his mouth, and spits most of the wine back out, onto his shirt and the floor. "That's gross."

"Smooth, O'Riley, real smooth," Patrick says.

Paul grabs the bottle from Sean and refills it with water to the tape line.

There is a noise from the front of the church. "What was that?" Paul asks.

"Somebody's here," warns Patrick.

"Don't panic, men," Paul says. He drops to his knees and crawls to the door. "Get down and follow me." He gives them a follow-me arm wave like Ward Bond's "Wagons Ho!" wave at the end of each episode of *Wagon Train*.

"Who's here? Is anybody here?" asks Agnes LeSalle, the housekeeper for the rectory. "Is anybody here?"

The boys crawl out of the sanctuary, past the altar, to the first row of pews. They hide under the seats. Agnes turns on the lights in the nave and walks down the middle aisle, checking the seats as she walks. The boys watch her feet as she strides past their pew. She checks behind the altar and walks to the sanctuary. She turns on the lights and spots the three opened wine bottles on the table and the puddle of wine on the floor. She wipes the puddle dry with a hand towel, replaces the corks, places the bottles in the closet, closes the closet door, turns off the lights, and exits the sanctuary. Then she walks back through the nave, turns off the lights, and says loudly, "I guess nobody's here." She leaves through the main entrance doors, checking to make sure the door is locked.

"Etslay, eetmay, at our ecretsay ideouthay," Paul whispers to the others.

The five of them crawl out from under the pew, slither on their bellies to the back door, and tumble through to the outside. Quickly, they rise and bolt, nonstop, from there to their secret hideout three blocks away. Agnes watches them run across the church parking lot and laughs to herself. She is holding Michael O'Riley's baseball cap in her hands. His name, street address, and telephone number are written on the underside of the lid. She checks the back door to make sure it is locked.

Their secret hiding place is a cardboard fortress under the O'Rileys' back porch. The boys have covered the ground, the walls, and the ceiling with cardboard. The ceiling is just high enough so they can sit up without hitting their heads. Several dozen *Playboys* are hidden in the ceiling.

"All right, men, don't tell anybody. Loose lips sink ships," Paul says.

"What's that mean?" says Patrick.

"I don't know. You're supposed to say it when you want to keep a secret." Paul holds his hand out for their secret handshake. "Ooselay ipslay inksay ipshay."

"Oooselay ipslay inksay ipshay," the others say together.

. . .

Sister Ryan is standing at her desk at the front of the classroom, reading a note from Monsignor Gauthier. "Mr. Fermonte, stand up," she says. He stands. "Mr. O'Riley—both of you—Mr. Colman, Mr. Nolan, stand up." She walks to them and examines each boy as if she were examining a horse for sale. "Boys, Monsignor Gauthier wants to see you immediately. I don't know what you did, but this can't be good news." She crumples the note and throws it into the wastebasket next to the desk.

"Eway are crewedsay," Paul whispers to Patrick.

"What was that, Mr. Fermonte?" Sister Ryan says.

"Nothing, Sister." He speaks so quickly that "sister" sounds like "stir." She sends them to the rectory.

Monsignor Gauthier, Father Symanski, and Father Anthony Cantone are sitting at the kitchen table. Symanski and Cantone share the first-floor apartment. Gauthier is holding Michael O'Riley's baseball cap in his right hand. "So, Michael, did you lose your cap?" Gauthier says. He hands the cap to Michael.

"Yes, Father, I guess I did."

"Do you know when?"

"Not sure, I musta left it on Sunday when I served Mass."

"Michael, you didn't serve Mass this week," Symanski says.

"Yes, I did, Father."

"No, you did not, let's not make this worse than it already is," Gauthier says.

Agnes walks into the room holding the three wine bottles from the night before. She places the bottles on the table in front of Gauthier. He grabs his bottle and peels the tape free from the glass. "Do any of you boys know why there's a piece of tape on this bottle neck?"

"No, Father," all five say.

"And tape on the other two bottles?"

"No, Father." Sean's voice trembles.

"Boys, boys, boys, cut the crap, you were in the sanctuary last night drinking our wine. That's bad enough, but what's worse is you ruined three bottles of wine. Never water down good wine."

Sean starts to cry.

"Mr. O'Riley, there's no reason to cry, nobody's going to hit you," Gauthier says.

"But you're going to tell my dad," Sean says.

"Maybe, maybe not, depends." He peels the tape from the three bottles, rolls the three pieces of tape together, and flicks the sticky ball into the kitchen sink. "How did you boys get in the sanctuary? The door was locked."

None of them say anything.

"My question is pretty simple—how did you get in?" He glares at them.

"If you jam your shoulder hard into the back door, it opens," Paul says.

"I guess we'll have to get that fixed," Gauthier says. He stands up and leans his face five inches from Paul's nose. His breath smells like rum, pipe tobacco, and mint mouthwash. "Here's what you're going to do, boys. You're going to clean the church, cleaner than it's ever been cleaned. You're going to mop the floors, scrub the pews, and polish the brass. I want you here, all five of you, after school today, tomorrow, and Friday, three o'clock sharp."

"We've got Boy Scouts today after school," Michael says.

"Apparently, I wasn't clear, Mr. O'Riley. You will be here today at three o'clock, here tomorrow at three, and here at three on Friday. You'll work each day until five, no breaks. Am I clear this time?" He speaks slowly and firmly.

"Yes, Father," Michael says.

"Now get out of here before I call your parents."

The boys turn to leave the room. "Mr. Colman, stay behind. I have something I need you to do," Gauthier says.

"Ou'reyay in eepday itshay," Paul whispers to Patrick.

"Paul, you're all in deep shit," Gauthier says, surprising the boys. He guides Patrick to his apartment. "How's the book coming, Patrick?"

"Almost done."

"Finish it tonight, I'll quiz you tomorrow."

"Um..."

"You haven't started it, have you, Patrick?"

"No, sir."

"Finish it by Monday. That gives you the weekend."

"Yes, Father."

"I've never thanked you for organizing all my records. You did a great job." He grabs the Chopin album with the cracked record from the shelf and holds it as if he were holding a baby. "Patrick, have you ever heard Chopin's Opus no. 9?"

"No, Father."

"Let me play it for you, it's beautiful."

"I can't stay, Father, Sister Ryan will miss me. I have a spelling test." His forehead is sweating.

"The test can wait." He pulls the record from the sleeve. "Oh my goodness, the record is cracked. Do you know how that happened, Patrick?"

"No, Father."

"Patrick, you dropped it, and then you tried to glue it together. Isn't that what happened?"

"It was an accident. I didn't mean to."

"I didn't say you did. Next time you break something by accident, just tell me. Can you do that?"

"Yes, Father."

"Finish *A Separate Peace*. I'm going to quiz you first thing Monday morning. Remember the opening scene, that's key."

"Yes, sir."

"Do yourself a favor. In the future, when Mr. Fermonte suggests something stupid, don't do it just because he says so."

"Yes, Father."

"Rule of thumb—if you can't tell your mother, you shouldn't do it." He waves him away. "Now, go finish the book."

Chapter 8

December 1928
St. Francis of Assisi Parish, East Providence, Vermont

Charles pulls John through the barn to the milk storage room. At the back of the room, next to the milk cans, is a large cardboard box, five feet high and three feet wide. The writing on the top of the box says "The Leonard Cleanable Refrigerator." Charles rips the box apart with a pocketknife and throws the cardboard pieces across the room. "What do ya think, Gauthier?"

"About what?"

"About the icebox. It's for the wife for Christmas. Best one on the market. What do ya think?"

"I don't know. You sure you want to give Audrey an icebox for Christmas?"

"It's top of the line."

"Top of the line would be an electric refrigerator."

"We don't got no electricity. This is a great gift."

"I don't think it's such a good idea. Jewelry maybe, or a dress or a new sweater, but not an icebox. You might as well buy her a new broom."

"What do you know? You're not married."

"True."

Charles walks back to the main section of the barn, grabs a shovel, and hands it to John. "Looks like you got a lot of manure to clean today, Gauthier. The girls were pretty active last night. Musta ate too much hay." He chuckles.

"What about you? Where's your shovel?"

"I'm management. Next thing you know, I'll be wearing a suit and tie." He scratches his nose and lights a cigarette. "Sunday is the second week in Advent. I want you to take the wife to Mass."

"Why me?"

"We've already gone over that, Gauthier. Because I'm the boss. The Catholic church's in West Providence. It's about an hour from here. If you leave by seven-forty-five you should make the nine o'clock service, easy. I'd go but every time I go ta church, I get a splitting headache and I gotta take a dump. The minute I walk through the door, bam, gotta take a dump. Happens every time."

"Then take a shit, there must be a bathroom," John says.

"Don't like taking a dump anywheres but here. Don't feel comfortable. When I was a kid, I could never shit at school. Held it all day."

"Looks like I'm going to church on Sunday."

"Looks that way."

. . .

Audrey is in the bathroom applying makeup and lipstick. She hasn't worn lipstick since her cousin's wedding four years ago. She clips on the jade earrings she wore then. She examines six dresses before she chooses the one to wear. She grabs a flapper's hat and dress shoes from her closet. The dress is much tighter than before she was pregnant. *My body's different since Little John*, she thinks. She looks in the mirror and sighs.

"You can't wear that hat, you'll freeze to death," Charles says from the doorway of the bedroom. He goes out to the living room, retrieves a wool toque and snow boots from the closet, comes back to the bedroom and tosses them to her. "This is Vermont, not Florida." He grabs a blanket from the couch and hands it to her. "You'll need this for your legs."

. . .

Gauthier is sitting on a kitchen chair that is next to the front door. He is wearing his new winter jacket and is holding his hat and gloves in his hands. He has been dressed and waiting for the past twenty minutes. His back and underarms are sweating. He checks the clock on the mantel above the fireplace in the living room. It is ten after eight.

Audrey and Charles enter the living room. She smells of roses. "Time to go, John," she says.

"Past time," Charles says. He points to the clock on the wall above the fireplace, steps to the front door and opens it. "Go, before it's too late."

Audrey kisses his forehead. "You're a grumpy man, Charles Doty, but I love you anyway."

"Go," he says. He smiles, and grazes her right hand with his left hand.

. . .

The sky is steel gray. It is difficult to tell the lower sky from the snow on the mountains. A mile from the house, Audrey removes her toque and replaces it with her flapper's hat. "Do you like my hat?"

"Yes, I do."

"Have you ever been to a speakeasy? I want to go to one someday. There's one in Providence. I've asked Charles to take me, but he won't. He says they're bad places, not fit for a good woman like me. I'm not that good, John." She adjusts her hat. "What are they like?"

"I've only been once."

"It must have been magical."

"I don't know about that. There was lots of cigarette smoke and jazz music and booze and dancing and women with hats like the one you've got on. The smoke bothered my eyes, and the music was so loud it gave me a headache. It was nearly impossible to talk to anyone."

"Did you dance?"

"I wanted to, but I didn't."

"Why not?"

"Too shy, I guess. I couldn't get up enough courage to ask anyone. There was a pretty girl who kept looking at me. I wanted to ask her to dance, but every time I got close to her, I lost my nerve and walked away and had another drink. By the time I asked her, I was so drunk I slurred my words and fell on my face right at her feet and puked on her shoes. Just missed puking on her dress. The bouncer picked me up like a rag doll and threw me out the front door. My face hit the dirt and I broke my nose. So, yes, speakeasies may be magical places for some people, but not for me."

Audrey laughs hard. "Sorry, John, I couldn't help it. Picturing you throwing up on the woman's shoes and then bouncing across the dirt, face-first, is funny."

"I'm glad you can laugh."

She lightly punches his shoulder. "It was funny." She punches him again. "Have you ever been to a Catholic Mass?"

"Not really. I went to a Catholic funeral once, but that was so long ago I can barely remember it."

"There're a lot of rules. You have to take your hat off when you enter the building. I keep mine on. Women wear hats, men don't. This hat should get some tongues wagging." She tugs it tighter on her head. "Before we enter our pew, we have to genuflect. Do you know how to genuflect?" He nods. "Good. When you genuflect you make the sign of the cross."

"The what?"

"The sign of the cross. You have to bless yourself. Do you know how to do that?"

"Yes."

She ignores what he said and shows him how to do it. "Remember to tap your left shoulder before your right shoulder. Forehead, chest, left shoulder, right shoulder."

"Audrey, I get it, it's the same in the Episcopal Church. Catholics don't have a lock on ritual."

. . .

There are about forty-five people in the pews. When they enter everyone in the church turns to look at them, even the priest, whose back was to the congregation. Several people cough. "Who's that with Audrey?" a little boy asks his mother. She places her hand over his mouth.

The priest turns back to the altar and resumes his prayer. "Per evangelica dicta deleantur nostra delicta," he chants.

"What's he saying?" John whispers to Audrey.

"I'm not sure, something about the Gospel and sin."

"If I remember Latin from college, I think 'deleantur' means to 'end' or 'terminate.' Probably means the Gospel ends sin."

An elderly couple in the pew in front of them turn and shush them. Audrey taps her lips with her right index finger in agreement. "Shhh," she says to John.

At the end of the service, the priest walks to the entrance door and greets everyone as they leave. "You must be John Gauthier," he says. "I'm Father LeFebvre, Dan LeFebvre." He shakes John's hand. "I've heard a lot of good things about you."

"I find that hard to believe."

"It's true." He grabs John's shoulder. "I noticed you didn't take Communion. You're not a Catholic?" the priest says.

"No."

"What denomination are you?"

"Actually, none."

"How can that be? Are you an atheist?"

"I don't think so. Haven't given it much thought, one way or another. When I was a small boy, my family attended the Episcopal church, but we stopped when I was eleven."

"Why'd you stop?"

"Just did."

The people in line behind John are getting anxious about the delay. Several are clearing their throats to make sure the priest gets their message. "I understand you spent two years in India. I was there for five years," the priest says. "We'll have to talk about that sometime." He looks at the anxious crowd. "I need to wrap this up, the natives are getting restless." He releases John's hands and motions him to move along. "See you next week."

The morning mist has cleared and the sky is deep blue with large, puffed clouds. "It's a beautiful day. You should take the sleigh to Providence. You haven't left the farm in over three months," Audrey says.

"Yes, I did, I went to town to buy new boots."

"That doesn't count. You should go to Providence and go to a movie. You can take my sister Charlotte. She lives two blocks from the movie theater. She'd love to go. You'll like her, she's fun. Take her to *The Jazz Singer*. It's a talkie. I've never been to a talking movie before."

"No, thanks, I'd rather not."

"You realize you're a very boring person."

"I do."

"So, why did your family stop going to church?"

"We just did?"

"Must be a reason?"

"My sister died. She was eight and I was eleven. Our cat was stuck on the window ledge of her bedroom, and she reached out to save it and fell to the ground and broke her neck. My mother blamed God."

"It wasn't God's fault. It was an accident."

"Tell that to my mother. She blamed God, and she blamed herself. She even blamed the cat. She cried for days. It's been sixteen years, and she still cries. I'm not sure if she'll ever get over it."

"Probably not. I wouldn't," Audrey says. She pulls the blanket off her legs and throws it to the back of the sleigh. "Don't need this, it's a beautiful day." She grabs Gauthier's right elbow and smiles coyly. "Are you as tired as I am? Little John was up all night. Half the time I'm so tired, I can't see straight. Some days, when you and Charles are in the barn milking the cows, I look at the clock and I don't know if it's five thirty in the afternoon or five thirty in the morning."

"I know the feeling. Little John sure does cry a lot."

"Can I rest my head on your shoulder?"

"Of course."

She tilts her head to his shoulder and quickly falls asleep. Her head slips to his lap. Her hat falls off. He stops the sleigh, replaces her flapper's hat with her toque, and tucks her hair into the wool. He stuffs the flapper's hat into her coat pocket and lightly rubs her cheek with his thumb. She doesn't wake up until they are about a mile from the house.

"I think I fell asleep," she says. "Sorry about that. Where are we?"

"We're about a mile from the house."

She rubs the sleep from her eyes with her thumbs. "You have a comfortable lap. Next time I can't sleep, I'll come into your room and put my head on your lap."

John blushes.

Charles meets them at the driveway. "Gauthier, it's a beautiful day. Go to Providence and go to a movie. I hear *The Jazz Singer* is in town. You can take

Audrey's sister, Charlotte. Take a horse. You'll get there in two hours, plenty of time. Stay overnight in a hotel. Audrey and I can do the milkin's tonight and tomorra morning."

"Audrey just said that an hour ago. You two think alike. Sounds good, but not this week, maybe next week."

"Could be a storm next weekend. Gotta go when the weather's good."

"I milk faster than you anyway," Audrey says to John.

"In your dreams. I can milk faster than you with one arm tied behind my back." He grins.

"In your dreams, John Gauthier," she says.

"Why don't you two go?" John says.

Charles shakes his head no. "I'm gonna make a management decision, Gauthier, since I'm the big boss, just like John D. Rockefeller. You're going to town and to a movie. And if you're gonna make the two o'clock show, you gotta leave now. I command it." He hands Gauthier a dollar bill. "And the popcorn's on me, Charles Rockefeller Doty."

"I can't take your money," John says.

"Consider it payment toward my loan." Both men smile.

"What loan?" Audrey says.

"No loan, That was a joke," Charles says.

John hands the dollar back to Charles. "Thanks, but no thanks."

"You're one boring son of a bitch. What are you gonna do, read?" Charles says.

"Probably."

Charles shakes his head, smiles, and pushes John toward the house. "Let's have lunch. You can do that, right?"

"I think so."

"Good. Next week, you goin' to a movie, whether you want to or not."

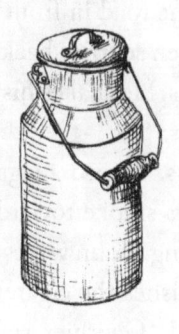

Chapter 9

*December 1928
Doty Farm, East Providence, Vermont*

Charles and John load twenty-six milk cans onto the big sleigh, then Charles hitches four horses to the front. He checks his pocket watch. "We should get to town by eleven. I want you to come with me," he says.

"Why?"

"Been thinkin'. You're probably right about the icebox. Gotta get Audrey somethin' nice. Haven't done that since we got married."

"You don't need me."

"Yes, I do. I'm the one who bought the icebox, remember? And I need your help with Audrey's grocery list. She wants to make you Indian food for Christmas. It's gonna be a surprise, so you don't know nothin'." He hands John Audrey's list.

John reads the list out loud. "I hope Audrey won't be disappointed, but I doubt Providence stores have these spices."

"You'd be surprised. Providence ain't as much of a hick town as you think it is."

John smiles. "Oh yes, it is."

The snow on the road is hard-packed, and the travel is fairly easy for December. Charles checks his watch and nods approval. Two miles from the farm, a bobcat scampers into the road in front of the sleigh, stops and looks at the men for a second, and then scurries back to the woods. "I'm gonna kill that son of a bitch," Charles says. He shakes his fist. A week ago, a bobcat had killed one of the three barn cats.

Charles hands John the reins. "I need a cigarette," he says. He offers one to John, who says no. He blows smoke toward John. "Nothin' better than a warm cigarette on a cold morning." John waves the smoke away from his face and coughs. When Charles finishes the cigarette, he lights a second from it and flicks the butt into the road. "Gauthier, you need a life beyond the farm. You been here since August, and you never leave—ever. You get two days off a week, but all you do is read and write. Go to Providence. It's only seven miles away—two hours and a half if you take the small sleigh, less if you ride one of the horses. Are you afraid of horses, Gauthier?"

"No, I'm rich, remember—or at least my parents are rich. Rich people ride horses."

"Then go. You need friends. You need a woman. I'll pay for a hotel room."

"I don't need friends and I sure as hell don't need a woman, they're just trouble."

"True, but you need one anyway."

. . .

Providence is crowded with shoppers, and the traffic on Main Street is barely moving. There are ten cars to every wagon and sleigh. A thirty-foot Christmas tree is in Depot Square and all the telephone poles on Main Street are decorated with six-foot-long, plywood candy canes. A Salvation Army bell ringer is in front of the Providence Bank and Trust, blowing warm air on his cold hands. The driver in the car behind Charles's sleigh blares his horn at a pedestrian who is crossing the road between his car and the sleigh. "Get out of the road, you stupid idiot, you got a death wish?" the driver yells at the man.

The walker pounds on the driver's hood. "Merry Christmas to you," he says.

"I hate cities. All that damn noise," Charles says.

John laughs. "This isn't city noise."

Charles ignores his comment. "What should I get her, Gauthier?"

"I don't know, whatever you want."

"I got no clue."

"Jewelry would work. Jewelry always works."

They deliver the milk to the creamery, and then drive to a livery barn. It is five blocks from the stable to the center of the downtown. A panhandler with urine-stained pants shoves his hat in front of the two men. "Please, mister, I'm hungry," he says.

Charles reaches in his pocket to retrieve a coin. "Don't give him anything. Don't even make eye contact," John says.

"Jesus, Gauthier, it's Christmas, have a heart." Charles hands the man a quarter, and three other men bump into each other as they present their hats to Charles.

"I told you so," John chuckles.

One of the men, the shortest of the three, says, "Listen, mister, give me a dime if I can tell you where you got them shoes?" He points to Charles's boots.

"Okay, I'm game. Where did I get my boots?"

"You got them on your feet," the man says. He smiles and holds his hand out for the dime.

Charles flips the man a nickel. "You win."

A tall, thin man, twenty paces behind Charles and John, waves to them and yells, "John, Charles. John Gauthier, Charles Doty, wait up, It's me, Father LeFebvre." He vigorously shakes both their hands. "Merry Christmas. Surprised to see you in town, John, Audrey said you never go anywhere."

"Apparently, that's the general consensus."

"Hope to see you at Christmas Mass," LeFebvre says to Charles.

"I don't know, Father, someone's gotta stay home with the baby."

"Bring the baby," LeFebvre says.

"You don't want that, believe me," Charles says.

LeFebvre walks with them for two blocks to the steps of St. Anthony's church. "I'd like to chat some more, boys, but I've got to see what the Italian church is up to—no farmers here." He waits a few seconds for a reaction to his comment but neither Charles nor John responds. "By the way, Charles, has Audrey made any of the Indian dishes from the cookbook I gave her?"

"Not yet. It's a Christmas surprise for Gauthier." Charles shows him the shopping list.

"Sorry about that. I didn't mean to spill the beans."

"Not a problem. I already knew," Gauthier says.

LeFebvre tells them where to get the spices and says Merry Christmas a second time. "See you on Christmas Day," he says to John. "Remember, we need to talk about India. What an amazing place . . . I've got to get back there someday."

John nods. "Me too."

The bell above the door in the jewelry shop tinkles when John and Charles, both dressed in their work clothes, enter the store. There are display cases along both walls and in the center of the store. Charles grabs a glass figurine from the top of a display case.

"Please don't touch that," says one of the clerks who wears a white shirt, green bow tie, and matching green vest.

Charles gently replaces the figurine. "Sorry."

"She's got one in her hand," John says to the clerk, pointing to a large woman wearing a mink coat. "Is she better than us?"

The clerk sighs and blinks for a long beat before saying, "She's going to buy one."

"How do you know we're not going to buy something?" John says.

The store owner, who was waiting on another customer, walks over toward Charles. "Can I help you two gentlemen?" he asks.

"Mr. Doty here wants to buy his wife a fine piece of jewelry. Might be the biggest sale of your day. Don't let these farm clothes fool you," John says.

"I can help you in one minute," the store owner says. He returns to his customer, sells her a man's watch, and steps back to them.

Charles points to a large, red glass brooch with a small diamond in the center and taps the top of the display case. The brooch is the size of John's fist. John grabs Charles's hand and pulls it from the glass. "No, absolutely not," he says and shakes his head.

"It's big and beautiful," Charles says.

"It is big, that's for sure," John says.

Charles selects six other brooches. John shakes his head at each one. "If I were you, I'd get her this jade necklace. It matches her earrings." He taps the case.

"Good choice, it's very beautiful," the store owner says.

"It's twenty-two dollars, Gauthier, a week's salary. Are you crazy?"

"Worth every penny," John says.

"I agree," the store owner says. He wraps the gift for Charles.

"The wife better like it, 'cause that sure were a lot of money for a frickin' necklace."

"She will," John says.

On their way back to the livery stable, John stops at a bookstore. "I need to get a few books."

"Big surprise. If I had a buck for every book you read, I'd be rich."

John selects *An American Tragedy*, *The Great Gatsby*, and six other books. He grabs copies of the *Providence Herald* and *Time* and hands Charles *The Portrait of A Lady*. "Here, wrap this when you get home and give it to Audrey with the necklace for Christmas."

"From you?"

"No, from you."

"Don't be stupid, Gauthier. She'd know it were from you." He hands the book back to John.

"I'm going to wrap it up, and I'm going to put your name on it," John says.

"You're stubborn for a little guy."

"You're stubborn for a big guy."

Three blocks from the livery stable, the man who had challenged Charles three hours earlier, yells, "Hey, mister, you got them shoes on your feet," and gives Charles a thumbs-up. Charles waves back to him.

The temperature has dropped considerably from this morning, and the trip back to the farm is cold, windy, and snowy. Charles grabs a blanket from the back of the sleigh and hands it to John. "If the snow gets too bad, bury your head in this."

"What about you?" John says.

"I'll be fine. I'm used to the cold, you're not."

"Yes, I am."

"You bitch every goddamn day." He shields his eyes from the snow. "Gauthier, there's somethin' I got to tell you, and you can't never repeat it."

"Is it something I want to hear?"

"Probably not, but you're gonna hear it anyway." He pauses, takes a deep breath, and stops the sleigh. "Little John ain't our first baby. Two years ago, we had another baby. She lived only three hours. She's buried in East Providence cemetery next to my mom. Audrey was holding her when she died. 'She can't be dead,' she screamed over and over. Her cries were awful. I didn't know what to do, I felt helpless. I tried to hug her, but she pushed me away. She didn't talk to me for a month, and then when she did, she acted like nothin'd happened, like we never had a baby, like she weren't never pregnant. She wouldn't sleep with me until I burned the bed and the mattress and the frame and the box springs."

"Why did you tell me this?"

"In case you're with her alone and she cries for no reason. She does that sometimes. It won't be your fault if she does. Some days she chops onions just so I won't know she's crying. When she cries, I don't know what to do. I'll never know what to do. That's why she goes to church. She'd go every day if it weren't so far."

"Why the Catholic Church?"

"I don't know why. It's just mumbo jumbo to me. I went to Mass with her the first year. All that Latin nonsense, no idea what they were talking about. Total gibberish."

"Good to know," John says. A blast of snow slaps his face. "I think I'll hide under the blanket."

"I knew you couldn't handle the cold."

"Nice and warm under this blanket. Too bad for you, sucker." He falls asleep and nearly tumbles off the sleigh.

Charles grabs him. "I just saved your life." He laughs.

"I owe you one," John says, and he tosses the blanket to the back of the sleigh. Snow blows in his face. "I can take it. I'm Vermont tough."

"Sure, and I'm the pope." He grabs the blanket and hands it back to John. "Here, put this over your head. I'm sick of looking at you."

Chapter 10

December 1928
Doty Farm, East Providence, Vermont

By the time the sleigh enters the driveway, Charles and John are coated with ice, even though the snowstorm had stopped two miles before. The ice on John's glasses is so thick he can barely see the house. He removes his gloves and melts the ice with his thumbs. When they are thirty yards from the front porch, Audrey waves to them, a big, bold, both-hands-over-her-head wave. The golden retriever is leaning its head against her legs, and Audrey's sister Charlotte is standing next to her, holding Little John.

The baby, wrapped in a blue wool blanket, is sucking on Charlotte's thumb. Charlotte is several inches taller than Audrey, but otherwise, she could be her taller twin. She has the same piercing blue eyes, the same seductive smile, the same long, red hair, the same freckles, and the same dimple—but on her left cheek. Charles stops the sleigh. "Oh shit, I was afraid of this. Gotta warn ya, Gauthier, Audrey's gonna try to set you up with her sister. She thinks you'd be the perfect husband. God knows why."

"I wouldn't be the perfect husband for anybody."

"No shit." Charles snaps the reins to tell the horses to proceed.

"Welcome back," Audrey says. John jumps to the ground and joins the two women. Audrey grabs his left arm and pulls him toward her. Her breath smells like rum. "John, this is my sister Charlotte. I've told you about her. She's staying with us until New Year's."

Charlotte timidly waves to him. He waves back.

"Gauthier would love to chat with you ladies, but we gotta unhitch the horses and milk the cows. The girls can't wait," Charles says. He points to the barn. John doesn't move. "Get in the barn before I fire your sorry ass."

. . .

The cows are restless. The men are an hour later than usual. They wash and lubricate their hands, then John walks to Cow One. Charles follows him and sets his stool at stanchion two. "We're gonna milk side by side today. I get ta tell you what's up."

"Is it bad?"

"No, not bad, you just need to be warned, that's all." Charles places his bucket under his cow, and then grabs a teat and squeezes a splat of milk to the ground. "Charlotte is Audrey's older sister. She's twenty-eight, maybe twenty-nine, not sure. When she were nineteen she were engaged to be married, but her boyfriend went off to war a month before the wedding. When he came home he were a different person. He was the nicest boy in the world before he left, but the war made him mean. Charlotte wanted to marry him anyway, but her father said, 'He's a nasty son of a bitch, you'll marry him over my dead body.' Charlotte and the boy, Ted Stevens, were set to run away but Charlotte's father caught them and tried to drag her back to the house.

"Ted grabbed him and beat him up, bad. He broke her dad's jaw and nose and cracked several of his ribs. Ted went to prison for fourteen months, and when he got out he just upped and left without a word to nobody. Not sure where he is now. Last I heard, he was in northern Maine, logging with a bunch of Frenchies from Quebec. She hasn't found anybody since, least not that I know of. Audrey figures you're Charlotte's last chance."

"Last chance, great. Just above a bum?"

"I didn't mean it like that. Audrey thinks high of you, in case you ain't noticed." They finish milking their cows and move to the next two cows.

"Charlotte is gonna sleep in the bedroom next to yours. There's a door between the rooms but no lock. Audrey is hoping one night you'll open that door and fall in love," Charles says.

"That's not going to happen."

"Well, if it does, just keep the damn noise down, I don't want to hear ya." He places his hands over his ears and shakes his head three times.

. . .

Audrey and Charlotte have spent most of the afternoon cooking a large meal for the men. There is chicken with potatoes, turnips, beets, pickled green beans, freshly baked bread, chocolate cake with chocolate frosting, and an apple pie. Audrey made eggnog with rum. She and Charlotte drank several glasses while they cooked. A nearly empty rum bottle is on the counter next to the kitchen sink. "We figured you two would be pretty hungry after your long trip," Audrey says when the men enter the house. She tries hard not to slur her words but fails.

"I second that," Charlotte says. She speaks slowly, with a pause after each word. She salutes the men.

"You're right. We didn't have time for lunch. I could eat a horse," Charles says.

"We don't have horse, just chicken," Charlotte titters.

"John, you must be famished," Audrey says.

John removes his fogged glasses and wipes the lenses dry with his shirt.

Audrey points to the table. "Let's sit, everything's ready." Little John is asleep in a crib next to the table. She gently rocks the crib with her right knee. "So, did you have a good trip, sell all of our milk?" She leans toward the crib and wipes spittle from Little John's chin. "Do you ever spit up your food?" she asks John. She and Charlotte laugh as if Audrey had just told the funniest joke they ever heard.

"Not usually." His comment makes the women laugh even harder.

"Looks like the rum's kicked in," Charles says to John. He plops three scoops of mashed potato onto John's plate. "Eat, Gauthier, you're too damn skinny."

"No, he's not, he's just right," Charlotte says. More chortles from her and Audrey.

"I think I need to hide the rum," Charles says.

"You can hide it in my room," John says. He grabs the bottle and pretends to walk to his room.

"Not so fast," Charles says. He grabs the bottle from John and smiles.

"My parents are coming on Christmas Eve and they're going to stay overnight. They want to see Little John's first Christmas," Audrey says.

"What a coincidence—my parents are coming too. The house will be very crowded," Charlotte says and laughs so hard she spits food from her mouth.

"Can't wait," Charles says.

. . .

Little John has been crying for two hours straight. Audrey and Charles have taken turns walking him through the house, from their bedroom to the living room and back, but without success. There is a light tap on John's door. "John, it's me, Charlotte. Can I come in? I can't sleep." She sits on his bed wearing a pink nightgown, the outline of her breast visible through the cloth. "How do you sleep through all this noise?"

"You get used to it."

"I want to apologize for this afternoon."

"Nothing to apologize for."

"Yes, there is. I was a bit drunk."

"Really? I didn't notice." They both smile.

"Charles probably told you about Audrey's grand scheme?"

"He did."

"I had nothing to do with it. In fact, I didn't know about it until I got here."

"I didn't think you did."

"Sometimes my sister drives me nuts. When she gets a plan in her head, she doesn't quit, even if the plan makes no sense."

"Planning never works."

"No, it doesn't." She taps his thigh. "She told me about the girl from India. Sounds sad."

"It was, very sad. Charles told me about your fiancé. That must have been awful."

"Yes, it was. Even if he was the right boy for me, we were way too young. We were only nineteen. That's crazy."

"Still, it must have been hard," John says.

"It was hard. But I'm happy now by myself. I have an apartment in Providence, and I'm a secretary for the vice president of the Providence Bank and Trust. I've got a good life. I pay my bills. I'm independent. I'm not looking for anyone."

"I'm not either."

"Didn't think you were. Audrey's never been alone. She was a junior in high school when she got engaged. She married Charles three weeks after she graduated. He's the only man she's ever known. She never had a boyfriend before him." Little John stops crying. "Hurray, it's over!"

"Not yet. Give him ten minutes and he'll be back, stronger than ever."

"This is going to be a very long two weeks."

"Yes, it is."

"In case you haven't noticed, Audrey's in love with you."

"She is not."

"John, are you blind? Are you in love with her?"

"No, of course not."

"Good. Otherwise, you'd have to leave."

"What does Charles think?"

"What he thinks is, Audrey is happy for the first time in four years."

"Since the death of her baby?"

"Yes, since the death of her babies."

"Charles said just one."

"I'm not surprised. He took the deaths as hard as she did. The first was a miscarriage, four years ago. He's blocked that out as if it never happened. Two years ago, their baby girl lived three hours. Audrey was holding her when she died. The little girl was as tiny as a kitten. I was at the hospital with them. We all cried—even the midwife cried. The next day Charles made a small coffin. He wanted to take the baby to the family plot in East Providence, but Audrey said no, she wanted Father LeFebvre to bless the baby before the burial. Do you know him?"

"I do."

"He's a good man. He helped her as much as anyone could, but it wasn't enough. For the past two years, she's been walking dead, barely living. I don't know what you've done, John, but she's alive again."

"I haven't done anything."

"Keep doing nothing, it's working." She grabs his right hand, kisses it, and places it on her breast. "If you decide to come through that door one of these nights, that would be fine with me."

"I might just do that."

"But not tonight."

"No, not tonight."

She rises from the bed and walks toward her room. "Make sure you knock first."

"I will."

"I'm not looking for love."

"I'm not either."

Chapter 11

May 1962
Sacred Heart Parish, Providence, Vermont

"What do you think, Patrick? Did you like the book?" Monsignor Gauthier asks. He reaches across his desk, grabs the paperback from Patrick, scans the cover, and places it on the desktop.

Patrick nods. "I liked it a lot. I read it in three days."

"What did you like about it?" Gauthier says. He drinks rum from a shot glass with one ice cube in it. The opened rum bottle is next to the typewriter. He holds a pipe in his left hand and the smoke smells like cinnamon and vanilla. Beethoven's Eroica Symphony is playing quietly in the background. He leans back in his chair and lifts his feet on to the top of the desk.

"I liked that Gene and Finny were friends even though they were so different," Patrick says.

"What about when Finny fell from the tree—was Gene to blame?"

"I think so."

"Why?"

"He shook the branch."

"Did he do that on purpose?"

"I think he did it on purpose because he was jealous. He felt terrible about what he did, but it was too late."

"Friendship is complicated." Monsignor Gauthier stands up from his chair, grabs the book from the desk, steps to the bookcase, and places it on the shelf. Patrick starts to leave the room. "Don't go yet." He searches the shelves, grabs a different book, and hands it to Patrick. "I want you to read this next—*Island of the Blue Dolphins*."

"What's it about?"

"It's the story of a young girl, just about your age, named Karana, who is stranded alone for years on an island off the California coast. It takes place in the 1800s. It's based on a true story."

Patrick tries to stuff the book into his back pocket, but it is too big. "Don't do that, Patrick, you'll break the binding." He shakes his head. "I'll give you five weeks this time. That will be the last week of school for this year." He scribbles a note and hands it to Patrick. "Give this to Sister Ryan." He refills his shot glass. "One more thing. I have an assignment for you. I want you to write a description of your living room. When I read it, I should be able to picture exactly what that room looks like. I want you to write one page—five hundred words or so. Can you do that? And print, don't use cursive."

"I think so. Why?"

"No reason. Just curious about how you write." He lifts a yellow legal pad from the bottom desk drawer and hands it to Patrick.

Patrick runs across the parking lot from the rectory to the school. The pavement is slippery from last night's rain. He trips on the curb in front of the school and tumbles face-first to the sidewalk. The paperback, the yellow pad, and the note to Sister Ryan fly from his hands and land in a deep puddle. "Damn, damn, damn," he says out loud. His hands are scraped, and his chin is bruised. He gets up, wipes the blood from his face with his jacket sleeve, and grabs the book, the note, and the yellow pad from the puddle. The book is soaked from cover to cover.

"Patrick, what happened to you?" Father Symanski says. He is standing in the doorway of the school, his right leg in the building and his left leg outside of the door.

"I tripped and fell down."

"I can see that," Symanski says. He pulls a handkerchief from his coat pocket, steps to Patrick, and wipes Patrick's chin. "Why aren't you in class?"

"I was with Monsignor Gauthier."

"I doubt that."

"I have a note." He hands the note to Symanksi, but the ink has run and the note is impossible to read.

"Good try, Mr. Colman."

"I'm telling the truth."

"We'll see about that." Symanski grabs Patrick's right shoulder and pulls him across the parking lot to the rectory. "Monsignor Gauthier, I have a young man here who says he was with you this morning."

"He was. What happened?"

"I tripped. I ruined your book." He holds up the waterlogged book and legal pad.

"Father Symanski, please go into the bathroom and bring back a wet washcloth—and grab a Band-Aid from behind the mirror," Gauthier says. He grabs the book and tries to flip through the pages, but they are stuck together in a wet lump. "You're right, the book is ruined," he says. He grabs the wet legal pad and throws both the book and pad into the wastebasket under the desk.

"I didn't mean to, Father, it was an accident."

"I'm sure it was. You are one clumsy son of a gun."

Symanski returns with the wet washcloth. Gauthier grabs it from him, wipes the dirt and dried blood off Patrick's face, and places the Band-Aid on the cut. The skin around Patrick's eyes is still slightly dark from when he hit the cement post with his sled two weeks ago.

"I'll get you another copy today. If I do, can you keep it out of a puddle?"

"Yes, Father. I think so."

"I'll leave the book with Sister Ryan." He reaches into the desk drawer, grabs another legal pad, hands it to Patrick, and waves him and Symanski away. Then he steps to the bookshelf, pulls *Fathers and Sons* from the shelf, turns up the volume on the stereo, sits in the recliner, and opens the book. Patrick leaves the building, but Symanski is still in the room. "Is there something I can help you with, Amand?" Gauthier says.

"Yes."

Gauthier cannot hear Symanski. He stands up from the recliner and turns the stereo volume down. "What do you want, Amand?"

"I am a bit concerned."

"About what?"

"You spend a lot of time with Mr. Colman. Are you sure that's a good idea?"

"What are you implying?"

"Nothing. Just that you shouldn't treat one boy differently than anyone else."

"I don't."

"Why did you give him that book?"

"Why not? It's a great book."

"That's beside the point."

"No, that is the point. The boy's a good writer, much better than any other kid in the school. Best writer we've ever had at this school, at least since I've been here. I read his essay for the seventh grade contest. How come he didn't win? You were one of the judges."

"It wasn't the best essay. Not even in the top five."

"Are you kidding me? None of the others were even close. I read them all, and most of them were terrible."

"He obviously had help. I wasn't going to reward him for cheating."

"You don't know that."

"Yes, I do, Sister Ryan said he cheated."

"What does she know?"

"She's his teacher, you're not. He's a B-minus student at best. Half the class gets better grades than he does. Sister Ryan says he barely tries."

"So let me get this straight—he lost the essay contest because he doesn't try hard enough in class and because he's a B-minus student. Is that about right?"

"Whatever you say." Symanski bites his lower lip.

Gauthier holds *Fathers and Sons* up to Symanski. "Ever read this book? I first read it when I was in college. It's brilliant."

"No, John, I haven't. Unlike you, I don't have time to read novels."

"You should make time."

"I read plenty."

"I know, I've seen your books. How many interpretations of the Gospels can you read? Doesn't that get a bit repetitious?"

"Never."

"Good for you. I wish I had your zeal. I had it once, I really did. Maybe I'll get it back, who knows."

"We can only hope."

"Don't hold your breath." He waves Symanski away, turns up the volume on the stereo, sits in the recliner, drinks a shot of rum, and opens his book. He is asleep in ten minutes.

Chapter 12

June 1962
Sacred Heart Parish, Providence, Vermont

Father Symanski paces the front of the classroom. He is wearing jeans and a light blue polo shirt, which is unusual for him. He stops under the flag mounted at the edge of the blackboard, sighs, and turns to face the thirteen altar boys sitting at the desks. Each boy has a copy of the St. Joseph Daily Missal opened to the chapter, "The Ordinary of the Mass." He coughs twice and dabs his lips with a handkerchief. He focuses his gaze on Patrick Colman. "Mr. Colman, what do you say when the priest says, 'Introibo ad altare Dei?'"

"Um . . ." Patrick says, looking at his desk as he speaks.

"Stand up, Mr. Colman."

Patrick stands.

"Stand up straight Mr. Colman."

Patrick rolls his shoulders and arches his back.

"Introibo ad altare Dei?" Symanski says. He glares at Patrick.

"Um . . ."

"You don't know your response, do you, Patrick?"

"Yes, I do, Father." He glances at his prayer book.

"Close the book." Symanski walks to Patrick, closes the book for him, and says, "Introibo ad altare Dei?"

"Key fee ... set ... column ... a ... train ... um," Colman says. He pauses between each word. His arms twitch as he speaks.

"No, that is not correct. That's not even Latin, it's gibberish. The correct answer is: 'Ad Deum qui laetificat juventutem meam.' When the priest says, 'Introibo ad altare Dei,' 'I will go to the altar of God,' the altar boys say, 'Ad Deum qui laetificat juventutem meam,' 'the God of my gladness and joy.' Your answer makes no sense."

Monsignor Gauthier, who has been in the hallway for the past fifteen minutes listening to Symanski lecture the boys, walks into the room. "Not the correct answer, Patrick, but not a bad answer, 'Qui fecit coelum et terram,' 'who made heaven and earth.' God did in fact make heaven and earth."

"The boys need to answer correctly," Symanski says.

"True, but if they said, 'ahmadee domadee do' for every response, no one would know it was wrong, or care." The boys laugh. "Don't laugh, boys, it's not funny." He chuckles.

Father Symanski shakes his head. "They need to answer correctly. They must memorize the text as it is written. The Mass is a sacred institution. An incorrect answer is an insult to God."

Gauthier smiles. "Father Symanski, I need Mr. Colman. I have a job for him."

Symanski waves Patrick away, turns his back to Gauthier, and grinds his teeth.

. . .

"I knew the answer, I just panicked," Patrick says to Monsignor Gauthier as they walk across the parking lot to the rectory.

Gauthier taps Patrick's shoulder. "I'm sure you did."

Gauthier's office smells like cinnamon toast and coffee. He grabs the record *Carnival of Animals* from the shelf and places it on the turntable. "If any music is more beautiful than this, I haven't heard it." He sets the volume to low. He opens the top drawer of the desk and pulls out a yellow legal pad. "I read your description of your bedroom. Not bad, not bad at all."

"Thank you, Father."

"I do have one question. What exactly did you mean when you wrote, 'The brown rug was eroded'?"

"It's worn out. In some places, you can see the floorboards through the rug."

"Why didn't you say that? Why didn't you say the rug was so worn you can see the floorboards?"

"Eroded sounded smarter."

"Don't try to sound smart, be clear. The simpler the word, the better." He stands up, searches his bookshelves for a few seconds, and pulls out *To Kill a Mockingbird*. He reads the first paragraph. "*When he was nearly thirteen, my brother Jem got his arm badly broken at the elbow. When it healed, and Jem's fears of never being able to play football were assuaged, he was seldom self-conscious about his injury. His left arm was somewhat shorter than his right; when he stood or walked, the back of his hand was at right angles to his body, his thumb parallel to his thigh. He couldn't have cared less, so long as he could pass and punt.*" He closes the book and places it on the desk. "What do you think?"

"I don't know." Patrick shrugs his shoulders.

"Can you see what happened? Can you picture Jem's arms?"

"Yes."

"That's what you want from your writing. You want the reader to see it, to smell it, to feel it, to taste it. A worn-out rug is a better description than an eroded rug. I can see a threadbare rug worn through to the floorboards, but I can't picture an eroded rug, can you?"

"No, Father."

"What did you think of *Island of the Blue Dolphins*? You did read it?"

"Yes, Father."

"What did you think?"

"It was exciting. I couldn't have done it. I think I would have starved to death."

"It's based on a real story about the life of a young woman who spent eighteen years by herself on San Nicolas Island in the Pacific."

"Wow, she must have been incredible."

"I'm sure she was." He returns the book to the shelf and grabs a new book, *My Ántonia*. "Are you up for another book?"

"Yes, sir."

"This novel tells the story of Ántonia Shimerda, the daughter in a family of immigrants in Nebraska at the end of the nineteenth century." He reads the opening page out loud, closes the book, and hands it to Patrick. "If I could have written only one novel, this would be it. It's an adult book, but you can handle it."

"Thank you, Father."

"I'll give you six weeks this time." He checks his calendar. "Tuesday, July twenty-first, ten o'clock, here. Can you remember that?"

"Yes, sir."

"When I was your age I wouldn't have remembered. I'll tell you what, I'll make sure you serve Mass the Sunday before, and I'll remind you then." Patrick nods. "Do you want another writing assignment?"

"Sure."

"Let's see." He pauses and thinks. "Do you know how to fly a kite?"

"Yes, sir."

"Describe how to fly a kite to someone who has never flown one before and who doesn't even know what a kite is. Don't miss a single step. It will be harder than you think. Can you do that?"

"I don't know."

"Just do your best. If it isn't perfect, who cares."

Gauthier looks at his watch. "You'd better go back to your altar boy studies. If you're lucky, it will be over by now."

Patrick smiles. "If I'm lucky."

"See you in July."

"Yes, sir."

"One more thing. Last Friday, when you and Paul Fermonte were the altar boys at the Gallo funeral, you both smirked through half the service. That was rude, don't ever do that again."

"I'm sorry, Father, we didn't mean to be rude. We couldn't help it."

"Why not? It was a funeral—a very sad occasion."

"John Gallo was at the back of the church making faces at us. He stuck his thumbs in both his ears, waved his fingers, and stuck out his tongue, and then he carved something into the back pew with a jackknife."

"I wondered who did that. Oh well, try not to laugh next time."

"I'll try, Father."

"Six weeks. I'll see you in six weeks."

Patrick starts to leave the room without the book. "Forget something, Mr. Colman?"

. . .

A New England boiled dinner is bubbling on the stove. Agnes LeSalle, the housekeeper for the three priests, turns the burner control knob from high to simmer. She rips off a piece of corned beef with a fork and knife, shakes it cool, and takes a bite. She adds several dabs of pepper to the pan. The meal is already a half hour later than usual. "Forty more minutes," she says to Monsignor Gauthier when he enters the kitchen. Her voice cracks.

"Relax, we're in no rush." He touches her shoulder when he speaks. "Scrabble tonight?"

She nods.

Agnes prides herself on being on time and on pleasing Monsignor Gauthier. Thirteen years ago, when Gauthier was the new priest at Sacred Heart, her husband Richard died unexpectedly from a massive heart attack. He was fifty-eight. He had been a heavy drinker, a chain smoker, and a compulsive gambler. He had gambled away their retirement funds and all of their savings and had to double mortgage their house to pay his debts.

After he died, she learned they were six months behind on the first mortgage and he hadn't paid a single payment on the second mortgage. The bank gave her three months to leave the house. She complained to a lawyer, but he showed her proof that the bank had warned her husband several times and had completed the legal work necessary to take the house. She had had no idea. She asked her two children to help her, but they refused. She had borrowed money several times from them, and they were sick of it.

At her husband's funeral, she sobbed. Everyone thought she was crying for him, even though he had been a miserable a son of a bitch, but she was crying for herself: *Where will I go? What will I do?* She hadn't had a job since high school and had no marketable skills. One day in confession she broke down and told Monsignor Gauthier about her woeful life. He hired her right there in the confessional booth to be the housekeeper at the rectory and to live in the third-floor bedroom. The parish council was not happy. Housekeepers had never lived at the rectory before and, more importantly, he had not run his decision by them.

When the dinner is set, Agnes tinkles a bell and calls the three priests to the table. The three men eat together in the first-floor apartment Monday through Friday nights.

. . .

"Smells wonderful," Father Symanski says. He says the exact line every night.

"It does indeed," Father Cantone says.

Agnes has a seat at the table but rarely sits with them for more than a few minutes at a time. Instead, she spends most of the meal serving the food as if she were their waitress. Gauthier constantly tells her to join them but she rarely does.

Father Symanski holds up his wine glass. "To another fine day." He takes a sip and says grace. Gauthier and Cantone bow their heads and say "Amen" at the end of the prayer. The three priests clink their wine glasses together.

Gauthier swirls his glass, sniffs the wine, and takes a drink. "I agree. To another fine day."

Father Symanski clears his throat as if he were getting set to make a speech. "John, I'd appreciate it if you didn't interfere with my Latin study sessions with the altar boys." He had practiced what to say ever since Gauthier left his classroom. He had even practiced in front of a mirror.

"What did I do?"

"You made fun of me, that's what you did. 'Ahmadee domadee do.' Why did you say that nonsense?"

"I thought it was funny?"

"It wasn't."

"Sorry about that, won't happen again."

"That's what you said last time. I know you don't take any of this seriously, but I do. The Mass is a sacred institution, the most holy sacrament. It goes back to the third century. Think about that, nearly two thousand years of worship, unchanged, unchangeable, exactly the same all over the world."

"I get it. I know the Mass is sacred, but whether a bunch of fourteen-year-old boys do or don't pronounce the Latin words correctly really isn't very important to anybody, let alone to God."

"It *is* important. We honor God when we do it right. When you make fun of me it undermines my authority." Symanski considers storming out of the room but stays seated. He takes a deep breath and silently counts to ten. "I agree—whether the boys pronounce the words correctly is not important, but what is important is they must try. We earn grace by our efforts. When you mock the Latin, the boys get the message that there's no reason to try, it's all a joke."

"If that's the message I sent, I am truly sorry. That said, I don't think the altar boys will be speaking Latin much longer. Are you following what's going on in Rome? The Latin Mass could be history."

"Never! It will never happen. Latin is the language of God."

"I'm pretty sure Christ spoke Aramaic."

"Christ spoke Aramaic, but Latin is the language of the church and has been for two thousand years and will be for two thousand more."

"Whatever you say, Amand."

Father Symanski shakes his head and leaves the room.

"He'll get over it," John says to Father Cantone.

"He will, but maybe you shouldn't mock him so often. He bruises easily."

"You're right. I need to be a better man."

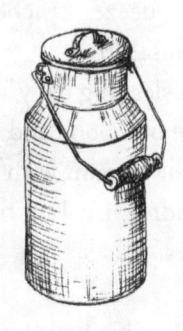

Chapter 13

December 1928
Doty Farm, East Providence, Vermont

J.ohn, Audrey, and Charlotte are decorating the Christmas tree. Charles is in the barn raking hay for the cows. Audrey grabs John's hands and places them on her sides. "Lift me up so I can put the star on the treetop," she says. He lifts her but not high enough—she still can't reach the top.

"I can't do it. I'm not strong enough."

"Are you saying I'm fat?"

"No, absolutely not."

"Relax, I was kidding," she says as she lightly swats the back of his head. She walks to the kitchen, carries a chair to the tree, and steps onto the seat. "Hold me so I don't fall into the tree. Can you do that?" She smiles, grabs his hands, and places them back on her hips. He clutches her dress when she leans toward the tree.

There is a knock at the front door. "Knock, knock, knock, we're heeeere," Audrey's mother, Claire, sings as she opens the door. Her husband, Tom, is behind her, carrying a tall stack of Christmas packages. He is having a hard time balancing the boxes and he has to squat to fit through the door. John rushes to him and grabs several boxes from the top of the pile.

"Where's that baby?" Claire squeals. She trots to the bedroom, grabs the sleeping baby, and kisses his face. "I love you, love you, love you, love you, you're so damn beautiful." She squeezes his cheek and nibbles his ear. Little John cries and tries to shake himself free.

"Mother, please, don't wake a sleeping baby," Audrey says. She grabs Little John from her, walks him to the bedroom, and places him back in the crib.

"He's my grandson, I'll do what I want with him."

The baby's cries continue. Audrey lifts him from the crib and feeds him.

"You must be John," Tom says.

"I am."

Tom places the packages still in his hands onto the floor and offers John his right hand. "I'm Tom, Tom Andrews." He crushes John's hand with his. He is nearly as big as Charles but has a flabby face, several chins and a big, pumpkin belly. "I've heard a lot about you."

"All good?" John says.

"Mostly," Tom says and grins.

Claire joins them. "You're not that skinny. Charles said you were as skinny as a stick. He's wrong." She removes her earmuffs, hat, and gloves and tosses them on the deacon's bench next to the front door.

"Thanks, I think," John says.

Claire and Tom remove their coats and take off their boots. "Tree looks nice. Could use a few more baubles on the window side. Too many on the top. I've seen better trees," Claire says, pointing to the tree. Audrey catches Charlotte's eyes. They both smile and lightly nod their heads in agreement. Claire steps closer to John, so close her breath warms his face. He considers moving away from her but stays put. "How come you're not with your own family? Christmas is family time. Don't you have a family? Don't you miss them? Are you Christian? You're not a Jew, are you?"

"No, I'm not a Jew."

"I'm sure Charles would have given you the week off. Why aren't you with your family?"

"It's a long story."

"We're his family this year," Charlotte says. She hugs her father. He rubs her hair as if she were a six-year-old.

"I hear you read a lot. We got you a book," Tom says to John.

"Jesus, Dad," Charlotte says, "that was supposed to be a surprise."

"When he sees the package, it will be pretty obvious what it is."

"That's not the point."

"I'm sure I'll love it. I'm sorry, but I didn't get you anything."

"We didn't expect you to. We want to hear about India, about that girl you almost married. That will be our gift. We want to hear all the gory details," Claire says.

"Mother!" says Audrey, who has returned from the baby's room. She stomps her right foot.

John glares at Audrey. "Not much to tell," he says.

"That's not what Audrey's been saying."

"She's wrong," John says.

Charles enters the house. "Gauthier, I need your help." He gives John a *Come here* finger curl. John grabs his hat, winter coat, and gloves and follows him to the barn. "What's up?"

"Nothing. Thought I'd save you from two hours of annoying chatter. Audrey's mother never shuts up. Too bad her jaw weren't held together with a bolt. If it was, I'd get a wrench and tighten it so hard she wouldn't be able to open her mouth."

"She seems fine."

"Give her time."

Charles hands John a pitchfork and points to the hayloft. "We need more hay." John climbs to the loft and drops several bales to the floor of the barn. One bale just misses hitting Charles. "You tryin' to kill me?" Charles says. He gives John a fake surprised look.

"Yes, that's part of my nefarious plan to take over your farm."

"You can have it—ain't worth a bucket of warm spit. But a hay bale won't do it, just make me mad. Next time throw the pitchfork. Make sure you get my neck."

"Got it, pitchfork to the neck and the farm is mine."

"By tomorrow you're gonna want a pitchfork in your neck, believe me. Twenty-four hours with Claire and you'll want to kill yourself. I know I will."

"Is she mean?"

"She ain't mean, at least not mean to me. But Audrey can't do nothin' right. Last year, when I were hiding in the barn avoidin' talking to her parents, Audrey came in spitting-blood mad. I said, 'Go back to the house, be with your family.' 'I'm not going back in there,' she said. She'd spent six hours cooking our Christmas dinner. She'd gotten up at five in the morning. We had a twenty-four-pound turkey. Claire followed her through the kitchen, watching her every move and telling her what she'd done wrong. 'The potatoes are lumpy,' she said. 'The squash needs more salt.' When Audrey turned her back, Claire salted the squash.

"The topper was when Audrey was in the barn helpin' me milk the cow. Claire scooped the dressing out of the turkey and replaced it with her own dressing. She hid Audrey's dressing at the bottom of the garbage can, under all the other trash. I didn't know what she'd done. At dinner, I said, 'Audrey, this is the best dressing you've ever made. You should give your mom the recipe.' Audrey didn't say nothing, but if looks could kill, I'd be a dead man and you'd be milkin' the cows by yourself. She didn't tell me what her mother'd done until we were in bed. When she told me, she hit my shoulder, bam, bam, bam, over and over—hard, real hard. By the time she were done complaining, my left shoulder were real sore. I could hardly move it."

John smiles.

"It weren't funny. My shoulder were so sore the next day I could barely raise my arm over my head. You try milkin' cows with a sore shoulder. Ain't easy." He tosses the last of the hay to the cows. "Claire wanted to come here after Little John was born, but I said no way. Audrey was furious with me. Last summer, Claire stayed for two weeks, just before you got here. She wouldn't let me smoke in the house. She made me take my shoes off ever' damn time I came in, even if I was just coming in to get something. Drove me nuts."

"My mother's pretty much the same. The only difference is she uses rich person talk. She cuts me down at my knees, but she's polite about it. When I brought my first girlfriend home from college, she said, 'She's a very nice girl for an Italian.' She sent me a letter last week. 'Are you sure working as a farmhand in Vermont is a wise choice for your life? You could do so much better. I hear the winters are very challenging.' That's rich-people talk for stop wasting your damn life in that backwater icebox. She thinks Vermont's at the ass-end of the world."

"It is," Charles says. He looks around the barn and checks his watch. "We done everything we need to do here. What we gonna do for the next hour?"

"We could go back inside the house?"

"You go. I'll stay here."

John hangs his rake on the wall, washes his hands, knocks manure off his boots, and walks toward the barn entrance.

"One more thing, Gauthier, whatever you do, don't mention Christmas Mass. Audrey's parents are Methodists, Methodists to the bone. When she switched, they were furious. They didn't dare say nothin' cause Audrey had just lost the baby, but they weren't happy, that's for damn sure. Still ain't."

"Why would I mention Christmas Mass?"

"Cause you're taking Audrey tomorrow morning. Better you than me, Gauthier. Besides, I hear the old ladies at the church are in love with you."

"Lucky me. Maybe I'll marry one of them."

"I'll be your best man, you and me and your eighty-year-old wife."

"Does she have teeth?"

"Not real ones."

. . .

The Christmas tree is so fat it is difficult to walk through the living room. The dog is sleeping in the middle of the room in front of the tree, his body twitching in a bad dream. Two of the three house cats are sleeping on packages under the tree, and the third cat is watching everyone from the shelf above the dish cabinet in the kitchen. This cat is angry that the tree is in the house. He tried to knock it down several times before Audrey hit him with the broom. Tom and Claire are asleep on the couch. Tom's left nostril wobbles as he snores. Claire's knitting needles and yarn are clutched in her hands. Charlotte and Audrey are cleaning the kitchen, and John and Charles are in the barn milking the cows.

"So what do you think, do I give the wife the icebox or not?" Charles says. The icebox is hidden under a pile of hay.

"I'm pretty sure she knows it's coming, so yes," John says.

"She don't know, no way."

"Think about it, Charles, there's a five-foot mountain of hay in the middle of the milk room. That doesn't make any sense. You don't leave a pile of hay for weeks sitting on the barn floor."

"Didn't think of that."

"She probably knows she's getting the icebox, but what she doesn't know is she's getting a jade necklace. Put the necklace inside the icebox."

"You're a genius," Charles says. He hugs John.

The two men clear the hay from around the icebox, and Charles polishes the metal with a rag. "That should do it." He retrieves the gift box from an empty milk jug, tosses it into the icebox, grabs the top of the refrigerator, and tilts it to carry it. "Gauthier, grab the bottom end."

"Christmas is tomorrow."

"We open one gift tonight. This will be Audrey's Christmas Eve gift."

John lifts the bottom. "Damn, this is heavy. Must weigh two hundred pounds."

"Stop whining. I carried it in here by myself."

"Do you have a handcart, Charles Atlas?"

Charles nods and flexes his arm muscles. "Charles Atlas ain't got nothing on me." He retrieves the handcart from the closet at the back of the barn. "Happy now?"

"Yes, sir, Mr. Atlas, sir." He salutes Charles.

Charles wheels the icebox to the barn door. The path from the barn to the front porch is thick mud. It's been raining for the past hour. "Help me, Don't just stand there like a dumbass," Charles says. It is a struggle for the two men to push the icebox across the soggy driveway.

"Doesn't make any sense. Got two feet of snow on Thanksgiving, and now it's pouring rain," John says.

"Last I knew, when it pours, it always pours rain, never nothing else," Charles says and chuckles. "This is Vermont, Gauthier, get used to it. The weather changes every day, sometimes twice a day. Tomorrow it might be twenty below zero and the ground will be solid ice. Last November, it rained for three weeks straight. Providence was six feet underwater. The East Crick bridge washed out, and I couldn't get my milk to the dairy for over a month. I'd rather have frozen ground than mud, that's for sure."

Audrey has placed several saucepans on the floor in the kitchen and living room to collect the water dripping from the leaky ceiling. The drops, pinging against the metal, wake Tom. "What time is it? Is it Christmas morning?" He has spittle on his chin.

"No, Dad, it's only eight o'clock. Still Christmas Eve," Audrey says.

"I must have dozed off for a couple of minutes."

"More like two hours, Dad," Charlotte says. She pokes Audrey's arm. Both women smile.

Charles rattles the door and opens it. "Coming through." He wheels the icebox to the kitchen and removes it from the handcart. "Merry Christmas!w What do you think, Audrey?"

"I think you're tracking mud all over the floor."

The commotion wakes Claire. "What's going on?"

John wipes raindrops and fog from his glasses with his shirt.

"It's top of the line," Charles says.

"That would be an electric refrigerator," Claire says. "We got one last month."

"Well, good for you," Charles says. He starts to open the icebox door but shuts it. "Audrey, open the door, there's sumthin' in there you'll like."

She opens the door and grabs the package. "What is this?"

"What do you think it is? It's a Christmas present."

She opens the package and throws the wrapping paper onto the kitchen table. "Oh my goodness, Charles, this necklace is beautiful." She hugs him.

"How much did that necklace cost? What, are you rolling in dough?" Claire says to Charles.

"Oh, Mother, it's beautiful," Audrey says. She hugs Charles again.

The angry cat drops an almost dead mouse next to the Christmas packages and runs off to the bedrooms. The mouse is alive but can't move—its neck is broken. Audrey sweeps it up with a dustpan and throws it out the front door. "I guess that's a message from kitty. Time to open our Christmas Eve gifts."

Claire hands John his gift. "You first. You're our guest."

He opens the book and scans the first page. *"Mother India*, thank you."

"We thought you'd like it, thought it would remind you of India. You haven't read it already? If you have, I'm sure the bookstore will exchange it," Claire says.

"No, I don't have it and I haven't read it. I've heard of it. It sounds like a very interesting book, for sure."

The heat from the wood stove is too high. Charles opens the front door. "Dammit, it's hot in here." He removes his sweater and shirt and tosses them on the couch. His undershirt is stained with sweat. After the gifts have been opened, Audrey pours eggnog for everyone. "I'll have my rum straight," Charles says. He retrieves a rum bottle from the kitchen and pours two shots into a glass.

"Same for me," Tom says.

"How about you, John, are you going to join the big, burly men and drink your rum straight?" Audrey says.

"I think I'll pass."

"Not gonna happen, Gauthier," Charles says. He pours John a two-shot drink. "Drink up, it's Christmas Eve."

John shakes his head.

"Who's the boss here, Gauthier?"

John swallows the rum in two gulps and grimaces. He holds up his empty glass. "Merry Christmas to my new family."

. . .

John's head is spinning. He drank three double shots. Charlotte raps lightly on his door and walks into the bedroom before he says anything.

"You don't look too good."

"I don't feel so hot."

"Are you going to throw up?"

He pukes into a wastebasket. "Yes."

She scrapes puke off the rim of his nose and flicks it to the floor. "You picked out the jade necklace."

"I did not."

"There's no way Charles bought it. I love Charles dearly, I really do, but, John, please."

"Maybe I did, so what?"

"My parents like you."

"I like them."

"They like you because they know you're rich."

"Good reason as any."

"They don't know why you're here."

"I don't either. When I do, I'll let them know."

John sprints to the bathroom, throws up in the toilet again, and returns. His legs are wobbly. "You're still here?"

"I am." She is sitting on the bed, her back against the headboard, her knees tucked to her chin, and she is holding her ankles. John sits next to her. She points to his chin to let him know he has a glob of vomit on it.

"You must think I'm a loser," he says, wiping away the dried puke.

"No, I think you're a man who doesn't drink much."

"I don't."

"How long do you think you'll stay?"

"A year, maybe two, I'm not really sure. Why?"

"Just wondering." She slips down the bed and lies flat on the mattress. Her nightgown clings to her body. "When Audrey and I were young girls, our dad was a farmhand like you. He'd leave the house at four thirty in the morning and get home at eight or nine at night. I never saw him, barely knew who he was. He was home on the weekends, but he spent most of the time sleeping. Finally, Mom told him he had to get a new job. But there weren't any jobs, at least not in East Providence. He got a job at Jefferson Iron Works in Providence. His hours were basically the same. It took him two hours to get to town and two hours back. He was gone from five in the morning until seven at night or later. So, we moved to Providence, into a five-room apartment above an Italian bakery. We woke up every morning to the smell of bread baking, even on Sundays. Audrey and I were the only kids in the neighborhood who didn't speak Italian. Mother hated every minute of her life there, at least at first. Just when things were getting better for her, Grandma got sick, and we moved back to East Providence so Mom could care for her. Grandma lived another year. Every afternoon. Dad made us go into her room, tell her about our day. and kiss her cheek. Her skin felt like beef jerky. I hated kissing her, especially toward the end when she barely knew who I was. What I remember most is the smell of the bedroom, similar to the smell of a big pile of dirty laundry, but worse."

"After Grandma died, Grandpa gave us the house. and he moved to Providence to live with his brother. Dad told him to stay with us, but he didn't want to. He died three years later, when I was nine. I don't remember much about him. Mostly what I remember is he had really bad breath. After he died, Dad started his handyman business and Mom started cleaning houses for rich people in Providence, people like your family."

"Probably not as rich as mine," John says.

"Probably not."

John grabs her hand and squeezes it. "I'd love to hear more, but I am so tired I'm afraid I'll fall asleep on you, and that would be rude. I want to learn more about you and your family, but not tonight."

"I'll be back in here tomorrow night." She grabs his hands and kisses his forehead. "Next time, I want to hear about you and your family and the girl from India."

"Not much to tell."

"Oh, John, please, I'm sure there's plenty to tell." She waves her hand in front of his mouth. "Your breath stinks. Don't get drunk tomorrow."

He nods in agreement.

"Sorry about the book my parents bought you. I told them not to get it. They're burning it in India."

"Yes, they are."

"They meant well."

"I'm sure they did."

"Don't forget, no drinking tomorrow. Be prepared to tell me everything."

"I will."

She kisses his forehead and leaves the room.

He lies on the bed and watches the ceiling swirl. *God, she's beautiful,* he thinks.

Chapter 14

Christmas Day, 1928
Doty Farm, East Providence, Vermont

Last night's rain is now ice. Charles looks out the kitchen window. "Can't go to Mass today," he says to Audrey.

"Sure I can."

"No, you can't, too dangerous for the horses. The ice'll cut their legs."

John slowly walks into the room. His gait is unsteady, and he is rubbing his eyes with his palms. His hair is rumpled.

"You look like a horse stomped on your face," Charles says. "How many times did you throw up last night?"

"Three, maybe four, lost count."

"Five times," Audrey says. She holds up the five fingers of her right hand. She is wearing her new jade necklace. She hands John a wet cloth and signals with her hands that he needs to clean his neck.

Tom and Claire enter the living room. "Rough night, John," Tom says. "Not much of a drinker?"

"Not much." He presses his palms against his forehead. "What time is it?"

"Ten thirty," Charles says.

"Damn, I missed the milking."

"Relax, Audrey helped milk the cows. She's faster than you anyways," Charles says. He smiles.

"I am," Audrey says. "I can drink more too—a lot more."

Claire sniffs the air like a dog. "What is that? Smells like a dead rat."

"We're eating Indian food today, Mom, a new adventure for all of us except John," Audrey says.

"Can't have Christmas without a turkey," Claire says.

"You can this year."

Claire grumbles and turns to John. "Tell us about India. I have to confess, I read some of the book we got you. Sounds like a terrible place."

"India isn't a terrible place. It's a wonderful place, just different from here—much different," John says.

Charlotte enters the house. She had smoked two cigarettes on the porch. Her cheeks are red from the cold, and there is a speck of tobacco on her bottom lip. She swipes it off with her finger and says, "It's a beautiful day, cold, but beautiful."

"John was just about to tell us all about India," Claire says.

"No, I wasn't. My head hurts too much to talk."

"Do they really force young girls to marry old men?" Claire says.

"Mom, stop it, John's head hurts," Audrey says. She points to the packages under the Christmas tree and looks at John. "We waited for you to open the rest of the presents. Didn't think you'd ever get up."

"Tell us about India," Claire insists.

"There's not much to tell. It's really hot. I was there for two years, but I am here now."

"And you fell in love?" Claire says.

"I did."

"Mother!" Audrey says. "Stop it."

Charles looks out the window and spots the bobcat near the barn door. "I'm gonna get you, you son of a bitch." He shakes his fist, grabs his rifle from the gun cabinet, loads it, and puts on his boots, coat, and hat. When he opens the front door, the bobcat looks at him the way a pet looks at its owner.

"You gotta be kidding me, bobcat. I'm gonna blow your stupid head off! Stop smiling," he says out loud. The bobcat trots around the side of the barn. Charles slips on the ice, falls on his butt, and drops the rifle. It discharges with a loud boom. The knuckles on his right hand bleed from crashing through the ice. He dries his bloody knuckles on his pants. "You're dead," he says to the bobcat. He shakes his fist.

The bobcat peeks around the corner of the barn as if he and Charles are playing a game of hide-and-seek. Charles gets up, retrieves his gun, and steps slowly toward the barn. He stops and aims the rifle at the bobcat's head. The bobcat disappears behind the barn and trots toward the chicken coop. Charles follows him. The bobcat stops thirty feet from the coop, turns about-face, and looks directly at Charles.

Charles aims the sight bead of the rifle on the center of the bobcat's head. The animal doesn't move. Instead, it stares at Charles. Charles lifts the gun barrel so the bead is aimed a few inches above the bobcat's right ear. He shoots and misses. "Next time, bobcat, you're dead." The bobcat doesn't move. Charles shoots a bullet into the ice a few inches in front of the bobcat's front paws. "Bobcat, are you stupid or what? Get the hell out of here." The animal takes one last look at him and runs toward the woods.

"I missed," Charles says to everyone in the house.

"You missed three times," Tom says.

"Yup, I did."

"Never were much of a shooter," Tom says and grins. Charles has won the rifle shooting contest three of the last five years at the East Providence Rod and Gun Club.

John is sitting on the couch between Audrey, on his right side, and Charlotte on his left. Both of their hips are touching his. Charlotte is clutching his arm. She whispers into his ear, too quietly for anyone to hear but him and Audrey. "Tell us about India. Tell us about the girl you loved." She pinches his arm and leans her head on his shoulder. He blushes.

"You're awful," Audrey says to Charlotte. She reaches behind John's shoulders and swats the back of her sister's head. When she brings her hand back to her side, she grazes John's neck with her fingertips.

"Awful? Awful about what?" Claire says. She is licking a candy cane she had picked off the Christmas tree.

"Nothing, Mom," Charlotte says. She reaches behind John and lightly pokes Audrey's shoulder.

"Girls, stop it, you're not kids anymore."

"Girls, stop it, you're not kids anymore," Charlotte mimics.

Claire shakes her head and points her right index finger at them as if she were annoyed with stubborn toddlers.

Charles hands John a small package. "Open it, Gauthier."

The present is a silver pocket watch. John opens the cover. The engraving on the inside says: *Not a Piss Hole in the Snow, Christmas 1928*. "Oh my, I didn't get you anything as nice as this." He remembers the watch from the jewelry store. Charles had held it up to the light from the window. "Beautiful watch, can't afford it, wish I could," he had said.

"Don't worry about it, Gauthier, I'm taking the cost out of your pay, next two weeks, half-pay." He grabs the watch from John and closes the cover. "Maybe you'll get up on time from now on."

"I doubt it," John says.

. . .

"Christmas dinner is chicken biryani. It's one of the most popular dishes in India. I hope everybody likes it," Audrey says as she walks to the dining room from the kitchen. The chicken dish is steaming hot. She fills everyone's plate.

"I'm sure it's wonderful," John says.

Claire stabs a piece of chicken.

"Wait, Mom, we need to say grace first," Audrey says. She and Charlotte retrieve the rest of the food from the kitchen and sit at the table. She closes her eyes, folds her hands, and bows her head. "Bless us, O Lord, for these, Thy gifts, which we are about to receive, from Thy bounty, through Christ, our Lord, Amen." She makes the sign of the cross as she speaks.

"Had to say the Catholic prayer," Claire says. She shakes her head in dismay.

"Claire," Tom says. He scowls at his wife.

"Yes, Mom, I did."

Claire pops a piece of chicken into her mouth, chews it, and grimaces as she swallows. "My goodness, this is hot." She grabs her water glass and drinks it empty. "My mouth is on fire."

"It's delicious," Charlotte says.

"It's not turkey. Christmas dinner is turkey and dressing and mashed potatoes and string beans, and squash and apple pie and plum pudding, not whatever this is," Claire says.

"Give it a rest, Mom," Charlotte says.

"I hear your parents are loaded," Tom says to John.

"Jesus, Dad, what kind of question is that? Sorry, John, sometimes my father speaks before he thinks," Audrey says.

"Not a problem. You are correct, my parents are loaded. We're old money, respectable money, part of the Connecticut gentry. But that wasn't always so. My great-great-great-grandfather was Jacques Bastien Gauthier of Quebec, a sometime fur trapper and full-time con man. He swindled several men out of their money and fled Canada one step ahead of the lynch mob. Jacques's evil deeds have long been forgotten. My family is now among a very select group of families who control Connecticut as if they own it, which they do."

"We've got a pretty select group right here at this table," Charlotte says. She instructs everyone to hold up their wineglasses. Little John is in his crib in his bedroom. He starts to cry. Audrey rises from her seat. "Sit down, Audrey, the baby can wait five minutes." She clicks her glass against John's. "A toast to the dynamic Andrews sisters, undoubtedly the two most beautiful and smartest women in the entire state. To their fine parents, Tom Andrews, handyman exemplar—if you break it, he'll fix it—and his lovely wife, Claire Wilson Andrews, Providence's best cleaning lady—she'll make your house shine, and she'll iron your shirts and wash your clothes. To Charles Howard Doty, the most successful farmer in all of Vermont, and, finally, the disgruntled ex-millionaire, John Randolph Gauthier, who has chosen a life of near poverty over riches and fame. Not the smartest decision ever made."

"To near poverty," Audrey says. She taps her glass against John's, sets it on the table, and answers Little John's cry.

The early afternoon sun is shining bright. Most of the ground ice has melted. Charles points to the window. "Looks like good news, Mom, you can be on your way after dinner. No problems for the horses." He had never called her Mom before.

"I'm not your mother."

"Sorry, Claire."

"You can call me Dad," Tom says.

"Okay, it's Dad and Claire Andrews."

"All right, you win, it's Dad and Mom Andrews." She steps to Charles and kisses the top of his head. "You're my favorite son-in-law."

"He's your only son-in-law, Ma," Charlotte says.

"He's still my favorite."

"To Mom and Dad Andrews," Charles says and taps his spoon against his wineglass.

Audrey is on the living room couch breastfeeding Little John. One of the cats is trying to get her attention by stroking her shoulder with his paw. She swats his face and pushes him off the couch.

Charlotte leans toward John and whispers into his ear. "You've got a story to tell me tonight. Don't get drunk. I want to hear everything."

"I'll tell you my story only if you tell me yours. I want to hear everything about you."

"What are you two talking about?" Audrey asks.

"Nothing," Charlotte says. She grabs John's arm.

"Less than nothing," John says. He taps his wineglass against Charlotte's. "To the stories we will tell."

Chapter 15

September 1962
Sacred Heart Parish, East Providence, Vermont

Monsignor Gauthier is sitting at his desk reading Patrick Colman's instructions on how to fly a kite. Tchaikovsky's *Serenade for Strings* is playing on the stereo. Patrick is sitting in a chair in front of the desk watching Gauthier read. Gauthier has a lit pipe in his mouth. A thick bead of spit is dangling from the bottom of the bowl of the pipe. Patrick is staring at the spit wondering if it will splatter onto the desktop.

The priest rolls his chair away from the desk and leans toward Patrick. "Your directions tell the kite flier to hold the kite above his head and then slowly let it go. What if the kite flier is facing the wrong way? Shouldn't you have added that the kite flier's back is to the wind?" His pipe bobs up and down as he speaks, and the spit blob plops to the floor. He grinds the spit dry with the toe of his right shoe.

"Isn't that obvious?" Patrick says.

"There's nothing obvious in directions. Assume the reader knows nothing. Before I knew how to cook, I read a recipe that said to fold the egg and flour mixture into the fruit. I had no idea what fold meant. Bakers knew but I didn't know."

"What does it mean?"

"To stir lightly—not obvious to someone who's never cooked before. Writing instructions on how to do something you know how to do so well that you don't even have to think about it is very difficult. You forget steps, you forget the reader doesn't know the terminology. Details are important. When I give directions, I always screw up. I forget a street or a traffic light. I never get them right. I'm always sending people down the wrong road. That's the story of my life." He chuckles at his comment.

"Mine too," Father Cantone says. He is standing in the doorway of Gauthier's office. Neither Gauthier nor Patrick knew he was there. Gauthier ignores him. Cantone lightly taps his right fist against the door and gives a fake cough. "Monsignor, we've got a big problem."

"Come back in ten minutes."

"The problem needs to be addressed now, not ten minutes from now."

Gauthier glances at Patrick's kite-flying instruction and tosses the paper into the top drawer of his desk. "We'll get back to this next week." He sucks deeply on his pipe and blows the puff of smoke above his head. "Have you read *My Ántonia?*"

"Some of it."

"Do you like it?"

"It's okay."

"Maybe not the perfect book for a thirteen-year-old boy. Finish it anyway. Finish it by next week. You've had plenty of time." He waves Patrick away, coughs into his fist, spits a wad of phlegm onto a handkerchief, and taps his pipe against the side of a black metal wastebasket next to the desk, knocking the tobacco into the basket. Turning to Father Cantone, he says, "What's the problem? It better be good."

"There's money missing from the Boy Scouts' cashbox—fifty-five dollars. Scout Master Bill is going crazy. Father Symanski is pretty sure Paul Fermonte took the money. He's grilling him now, him and the two O'Riley boys and Maurice Nolan. He sent me here to get Patrick. He figures Patrick's involved. Maurice is bawling like a three-year-old. Sister Ryan is ready to call the police. If I hadn't stopped her, she would have."

Gauthier sighs and shakes his head. "Oh, for goodness sake. They didn't take money, I did. I should have left a note in the box. Polly Bove couldn't pay her oil bill, so I gave her the cash. I meant to replace the money, but I forgot. I didn't have any cash, and I couldn't find my checkbook." He grabs his checkbook from his desk and follows Father Cantone to the school.

Gauthier is a soft touch. Everyone in church knows his family is rich. Several members of the parish council call him "The Bank." They want him to stop giving out money so easily. Three years ago, they set up an emergency fund he could use. They approved a complicated set of rules that required signed statements explaining why the money was needed, a detailed plan on how the money would be paid back, and limits on the amount he could give out each week. He routinely ignores their form and their rules, never asks anyone to repay anything, and often exceeds the weekly amount authorized. When he does, he uses his own money to pay the extra.

. . .

"Good morning, Father," Gauthier says to Father Symanski. "Good morning, boys." He steps into the principal's office. "Boys, why don't you go back to your classroom. I have business with Father Symanski." He points to the door.

"I'm in the middle of something very important, Father," Symanski says.

"Boys, go," Gauthier says, pointing to the door again. The boys amble to their classroom, punching each other as they walk down the hall.

"I screwed up big time. I took the Boy Scout money. Polly Bove needed the money to pay her oil bill." Sister Bartholomew is listening from the doorway. "Thank you, Sister," he says and closes the door.

"Why didn't you leave a note?" Symanski asks.

"I meant to, I just forgot. Sorry about that. No excuses."

"It's early September. Mrs. Bove doesn't need oil now."

"Tell that to the oil company."

Gauthier hands Symanski a check for a hundred dollars. "Give this to Bill. This should more than cover what was in the box. I'll call him and apologize."

"You can't just buy your way out of trouble."

"I'm not and there was no trouble. Nothing was stolen, I just forgot. I really am sorry."

Symanski folds the check and stuffs it into his shirt pocket. Sister

Bartholomew greets him when he leaves the office. "Sometimes the Monsignor makes life difficult, but he is a good man, a very good man," she whispers to him when he enters the hall.

. . .

When John was fifteen, there was a terrible accident at one of the job sites at his father's construction company. A workman slipped off a steel girder and fell forty feet to his death. He was wearing a safety harness, but he hadn't fastened it correctly. A story about the accident was featured in the local newspapers. "Tragedy at the Worksite," one headline read. His father, Julien, was quoted as saying how sorry he was for the family and that his company would make sure the family was compensated for their loss.

"My heart goes out to Mrs. Cato and her children. No amount of money can replace a lost husband, a lost father, or a lost friend, but we will make things as right as we can," he said. One of the papers ran a picture of him handing a check to the widow. There were tears in his eyes and hers.

Six months later, the dead man's wife and her five children showed up at the front gate of the Gauthier home in Greenwich, Connecticut. It had taken them over four hours to get there from Brooklyn. Julien thought they were beggars and told his butler to give them food and two dollars. The widow threw the food and the money to the ground and stormed past the butler to the front door of the house.

"You said you'd help us, you'd make things right," she yelled as she marched toward Julien, who was standing at the door.

"I did help you," he said.

"Five hundred dollars! Five hundred measly dollars for a man's life! That's nothing—less than nothing. You should be ashamed of yourself. I have no place to live. I've been kicked out of my apartment, we're homeless, and my children are starving." She shook her fist at him. "You think five hundred dollars is enough? You try living on five hundred dollars." She grabbed a handful of pebbles from the driveway and threw them at him. He covered his eyes with his left arm and swatted the flying pebbles with his right forearm.

"Either you leave here or I will call the police," he said. He stepped back into the house and slammed the door shut. "It was her husband's fault. He was careless," he said to his wife, Pauline. John was at the top of the stairs listening to his father argue with the angry woman. Her oldest boy was his age. The boy's pants and shirt sleeves were too short for his arms and legs.

The woman pulled a brick from the border of the flower bed next to the entrance stairs and threw it through the front window. Ten minutes later, the Greenwich police arrested her and her children.

"You could have given her more money," Pauline said to Julien at dinner that night.

"I gave her plenty. I didn't have to give her a dime. It was her husband's fault. He didn't buckle his safety belt. You make a mistake, you live with it—or die with it, in his case."

"It wasn't the children's fault," John said.

"If I want your opinion I'll ask for it." He ordered his son to his room.

Five weeks later, on the Wednesday before Thanksgiving, Julien and several men from his company volunteered at a Thanksgiving dinner for the homeless in Hartford. The *Hartford Courant* ran a story about the dinner that featured a picture of him and his men. The headline said: "Local Businessmen Lend a Hand." The article said Julien was a well-known philanthropist who frequently donated his time and money to worthy causes. Several of the people who organized the dinner said he was a very good man. "I am just trying to give back to those in need," he told the reporter.

At breakfast the next day, John read the story to his parents and reminded his father about the mother and her five hungry children. Julien slapped his face. "You don't know a damn thing about the world. You'll change your tune when you're older."

"I won't change my tune, ever," he said. He jumped up from the table, threw his napkin at his father, and stormed out the door to the horse barn. Whenever he was upset, he brushed the horses and cleaned the stalls. By the time he was done, the stalls were spotless.

Chapter 16

February 1929
Charlotte Andrews's Apartment, Providence, Vermont

"I didn't think you'd come," Charlotte says.

"Why not? I said I would," John says.

"I don't know, I just didn't think you would." She grabs his left arm and pulls him into her apartment. "What do you think?"

"It's nice."

Her apartment is on the third floor of the six-story Grantham building on Center Street in downtown Providence. There are three stores at street level: a women's hat store, a jewelry store, and a stationery store. The law firm of Wilson, Struthers, and McCabe takes up the entire second floor. There are four apartments on each of the third and fourth floors and six one-room apartments on the top two floors.

She tells him to take off his hat, coat, and boots and put them in the bedroom closet. She points the way. The apartment has three rooms—a small kitchen with a table for two, a bedroom, which has the only closet in the apartment and is barely big enough for the bed and bureau, and a living room with a couch, two chairs, a radio, and a bookshelf. She shares the bathroom at the end of the hall. There is a large steam radiator in each room. The radiator in the living room is hissing steam, and the apartment is very hot. The living room window is held open three inches by a piece of wood. The wallpaper in all three of her rooms is golden brown with large flowers, the same wallpaper as in the hallway. The walls are twelve feet high. A fan hangs from the ceiling in the middle of the living room. There are two large windows in the living room and one in the bedroom. The window in the bedroom is rattling from the wind.

"What are we going to do today?" John says.

"First, we're going to have sex."

"Now? It's ten thirty in the morning?"

"Why not now? You need practice."

"What do you mean I need practice? Are you saying I'm not good?"

"I'm saying you've got a lot to learn."

"So I'm terrible."

"No, you're not terrible. You've got potential. If sex were baseball, you'd be a rookie who sits on the bench. By the time you leave here Monday morning, you'll be Babe Ruth."

"Sixty home runs?"

"Not sixty. I'll settle for two a day, maybe three."

"I don't know if I can do that."

"You can."

"What else are we going to do?"

"I'm treating you to lunch at Berlusconi's Italian restaurant. They have the best bread I've ever eaten. And the pasta is unbelievable. Hope you like garlic and olive oil?"

"I can pay."

"No, you can't, I know what you make."

"I'm rich, remember."

"Your parents are rich. You make twenty-five dollars a week."

"I've got no expenses, none. I'm paying for lunch, that's the end of it." He makes a fist and gently taps her nose. He wants to kiss her, but he doesn't.

She pulls him to her by his belt buckle, unbuttons his pants, and drops them to his ankles. "A tough guy, I like that," she says.

"What else are we going to do?"

"Tonight we're going to a speakeasy and we're going to dance." She grabs his hands, shakes his arms, and sings the words, "Do the Charleston" three times.

"I don't like speakeasies, they're too loud." He covers his ears with his hands. "And I don't dance."

"I know, Audrey told me. You'll like this one. The music is fantastic, and the booze is delicious. My friends want to meet you. You don't have any choice. And you will dance." She tells him to lift his left foot. She pulls his pant leg over his foot and tickles his ankle. She does the same with the right pant leg. She tosses the pants, socks, and underwear across the room toward the couch. She steps back, slowly removes her blouse, and drops it to the floor. She is wearing nothing under her shirt.

"Aren't you worried about . . . you know?"

"You know? You know what? Getting pregnant?"

"Yes."

"You didn't have a problem last time."

"I wasn't thinking last time."

"Not to worry. Unfortunately, it's not a problem."

"I'm sorry."

"I am too."

"What are we going to do tomorrow?"

"John, focus on this moment. What are we going to do right now?"

"We're going to have sex."

"Good man. You're a little slow on the draw but you can learn, right?"

He nods.

She removes his shirt and drops it to the floor and removes her stockings from her legs. She kicks her skirt, stockings, and underwear away from her feet, grabs his right hand, and guides him to the bedroom.

"Apparently, I've got a lot to learn," John says.

"You do, but I'm a good teacher, a very good teacher."

"I'm ready to learn." He picks her up and carries her to the bed. She kisses his neck.

. . .

Piero Berlusconi greets John and Charlotte at the front door of his restaurant. He is short, five foot three at the most, and has a fuzzy gray mustache and wild, thick eyebrows. He grabs John's right hand and shakes it vigorously.

"Welcome, welcome, welcome," he says with a thick Italian accent. His voice is loud, and his face is very close to John's face. He taps John's cheek with his index finger each time he says "welcome." It is three in the afternoon. There are no other customers in the restaurant. He hugs Charlotte. "I see you brought a friend."

"I did. John Randolph Gauthier. He's a farmhand at my brother-in-law's farm."

"Welcome, Mr. John Randolph Gauthier. Farming's hard work." He grimaces to emphasize the truth of what he just said. "Charlotte's our favorite customer. We love her," Piero says. He kisses Charlotte's right cheek.

Piero's wife, Assumpta, joins them from the kitchen. She is the same height as her husband and looks almost like she could be his sister. They both have dark, piercing eyes that dominate their faces, large noses, and skin the color of a leather boot. She wipes her hands on her apron as she crosses the dining room. She hugs Charlotte and kisses both of her cheeks.

"This is my friend John," Charlotte says.

"Is he a special friend?" Assumpta asks.

"Yes, a very special friend."

John smiles.

Assumpta grabs John's right hand and squeezes it. She pinches his left cheek so hard his skin turns red. "You treat her good. You be gentleman. We love Charlotte." John has a hard time understanding her words.

"He's very good, Mrs. Berlusconi, and he's getting better every day, that's for sure." She looks to John for a reaction. He closes his eyes, places his right hand on his face, and slowly shakes his head.

"Good boy," Assumpta says. She pinches his cheek a second time, even harder than before.

Piero leads John and Charlotte to their table. "Sit," he says. He tenderly grabs Charlotte's left shoulder. "You good girl." He joins his wife in the kitchen.

"Don't mind Mrs. Berlusconi, she likes to squeeze cheeks," Charlotte says.

"I'm used to it. I dated an Italian girl in college. Her mother squeezed my cheek just about every time I saw her. One time she bit my ear. That took me by surprise."

"What happened to the girl?"

"I went to India. I asked her to come with me, but she said no. Last I heard, she was married to a doctor and has three children. She'll probably have ten by the time she's done."

"Did you love her?"

"I don't know. I don't think so, not really sure. What about you? What happened to the Army boy you were going to marry? Did you love him?"

"I thought I did, at the time anyway."

"I hear he was mean."

"Not at first. Not before the war. He was kind and gentle. The war changed him. He was a sweet boy when he left. He came back mean. He beat up my dad."

"Charles told me."

"What else did Charles tell you?"

"Not much. Have you loved anyone since?

"Yes and no."

"What do you mean, yes and no? Either you have or you haven't."

"It's not that simple, John. Love is complicated. I was involved with one of my bosses at a law firm. He got me this apartment. He paid the rent. He had a wife and two children. He told me he would leave them, but he never did. I stayed with him for almost three years before I smartened up. Never get involved with a married man."

"I'll remember that. I will never get involved with a married man."

"You're very funny." She kisses his right hand.

Piero and Assumpta return from the kitchen, each holding a steaming bowl of soup. "We haven't ordered yet, Mr. Berlusconi," Charlotte says.

"No need. Dinner on us. We start with a tomato soup with steamed mussels. For main meal,"—he kisses his fingertips—"chicken. Sicilian style."

"This is too much, Mr. Berlusconi, way too much," Charlotte says.

"Not too much. We celebrate. You been alone too long. John nice boy," Assumpta says.

"He is indeed a nice boy." Charlotte pokes John's arm again.

"You get married, you invite us," Assumpta says.

"I will. We'll have the reception here."

"Wow, things are moving fast," John says.

"Relax, John, nothing's moving anywhere." She reaches across the table, pulls his head to her, and kisses his forehead.

Assumpta claps her hands. "You be good to her."

"I will," John says.

"Oh, he will, that's for sure, he'll be very good," Charlotte says.

"Stop it," John says. His face is red.

"Stop what?" She removes her right shoe, lifts her foot to John's crotch, and rubs him with her toes. He is startled. She leans her face to his and whispers, "Are you ready for round two?"

"I think so. I'm not sure," he whispers.

She grabs his head and kisses his forehead. "I could get used to you, John Gauthier."

"I could get used to you too, Charlotte Andrews." He kisses her hands.

Chapter 17

February 1929
St. Francis of Assisi Parish, East Providence, Vermont

Father LeFebvre is staring out the window of the sacristy. The sun is shining brightly on the snow. From inside the church, the day looks perfect. There are no clouds and the sky is deep blue. But looks are deceiving. The outside temperature is twenty-eight below zero. The radiator at the back of the room is pumping so much steam there is a cloud above the vent. During Mass, he could see his breath. The chalice was cold in his hands. No one took off their coats.

He pours a glass of wine from the altar wine bottle, swirls the glass several times, and takes a big gulp. He sits at his desk at the back of the room and stares out the window. Only nine people showed up for the service. There is a light tap at the door.

"Hello, Father, do you have a few minutes?" John Gauthier asks.

"Of course I do. I was surprised to see you here without Audrey."

"She didn't feel well."

"And you came anyway."

"I did."

"Why?"

"I'm not sure why. But I'm here now."

LeFebvre pours Gauthier a glass of wine. "Not the best wine in the world but not too bad." He finishes his glass and refills it. "So, what's on your mind?"

"I thought we could talk about India."

"Don't get me started, I could go on all day."

"So could I."

"Did you see the Taj Mahal?"

"Of course I did. Can't be an American tourist without seeing the Taj Mahal. You were in India for five years. Why so long?"

"I was there to teach the heathens about Christ." He laughs as if he has just told a joke.

"Did it work?"

"Not really. The only people who came to the church were people who were starving. They didn't want to be saved, they wanted food."

John nods in agreement. "I never did get used to beggars. One day I gave a dollar bill to a man with no legs. When the other beggars near him saw what I had done, they surrounded me and wouldn't let me go free. I was afraid for my life. I ended up giving them everything I had—thirty-two dollars. I was an arrogant, rich American with thirty-three dollars in my pocket. Totally ridiculous. When my pockets were empty, I told them I had nothing left to give them, but they didn't believe me. One man threatened to break my arm. They let me go only when I pulled out my empty pockets and proved I had no more money. I never gave beggars anything after that, not a dime."

"Pretty much the same thing happened to me, except that I got violent. I pushed several beggars to the ground and punched one man in the face. I broke his nose. Can you believe that? A young Catholic priest punching a beggar in the face—not a good advertisement for the Church. Good thing I wasn't wearing my robe or collar."

"Were your five years a failure?" Gauthier asks.

"Not at all. We fed a lot of very hungry people. Food trumps God. We had a medical clinic. It was pretty obvious that medical care was more important than Mass. Did we convert any of them? Maybe a few. A handful at best. They had gods already—they didn't need another. If I learned anything in India, I learned that one god is no better or worse than any other. I was intrigued by Hinduism. Still am. They believe in reincarnation. After death, the soul returns in a new body. Each soul completes this cycle many times, learning new things each time and working toward spiritual perfection. Think about that. Basically, you keep trying until you get it right. Not a bad message, pretty much what Christ said—keep trying until you get it right. A simple message but a good one."

"Why'd you become a priest? When I think of priests, I think of old men with double chins and ear hair. You're not much older than me."

"We're not all old, whippersnapper," LeFebvre says in a fake old man's voice. He covers his teeth with his lips and pretends he has no teeth. "I'm not old, but I'm not young either. I'm forty-one years old, and I've been a Catholic priest for almost half my life. It seems like just yesterday I was a twenty-seven-year-old know-it-all priest, hellbent on saving the world. The older I get, the less I know." He corks the wine bottle and puts it into the storage closet. "Why did I become a priest? You don't want to know, believe me."

"I do."

"Why?"

"I just do."

"If I tell you, you're going to think I'm a phony. Maybe I am, who knows?"

"I doubt that."

"I became a priest to get out of poverty. I realize that makes me sound like a hypocrite, but that's the reason—not the only reason, but the main reason. I wish I had a more noble motive, but I don't. I was sick of being poor. Me and Julien Sorel—*saved* from poverty by the Roman Catholic Church. Have you read *The Red and the Black*?"

Gauthier nods.

"Great book. Maybe if I had read it before I became a priest, I would have gone down a different road."

He pulls off his robe and hangs it in the closet. "I lived on a small dairy farm in Orleans County. There were ten of us, eight kids and my parents. I was the oldest child and one of only two boys. The farm could barely support my parents, let alone eight children. We were always hungry, especially in the winter. Everybody in our town was as poor as we were, so poverty seemed normal. I started milking cows when I was nine years old. By the time I was fifteen, I was pretty much running the farm. My father was sick more often than he was well. He had a heart attack when I was ten and another when I was fourteen. Somehow—I'm not sure how—I finished high school.

"I was first in my class, class valedictorian. Sounds pretty impressive, except there were only thirty-nine of us and most of the others, like me, rarely attended. The best of thirty-nine—definitely not a big deal. My father died my senior year, two weeks before my graduation. Mom thought I'd take over the farm, but I said no, I was going to college. She was furious. I had won a full scholarship to Dartmouth. She is an Abenaki, and that helped me get the scholarship.

"I knew nothing about Dartmouth or the scholarship, but the local priest guided me as if I were his son. One day after church, he took me aside and said, *'Daniel, you need to leave the farm and see the world. You're a kid, you work like a man. Time to take a break from farming.'*

"He told my mother to go home, he had a job for me—he'd pay me five dollars, and he'd get me home after the job was done. Five dollars was a lot of money for a half day's work. I couldn't say no. He had the Dartmouth application in his hand and had pretty much already filled it out. He had written my letter to the college and a letter of recommendation. His letter was so glowing it embarrassed me. He said I was brilliant, which definitely was not true. He told Dartmouth I was running the farm by myself, which also was not true. My brother Clem and my older sisters worked as hard as I did.

"He refused to change the letter. He had typed both letters the day before. All I had to do was sign my letter and fill in a few blanks on the application. I don't know why he did it. We weren't very close. I had missed Mass most Sundays because I had to finish milking, and I rarely attended catechism. He said I could always go back to the farm after graduation, but I should go to college first. He said if I didn't sign the letter, he'd sign it for me. A forger-priest, can you believe that? I never told my mother about the application. She didn't know about it until the day I got the letter of acceptance from the school. When I graduated from Dartmouth, I went right into the seminary. I suppose I had other options, but I didn't see them. I was too much of a hick to see what was beyond our farm. I suspect the priest, Father Dusablon, had more influence on me than I had thought. The rest, as they say, is history."

"Do you believe in God?" Gauthier asks.

"I do. I have doubts, but I suspect every priest, or at least most priests, have doubts. I don't know how it could be otherwise." He finishes the wine in his glass. "When I was a young boy, nobody I knew questioned God, or at least nobody at our church, Saint John of the Snows. We children had to memorize the *Baltimore Catechism* word for word, every rule, every question, every answer. 'Who made the world? God made the world. Who is God? God is the creator of heaven and earth, and of all things. What is man? Man is a creature composed of body and soul, and made to the image and likeness of God.' I can still recite that nonsense, word for word, thirty years later."

"We had a similar catechism at the Episcopal church, but we didn't have to memorize anything. Catholic lite," John jokes.

LeFebvre chuckles. "Catholic lite, I like that. I thought you didn't go to church?"

"I did—every Sunday until I was eleven. Didn't miss a single Sunday for seven years, not even when I was sick."

"Why'd you stop?"

"It's complicated." He finishes his wine, washes the glass at the sink, and dries it with an altar cloth. "Do you ever regret your decision?"

"Not at all. I think I was predestined to become a priest. I just didn't know it. Sometimes the politics of running a church gets to me. The pettiness of some of the parishioners can be mind-numbing. Please don't tell anybody I said that. I like it here, and I want to stay."

"My lips are sealed."

"They better be," Father LeFebvre says. He smiles. "Every job has a routine. It doesn't matter what the job is. Sometimes the routine here can feel like getting crushed by a gristmill, but mostly it's okay. I don't think that's unique to the priesthood."

"My father runs a construction company. He says the same thing."

"Don't get me wrong, I love this job, I love being a priest, and I love it here."

"Do you miss, you know . . ."

"Sex?"

"Yes, sex."

"Of course I do. It was very hard at first, but after a while, you get used to it."

"Have you ever been in love?"

"Once?"

"What was she like?"

"That's a tough question."

"Why?"

"I can't tell you."

"Why not? Except for Charles and Audrey and Audrey's family, I don't know a single soul in this town. Who would I tell?"

"I had several girlfriends in high school and one girlfriend my freshman year at college, but I knew pretty early on—when I was twelve, maybe thirteen—that I wasn't interested in girls. When I was with them, nothing ever felt right. It was as if I was a stranger in a strange land that I didn't understand."

"I thought you said you were in love?"

"I was." He slowly shakes his head to let John know he needs to listen more carefully.

"Oh, sorry, sometimes I'm slow on the draw."

"You are. It was my junior year at Dartmouth. My friend was a senior. We were planning to go to Boston after I graduated, but he moved back to Portland, Maine, with his parents. He sent me a letter—'I can't do this, I'm sorry.' That's all the letter said, nothing else. Last I knew, he was married and had two children. I hope he's happy."

"I hope so too. If you could go back in time, knowing what you know now, would you still be a priest?"

"Yes, I would. I get to help people in need. I'm someone they look to when they have no one else. I celebrate their best days with them—their marriages and their baptisms—and I grieve with them when their loved ones die. Before I was a priest, I thought confession was silly, and it often is, but one thing I've learned is most people, when they know they've done wrong, want to confess to someone, to me or to God, it doesn't really matter to them. What they want is an ear, someone to listen to them, to hear them out, to forgive them. They need to tell their story to somebody, but they can't tell it to their family. And they need someone to tell them they will be okay, that God has forgiven them. That's what I do. I tell them God has forgiven them, and I mean it, and I never judge them, no matter what they've done."

"You helped Audrey a great deal."

"Thank you for saying that. She's a hard woman to read. Sometimes I feel I am doing her more harm than good."

"More good, for sure. When I think about her losing two babies, I think, why her? She never did anything to anyone. She's the nicest person in the world, she and Charles both. Life is not fair," John says.

"I can't talk about Audrey. A priest is like a lawyer—what happens between a priest and a parishioner is confidential, a sacred trust that can't be broken. But you're right, life is unfair. Bad things happen to good people all the time, why not you, why not me, why not anyone? It's all a crapshoot. I've been trying to make sense of woe and sadness ever since I took my vows. If you know the answer, please let me know because I sure don't."

"I don't either." John stands up, walks to the window, and scrapes ice off the glass with his thumb. "How did you end up here?"

"Nobody else wanted this parish. It's too small and the people are too poor and too uneducated for most priests. We've got only forty-seven families, and it's a rare Sunday when everybody shows up. Most of them are farmers, and unless the milking is done, they can't come."

"Has there ever been a Sunday when nobody showed up?"

"One Sunday, only six people came to Mass. It was in March, three or four years ago. The roads were a muddy soup, nearly impossible to go anywhere. The LeSalles were the only people who made it." He points out the window to the house two hundred yards down the road. "That's their house."

John returns to his seat. "Do you wish you were somewhere else?"

"Absolutely not. I love these people. They may not be educated, but they're smarter than I'll ever be. They struggle and they survive, and they love each other. They take joy in what matters—family, friendship, honesty. I wish I were more like them. I am humbled by them." He stands up and puts on his coat to let John know the conversation has come to an end. "We'll have to talk more about India. One of these days I'll have you and Audrey and Charles over to the rectory for an Indian meal. I've gotten to be a pretty good cook. That reminds me, how'd the Christmas dinner go?"

"It was okay. Audrey's got a lot to learn about Indian cooking. Maybe you can teach her. The meal was so hot I could barely breathe."

"Good to know. I'm on it. Cooking lessons will start next Sunday after church. Tell Audrey what's up. See you next week." He looks at a thermometer on the outside of the window. "We've had a regular heatwave since this morning—it's only two below now."

"We'll be swimming by next week."

"Bring your ice auger, you'll need it," Father LeFebvre says.

Despite the cold, the trip back to the farm is pleasant, as the sunshine is bright and soothing.

. . .

"Jesus, Gauthier, didn't think you'd ever come back," Charles says when John enters the house.

"It's two below zero, where would I go?"

"When you do go, leave the wagon at the livery stable in Providence." He smiles.

"Sounds like a plan."

"You're not leaving us, are you, John?" Audrey asks.

"Nope, you're stuck with me."

"Good. I don't want to look for nobody else. You're not terrible," Charles says.

"If I die, put that on my gravestone— John Randolph Gauthier, he wasn't terrible."

"How about 'J. Randolph Gauthier'? Sounds classier," Audrey says.

"All right, J. Randolph Gauthier it is. Granite, not marble—marble's too soft—and definitely not slate, slate cracks."

"As long as you pay, Gauthier," Charles says

John removes a ten-dollar bill from his wallet and pretends to pay Charles. "J. Randolph Gauthier, he wasn't terrible."

"Not terrible," Charles says. He grabs John's arm. "No rest for the weary, Gauthier, we got cows to milk." He points out the window to the barn.

Chapter 18

February 1929
St. Francis of Assisi Parish, East Providence, Vermont

Father LeFebvre leads Audrey and John across the church parking lot to the rectory. He is talking fast and waving his arms as he speaks. His words are lost in the wind. The white paint on the building is peeling badly, and the porch roof is sagging under three feet of snow. The walkway is very narrow, not much wider than the blade of a snow shovel. The ice on the three steps to the porch is covered with ash from the wood stove.

All the ingredients needed to make chicken curry are lined up on the kitchen counter. Two nights ago, Father LeFebvre cooked a test run to make sure he'd get it right. At six this morning, he cleaned the kitchen spotless and lined up the spice jars as if he were a young child playing with toy army men, making sure each jar was in exactly the right position for battle. Last week he told John he was a good cook of Indian food. That was not true. He can cook a few simple dishes with one or two spices, but usually he fails miserably when the recipe is complicated.

"This curry chicken recipe is one of my favorites," he says. What he doesn't tell them is he had never cooked this meal before two days ago.

"Not to worry, I'll keep it pretty mild. I don't want to burn your throats." He laughs as he speaks. The chicken he cooked Friday night was too hot. Today he plans to cut the spice by a third.

John and Audrey remove their coats and hats and place them on a chair to the left of the door and set their boots on the straw mat next to the chair. LeFebvre hangs his coat on the rack in the hallway closet and tosses his boots to the closet floor. When he turns away from them to walk to the closet, Audrey lightly bumps John with her hip and pokes his arm.

"I'll get you," he whispers. His face is so close to hers that his lips nearly touch her right ear.

"Not if you can't catch me." She steps quickly away from him. He pumps his arm, pretending to chase her.

LaFebvre guides them to the kitchen. "The key is to have a hot oven, about twenty degrees hotter than needed for baking bread," he says. The wood in the cookstove is burning. He had lit it before the church service. He checks the temperature and adds two small logs to the fire. He offers them wine. Audrey says no. If John had answered first, he would have accepted, but instead, he waves no with his right hand.

"The first thing we need to do is heat two tablespoons of olive oil and fry the onion slices until they soften." He hands the onion, knife, and olive oil to John and a skillet and wooden spoon to Audrey. "How long are you staying here in East Providence? It must be much different from life in Connecticut." he says to John.

"It is, and I don't know how long," John says.

"Does Father LeFebvre know something that I don't know? Are you leaving us, John?" Audrey grabs his left arm as she speaks and tugs him to her.

"Father LeFebvre doesn't know anything you don't know. I'm not going anywhere."

"I'm starting to wonder," Audrey says.

LeFebvre grabs garlic, ginger, olive oil, and curry powder and tosses them into the hot pan. "You need to fry these for about a minute. Then you cook the sauce until it's thick but still moist. Keep the lid on it for the first ten minutes." He dumps the fried onions and hot spices into a Dutch oven. Completing the rest of the recipe takes about twenty minutes. "Voilà, that's it." He places the pan in the oven. "Now we wait." He drinks his wine and refills the glass. "John, how do you say voilà in Hindi?"

"I don't know. Never came up."

LeFebvre ponders for a few seconds. "It's *dekha*." He raises his arms and says, "Dekha, we wait."

"Dekha, we wait," Audrey says.

LeFebvre fills two glasses with wine and hands one to Audrey and the other to John. "I'm not taking no for an answer. This is the best wine I've had in years. I haven't had anyone to drink good wine with since I moved here six years ago." He walks them to the living room. "Sit." He points to the couch. "How's your son?" he says to Audrey.

"He's good. He slept through the night for the first time last week. It's been only once but hopefully, that was the start of better nights."

"Hopefully," John says and smiles. Audrey gives him a fake annoyed face.

"I grew up on a farm with eight kids. I don't think my mother had a single night without somebody crying for fifteen years. I was the oldest. My brother Clem and I were Irish twins. He arrived eleven months after me, and he cried every night for two years. I was so used to noise I couldn't get to sleep unless one of the babies was crying. When I went off to college, everybody in the dorm thought it was too loud but me. I remember waking up the first night at three in the morning. My roommate was breathing lightly, but otherwise, there was no noise. I couldn't get back to sleep—it was too darn quiet."

"I didn't know you grew up on a farm," Audrey says.

"I did. By the time I was fourteen I was milking cows every morning and every afternoon, seven days a week. Or as my father would have said, *I were blank, blank milkin' kayows every blank, blank morning and every blank, blank afternoon.*"

"Your father sounds a lot like Charles," Audrey says.

"He was. He was a good man, a hardworking man. I will never be half the man he was."

"You're a good man, Father," Audrey says.

"Maybe. Sometimes I wonder. We had four bedrooms in our house. My brother Clem and I slept in the smallest bedroom, barely big enough for two small beds. Three of my sisters were in the biggest bedroom and the other three in the other bedroom. My sisters' rooms were so crowded with beds and dressers it was impossible to walk from one end of the room to the other without stepping on a bed."

Audrey smiles. "My sister and I slept together in the same bed until I left the house to marry Charles. On the night before my wedding, she said, 'It's gonna be odd sleeping alone,' and I said, 'It's going to be odd sleeping with a man.'" She chuckles at her last line.

"My childhood was really hard, much worse than either of yours," John says. "We were the poorest family on our road. Dirt poor compared to everybody we knew. My parents are worth only about fifteen million dollars. Most of our neighbors are worth twice as much. We were so poor it was embarrassing." He pauses to make sure they get his sarcasm. "I had to share a wing of the house with my sister. Can you believe that—share a wing of the house? So sad. I got only two rooms to myself, my bedroom and my playroom. My playroom was filled with so many toys it was hard to move around—very annoying. My sister and I had to share a library, just one children's library for two children. Can you imagine sharing a library with your younger sister? She destroyed all my books. If I could write like Dickens, I would write my sad story."

"I'm so sorry, John, how awful it must have been, you poor little rich boy." Audrey grabs a couch pillow and lightly bashes his head with it.

He grabs it from her. "I'll have you arrested for assault. You're a witness, Father. Audrey assaulted me."

"Audrey, if you confess your sins next week, I won't have you arrested. God will forgive you," Father LeFebvre says.

The cook timer rings. "*Dekha*, it's done," LeFebvre says.

"*Dekha*, it's done," John and Audrey say in unison.

LeFebvre stabs a piece of chicken with a fork, waves it cool, blows on it, and takes a bite. He kisses his fingers. "Perfect," he says. He and Audrey set the table.

Father LeFebvre blesses the food. "Thank you both for joining me in this wonderful feast." He holds up his wineglass, and the three of them clink their glasses together.

When the meal is done, Father LeFebvre tells John and Audrey not to worry about the dishes, he'll wash them later. He ushers them to the living room.

John checks the books on LeFebvre's bookshelf. He grabs *The Great Gatsby*, reads the first two paragraphs, and places the book back on the shelf. He often imagines himself as Gatsby and Audrey as Daisy Buchanan.

He checks his watch. "We need to get going. I've got a milking to do in about two hours."

"Kayows nevva take a day off, that's for showa, ayuh," LeFebvre says. He looks for a laugh and scratches his chin. He walks with them to the sleigh. "I have something for you," he says to John. He motions for John to return to the house with him. Once inside the house he says to John, "You need to be careful."

"Careful about what?"

"What do you think? You and Audrey are very close, too close for your own good."

"I don't think so, Father. She's my friend, nothing more."

"John, I've been a priest for a long time. I've seen this play before. It never ends well."

John returns to the sleigh with a copy of *The Good Soldier* in his right hand. "He wants me to read this," he says.

Audrey tucks her ears into her hat, covers her legs with a wool blanket, and extends the blanket to cover John's legs. "I want to read some of your books. You have twenty-three."

"You counted?"

"I did. What book should I start with?"

"What do you like to read?"

"Do you have any love stories?"

He thinks for a few seconds. "I think you'd like *Women in Love*."

"What's it about?"

"It's about two sisters, Gudrun and Ursula. Gudrun is an artist and she falls in love with the wrong man. Ursula falls in love with a man who is in love with her sister's lover."

"Sounds complicated."

"It is."

"I'll start reading it tonight." She covers her head with the blanket. "If I fall asleep on the way home, can I rest my head on your lap?"

"Do you think that's a good idea?"

"I do."

"What if I charge you a lap-resting fee?"

"How much?"

"A dollar a mile."

"A dollar a mile it is. Let's see, that's three dollars and twenty-five cents. It's a deal." She shakes his hand. "I'll have Charles add it to your pay." A half mile later she leans her head against his shoulder and falls asleep.

Chapter 19

*September 1962
Sacred Heart Parish, Providence, Vermont*

Bishop Robert James is standing in the shadows at the back of the stage at Sacred Heart School, reading his notes. He tucks them into his right pocket, checks his watch, and clears his throat. It is ten minutes before seven. He will begin speaking precisely at seven—he is a very punctual man. The auditorium lights are off and the stage is lit. He shades his eyes and squints to see the crowd. All he can see are the exit signs and the lights in the hall. He walks to the lectern, removes his watch, places it next to a Bible on the top of the podium, and taps the microphone two times.

"Welcome," he says. He waits a few seconds for the crowd to be still. "Welcome, ladies and gentlemen, moms and dads, boys and girls, Sisters, janitors, friends, and everyone else associated with this wonderful school. I've come to you in Christ." He closes his eyes and bows his head. "Most of you probably don't remember, but I was a parish priest here, fifteen years ago. Seems like just yesterday. I love this school." He is wearing a black cassock with red piping, a red shoulder cape, and a red miter. A silver cross the size of his fist is on a chain around his neck. "This is an exciting week for our sixth and seventh graders—confirmation week, the week your children become soldiers in Christ." He grabs the cross, holds it in front of his face, closes his eyes again, and kisses it.

He steps away from the podium and walks to the edge of the stage, the microphone still in his hands. He is careful not to trip over the cord. He fancies himself Vermont's Bishop Fulton Sheen. "Before I get into the details about the confirmation, I need to tell you a story about what happened to me early this morning." He pauses to make sure everyone is listening. "I left Burlington at five o'clock, too early to eat breakfast, so I ate at the Midway Diner on Route Seven."

He pauses, looks directly at the audience, and points to the back of the auditorium as if he were pointing to the diner. "I asked for toast, two eggs, a cup of coffee, and a few kind words." He pauses after the words "toast," "eggs," and "coffee" and smiles at the crowd when he says each of them. "The waitress brought me the toast, the eggs, and the coffee, but said nothing." He pauses again, looks at the audience, and grins. "'What about a few kind words?' I said." He pauses, even longer than before, and scans the audience again. "'If you know what's good for you, you won't eat the eggs,' she said." He flashes a slight smirk. The audience roars with laughter.

"Boys and girls, I expect great things from you." He slowly paces back and forth across the stage as he speaks, and he stops after every thought to make eye contact with the audience he cannot see. "One priest and two or three nuns, at least," he says. He repeats himself but much slower. "One priest and two nuns from these two classes." A long pause and more intense eye contact.

He returns to the podium. "What does it mean to be a soldier in Christ?" He strokes his chin as if he were in deep thought and opens the Bible to Timothy. "As always, the Bible has the answer." He holds the Bible up to the audience and reads from it. "*Now teach these truths to other trustworthy people who will be able to pass them on to others. Endure suffering along with me, as a good soldier of Christ Jesus.*" He places the Bible back on the podium and returns to the front of the stage. "*If we die with him, we will also live with him.*" He wipes his brow.

"Ladies and gentlemen, confirmation is the sealing of the covenant created in baptism. It is an affirmation that Jesus Christ is our savior." He glances down at his watch. He has eight minutes left. He speaks for fifteen minutes, never longer. He knows from experience that no one listens beyond fifteen minutes and most lose interest after ten. He explains the details of the confirmation. His notes are illegible, so he repeats details from the confirmation address he gave two weeks ago in Newport. "It will be a great day."

Monsignor Gauthier follows him with the information Bishop James had forgotten and corrects the details that were wrong. "Confirmation is Monday, October twenty-second, not Sunday, at seven, not seven thirty, and please have your child here by six thirty, not seven, and in the cafeteria, not here in the auditorium."

"Sorry about that," Bishop James says when Gauthier exits the stage.

"Not a big deal."

James leans toward Gauthier and whispers, "We need to talk."

"Now?"

"No, later tonight in your apartment." He is sleeping in Gauthier's extra bedroom.

Sister Bartholomew approaches the two priests. "Tremendous speech, Bishop, I haven't laughed so hard in years. You had the crowd in the palm of your hand."

"That gets pretty heavy some days," he says.

"I bet it does," Gauthier says.

Several parishioners tell the bishop they loved his speech. One woman hugs him. He is surprised and his body stiffens. "Thank you, you're so kind," he says to her.

When the auditorium is mostly empty, Gauthier leads the bishop to the rectory. Two of the three streetlights in the parking lot are out, and there are several potholes that must be avoided.

"Sorry about the lights. Someone smashed them two nights ago," Gauthier says.

"We're pretty sure we know who did it," Father Symanski says. He and Father Cantone are walking directly behind Bishop James and Gauthier.

The four men enter the first-floor apartment. Symanski offers Bishop James a glass of wine. "Thank you so much, but John and I have some business to finish. Work never ends." He and John climb the stairs to John's apartment.

"So, what's the issue?" Gauthier says when they step into the living room.

"Let's get some wine first. Better yet, do you have whiskey?"

"I do."

"Double shot, two ice cubes."

"Sounds good." Gauthier returns with two filled shot glasses—his has no ice. "Is there a problem I should be aware of?"

"Father Symanski . . . he's a very busy man."

"He is indeed. Anything I need to worry about?"

"Not really. He sends me a letter every other month or so, sometimes about you, sometimes with a lamebrain idea about what the church should be doing differently. My secretary calls him 'The Ideas Man.' To be honest, I don't read most of them." He finishes his whiskey and refills his glass. "Tell me about Patrick Colman."

"What do you want to know?"

"Amand is worried."

"About what?"

"He thinks you spend too much time with the boy."

"I don't."

"That's not what he says. He says you have the boy up here alone in your apartment once or twice a week."

"Did he accuse me of . . ."

"No. Even if he had, I know you better than that. But it's best that you don't have the boy up here again, not alone anyway."

"I'm teaching him to write, that's all. Totally appropriate."

"That wasn't a suggestion, it was an order. Don't have the boy up here. You're not his teacher. Leave that to the nuns. If you continue, I'll have to transfer you. And I'm tired of transferring priests. It's getting old. If you're not careful, I'll send you to northern Maine, to moose country." Both men laugh. "I don't want to do that. You've done a good job here."

"You're the boss."

"I am."

"What else you got?"

"Amand is wondering if you believe in God."

"I do. I think it's self-evident God exists. Nothing else makes sense."

"Atheists would disagree."

"Yes, they would. I do have faith God exists, but sometimes I can't explain why I believe. Mostly it's a feeling I get in my gut. What I do know is I need God, more and more every day. Does it matter if I believe or not?"

"Probably not. Just do your job and keep your doubts to yourself."

"I will."

James holds up his glass. "How about a refill?"

"Sounds good."

"Do you want me to transfer Amand?"

"No, he's okay. He can be a pain in the butt, but mostly he's a good man. I think I need him around to remind me of what I should be doing here. Sometimes I forget."

"Yes, you do." He swirls a mouthful of whiskey around his mouth and swallows. "I don't know how you do it. He'd drive me nuts. When he's not sending me complaints or suggestions, he's sending me news clippings. He even sent me a clipping about Marilyn Monroe's suicide, as if I lived in a cave and knew nothing about it. He thought I should make suicide prevention the topic for the month."

"He means well, he really does. You'll get used to him. He's like a cheap wine. If you drink it often enough, you start to like it."

"I guess I better drink more."

Gauthier thinks back to their first meeting nineteen years ago. They met at Camp Holy Ghost, the Catholic summer camp for boys. Gauthier was a new priest, in his third year, and James was in his sixth year. Young priests got stuck with camp duty. James was sitting on his bed reading a letter from his brother Michael. He was so involved with reading the letter he hadn't heard Gauthier enter the room.

"You okay?" Gauthier remembers asking James.

"What?" James had answered.

"Are you okay? You look worried."

"I'm fine, just reading a letter from my brother." He folded the letter and tucked it into his shirt pocket. "Who are you?"

"John Gauthier, Corpus Christi, St. Johnsbury."

"Robert James, Sacred Heart, Providence." He walked to the closet and retrieved an Indian feathered headdress. "This is for you."

"What's it for?"

"We play Indian chiefs tonight around the campfire. We get all the campers in a line and dance them around the fire as if we were at a war dance. We whoop and we holler and we stomp our feet. The boys love it." He started stomping around the room.

"I'm pretty sure Indians didn't dance like that, and I'm pretty sure nobody in this part of the country ever wore a headdress like that either."

"True—the Sioux, Crow, Cheyenne, a couple others, but not the Abenakis. We're not recreating history. We're just having fun. Accuracy is for historians, not for young Catholic boys." He stomped around the room a second time. "If you're still wondering what upset me, my brother Michael wrote me a sad letter from the war, from Italy."

"Is he injured?"

"No, he's fine, at least physically. Two weeks ago, his wife sent him a Dear John letter. She has a new man, and she's filed for divorce. Their two-year-old daughter calls the new man 'Daddy.' Michael's devastated."

"I would be too."

"I'm afraid for him. I am afraid of what he might do. He could just up and leave or try to leave—not sure where he'd go—and then he'd get arrested and go to jail."

"I'll pray for him," John says.

"It's going to take more than prayers. I am going to Italy next month. I've asked the bishop to assign me to Michael's post. I nearly begged him. He said no, that wouldn't be a good idea."

"He's probably right."

"I know he's right, but I'm going to go see my brother anyway. I was a brother long before I was a priest."

"I hear ya."

"What about you. Why aren't you in Europe?"

"I wanted to go. I've asked the bishop a dozen times, but he keeps saying no."

"Why?"

"I don't know for sure, but I think my dad made a pretty substantial contribution to the cathedral in Burlington with the understanding I'd stay here in Vermont, at least until the war ends."

"Who's your father?"

"Nobody, just a rich guy who doesn't want his son to die. Apparently, you can buy anything, even the church." John places the headdress on his head and looks at himself in the mirror above the clothes dresser.

"Last month, my brother's best friend died in his arms. He was shot in the face and died quickly. Michael was on the ground next to him. 'It could have been me,' he said in his letter. 'It should have been me. Why didn't I die?' If the bullet had been ten inches to the left it would have hit his face. I wouldn't have a brother. Some nights I dream about him getting shot in the face. In one dream the bullet went through his head, but he was a cartoon character. His head was deformed from the shot. It looked like a watermelon. He just took his hands and popped his head back to the correct shape, pulled the bullet out of his forehead, examined it, flicked it to the ground, and said, 'I'm fine.' I couldn't get that picture out of my head for days."

"Maybe it's best we focus on our Indian dance," John said.

Chapter 20

November 1962
Sacred Heart Parish, Providence, Vermont

Monsignor Gauthier is slumped in his recliner. He should write his sermon for tomorrow, but he is not in the mood. He'll write it later this afternoon—either that or he'll rewrite one of the sermons he's given before. He has an extensive file of old sermons sorted by gospel. If he does reuse an old sermon, he'll make just enough changes so the few who actually pay attention won't recognize the recycled message. He's been called out several times for repeating sermons.

He is reading *The Idiot* but is too sleepy to follow the plot. He keeps rereading the same two pages. "Simple Gifts" from *Appalachian Spring* is playing softly on his stereo. A shot glass, filled with rum, is on the floor next to the recliner. He tries to focus on the text, but he is too tired. His head hurts, and his eyes burn from the need to sleep. He drops the book to the floor and closes his eyes. He falls asleep instantly. The ring from the telephone jars him awake.

"We have an emergency. Come quick," Sister Bartholomew says. She hangs up before he has a chance to speak.

Sister Ryan is waiting for him at the front door of the school. She is rocking back and forth and strumming her fingers on her hips. "Maurice Nolan is stuck in the heating tunnel."

"What?" Gauthier says. He is barely awake. He shakes his head to clear the fog.

She repeats what she just said.

"How can that be? The tunnel is plenty wide. What's he stuck on?"

"He's not stuck on anything. He's frozen with fear halfway between the church and the school. He won't go one way or the other."

The furnace in the basement of the church heats both the school and the church. It is a huge, coal-fired furnace nearly as big as a pickup truck. Three heating pipes run underground, below the parking lot, sixty-five yards from the furnace to the school. Each of the three pipes is covered with an asbestos shell that was white twenty years ago but is mostly pale yellow now. All three asbestos sleeves are repaired in several places with silver duct tape. There is a crawl space next to the pipes, three feet high and four feet wide. Access to the tunnel from the school is through a child-sized door under the stage in the auditorium.

Paul Fermonte, Patrick Colman, and the O'Riley twins are standing next to Sister Bartholomew, staring at the floor, their heads bowed in shame as if they were scolded puppies. Their hair is covered with cobwebs, and their faces, arms, and pants are soiled with dirt from the tunnel. Earlier that day, Paul had challenged the other four musketeers to crawl through the tunnel from the school to the church. They had been thinking about crawling through it for several weeks, ever since Ted Potter, an annoying sixth-grader with crooked teeth, bad breath, and a squeaky voice, boasted that he had crawled through it and had killed a rat the size of a cat with his bare hands. Nobody believed him, but the challenge was out.

. . .

Patrick was so fidgety at breakfast that his mother knew something stupid was planned. "Why are you up so early? It's Saturday. Usually, you sleep till noon," she said.

"Nothing. Just hanging out with the gang."

"I wasn't born yesterday. Something's up—probably something inane."

"Nothing's up, Ma. We're gonna play touch football, that's all. Leave me alone."

"It's too cold to play football."

"No, it's not." He ran up the stairs to his bedroom and grabbed his football and a flashlight.

"What's with the flashlight?"

"Our clubhouse is dark."

"Can't read your girlie magazines in the dark?"

"We don't have girlie magazines, Mom." He rolled his eyes. He said Mom as if there were three syllables in the word.

. . .

"All right, men, here's the plan," Paul said to the other musketeers when he told them about his plan to crawl through the heating tunnel. "We're gonna get into the school through one of the windows in the auditorium. I unlocked it yesterday after school." He paused to make sure the others were listening and glanced at his wristwatch. "Let's synchronize our watches."

"Why?" Patrick Colman said.

"I don't have a watch," Sean O'Riley said.

"I don't either," his brother Mike said.

"What does synchronize mean?" Maurice said. He looked at his watch.

"Forget it," Paul said. "Let's check our flashlights." His flashlight worked, but the batteries in the other four were dead. He slapped his head. "Good thing one of us has a brain."

The boys hid their bicycles in the lilac bushes behind the church, between the church and the rectory, and scurried from the bushes to the school parking lot like spies in a cartoon caper. "This is gonna be colossal, men, truly colossal," Paul said.

"Colossal? Seriously? Do you even know what that means?" Patrick said.

"Of course I do." He rolled his eyes.

"Okay, genius, lead the way," Patrick said.

Halfway through the tunnel, Paul's flashlight went dead. The tunnel was totally dark. They were too far from either end to see any light.

"Damn, damn, damn," Paul said. He banged the flashlight with the heel of his right hand, hoping it would turn back on, but nothing happened.

"What are we going to do? We're gonna die," Maurice said.

"We're not gonna die, you stupid idiot," Paul said.

A mouse bumped Maurice's arm with its nose. He screeched a piercing scream. "A rat just bit me."

"Shut up, or *I'll* bite you," Paul said. His voice cracked, and his legs twitched.

"What do we do now, Paul?" Patrick said.

"What do you think we do, numbnuts? We get out of here."

"What about the rats?" Maurice said.

"There aren't any rats. They're just mice," Patrick reassured Maurice.

"I saw one. A big, huge rat, bigger than my cat."

"I saw it too. It was a mouse, smaller than Buddy," Patrick said. Maurice has two hamsters. Buddy is the smaller of the two.

Patrick, Paul, and the O'Riley twins crawled back to the school. They hadn't noticed Maurice wasn't with them. Sister Bartholomew and Sister Ryan were waiting for them at the tunnel door. Sister Ryan had heard Maurice's scream. Sister Bartholomew grabbed each boy by his ear when he got to the entrance and pulled him out of the tunnel. "What's going on, boys?" she said.

"Nothing, Sister," Patrick said.

"Where's Maurice?" Paul's voice trembled. He stuck his head in the tunnel. "Maurice, where are you?" he yelled. There was no answer. "Sister, Maurice is still in the tunnel. We gotta go get him."

"You'll do no such thing." She grabbed Paul's ear again and pulled him to the first row of seats. "Sit." She pointed to the seat. "You three, sit," she said to the others. "I'm going to call Monsignor Gauthier. Do not move from these seats. Is that clear?" All of them mumbled yes.

. . .

Gauthier, half asleep, stumbles down the hallway to the auditorium. "So, what do we have here?" He runs his right hand through his hair.

The four boys scuff their feet nervously. "Nothing, Father," they say, almost in unison.

"Maurice is still in the tunnel," Sister Bartholomew says.

"I guess we'll have to do something about that," Gauthier says. He sticks his head through the door. "Maurice, can you hear me?"

"Yes, Father!" Maurice yells back.

"Just crawl out."

"I can't, Father. I can't move."

"Sure, you can."

"No, I can't. There are too many rats. I'm too afraid."

"There aren't any rats. A few harmless mice but no rats."

"Ted Potter killed one just a few weeks ago," Paul says.

"Ted Potter didn't kill anything. He had only got about thirty feet when he turned back," Gauthier says.

"Figures," Paul mutters. He punches Mike O'Riley's ribs. "I told ya so."

Father Cantone and Father Symanski have joined them. Symanski has a flashlight in his left hand. "Another boy frozen in the tunnel?" he says.

"'Fraid so," Gauthier says. "Who's going to crawl in there this time? I'm too old for this nonsense. If I get in there, I'll never get out. My body's too stiff."

"I'll go. You went in last time," Symanski says to Cantone.

David Kennedy, the school janitor, joins the group. "I'm gonna get a lock for the tunnel door this afternoon. Shoulda done that a month ago." He is as short as the boys and nearly as skinny. He has a cigarette balanced on his right ear.

"Good idea," Gauthier says.

Symanski quickly returns with Maurice. Both are covered with cobwebs and dirt. Maurice is sobbing. He has pissed his pants, and his nose is dripping snot and blood. He covers his mouth and bolts toward the door. He pukes under the exit sign. There are three raisins in the vomit. He drops to his knees and throws up again. Six more raisins float in the steaming goo.

"Ah, jeez," Kennedy says. He leaves the room and returns with a bucket of green sawdust and sprinkles it over the vomit.

"Boys, boys, boys, what should I do with you?" Gauthier says.

"I don't know, Father," Patrick says.

"Let's deal with this on Monday. I'm not in the mood right now. I've got a sermon to write. Sometimes you boys drive me insane." He waves them away. "Patrick, stay behind. I need to tell you something."

"Am I in trouble, Father?" Patrick says after everyone except the janitor, who is cleaning the floor, has left the auditorium.

"Yes, big trouble, but we'll deal with that on Monday. I don't have the patience right now."

"Sorry, Father."

"You should be. I expect better from you."

"I'll do better. I really will."

Gauthier places his left hand on Patrick's right shoulder and guides him toward the door. "What did you think of *To Kill a Mockingbird?*"

"I loved it. Best book I've ever read."

"I thought you'd like it. I can't give you any more books."

"Why not?"

"Just can't, at least not directly. What I'm going to do is set up a special shelf in the library open to everyone. I'll call it "Books Monsignor Gauthier Recommends." What do you think?"

"I don't know, Father. I'm not sure anyone would take your books. You're kinda old."

"You're probably right. I'll come up with a better title. In the meantime, use your head. Next time Paul comes up with something foolish, just say no. Can you do that?"

"Yes, sir."

"I'm serious, Patrick. You're a smart young man, but sometimes you're so stupid it scares me."

"My father says the same thing."

"I'm sure he does. Think for yourself Patrick. Don't let Paul think for you."

"Yes, Father."

"Now get out of here."

Patrick turns toward the exit. "Patrick, wait," Gauthier says. "I'll put two great books on the shelf on Monday, *Where the Red Fern Grows* and *Lord of the Flies*. You'll like them, I promise. I'd add *The Catcher in the Rye*, but I'm afraid your parents wouldn't be happy with me. Read *Lord of the Flies* first. I'd hate to see what would happen if you and your buddies were stranded alone on an island." He gently pushes Patrick toward the exit sign. Patrick sprints to the door, up the six stairs to the first floor, and down the hall to the main entrance. His friends are in the lilac bushes standing over their bikes.

"What'd he say?" Paul says.

"Nothing."

"What's he going to do to us?"

"I don't know."

"Do you think he'll call our parents?"

"Probably not."

"If he does, I'm in deep shit," Nolan says.

"Paul, next time you have a stupid idea, keep it to yourself." Patrick bikes in the opposite direction from the others.

"You're going the wrong way, dirtbag," Paul says.

"No, I'm not."

Chapter 21

March 1929
Doty Farm, East Providence, Vermont

John Gauthier is sitting on Charlotte's bed, his back resting against the headboard. He is naked. The top sheet is pulled to his waist. Charlotte is lying next to him on her side. Her head is on his lap. She is wearing his flannel shirt and nothing else. Her eyes are closed. She is half awake and half asleep. Her breaths sound like an old cat snoring. Two half-filled glasses of wine are on the end table next to the bed. Several cigarette butts are crushed in the ashtray on the table. The morning sun is streaming around the edges of the window shade. John is stroking her hair with his right hand and holding *Leaves of Grass* in his left hand.

He reads to her.

> *I mind how once we lay such a transparent summer morning,*
> *How you settled your head athwart my hips and gently turned over upon me,*
> *And parted the shirt from my bosom-bone, and plunged your tongue to my bare-stript heart,*

And reached till you felt my beard, and reached till you held my feet.

He lightly taps her head with the book. "Wake up. You're asleep."

"It's seven in the morning, I should be asleep. It's Sunday, remember? Not everybody gets up at five thirty in the morning to milk cows. I'm tired . . . let me go back to sleep."

He reads the poem again. "What do you think?"

"You don't have a beard, and it's not summer. Leave me alone."

He taps her head. "Very funny. What are we going to do today?"

"I know what I'm going to do today, I'm going to go back to sleep."

"No, you're not." He squeezes her nose.

She swats his arm away from her face. "Stop it."

"What are we going to do?" He kisses her forehead and yanks her ears.

"You sure are annoying in the morning. Don't speak to me until I've had my coffee. How many times have I told you that?"

"What are we going to do today?"

"What about 'Don't speak to me' don't you get?"

"You love me, you know you do."

"Maybe, but not at seven in the morning and not before I've had my coffee. And stop touching me." She slaps his hands.

"What are we going to do today?"

"My god, man, shut up." She covers her ears with her hands. "I told you yesterday. We're going to go snowshoeing after lunch, and then we're going to tap maple trees, but that's six hours from now. It'll be fun. Now let me go back to sleep for one more hour, please. Just one more measly hour without you talking."

"I don't want to tap maple trees. I did that last week. It's not fun, it's work. Hard work. This is my day off. My wrist is still sore from drilling the trees."

"Audrey is right, you sure do whine a lot."

"I do not. I spent five days last week slogging through snow and mud tapping maple trees. On Tuesday it rained all day, but that didn't stop Charles. I froze my ass off. A wet, cold rain is worse than below zero." He jumps out of the bed. "I'll make you breakfast."

"I don't want breakfast. I want to go back to sleep."

"You're not going to go back to sleep, you're getting breakfast."

She throws a pillow at him and pulls a second pillow over her head. "You drive me nuts."

He walks to the kitchen and grabs bacon and eggs from the icebox. "Put something on, bacon grease splatters," she says. The pillow muffles her voice.

He trots to the bed, grabs her head-shielding pillow, throws it across the room, rolls her onto her back, and unbuttons her shirt. "You're beautiful," he says. He kisses her chest. "I know what we can do for the next five minutes," he says.

"Five minutes? I don't think so. Twenty minutes, minimum." She kisses him.

"Fifteen. I'm really hungry."

"Twenty or nothing. We're not negotiating."

"Twenty it is." He removes her shirt and tosses it toward the pillow on the floor.

"This better be worth it."

"It will be."

She grabs his head, pulls him to her, and kisses him. "I do love you, but sometimes you drive me crazy."

"That's part of my charm."

. . .

The snow is wet and heavy and clumps to the rawhide webbing of their snowshoes. After a hundred yards, there is so much wet snow on the tops of their shoes that lifting their feet is difficult—as if they were lifting a ten-pound bag of sugar with each step. There are eight people in all, two men—Gauthier and Charlotte's cousin Arnold Erickson, a tall redhead who towers over the other seven—and six women—Charlotte and five of her friends. All five friends are married, but none of their husbands would join them. Each person is holding a sap bucket, and Arnold and John are carrying hand drills. Arnold's knapsack is filled with taps. The maple trees are on his land, a half mile west of his house, just past a stand of birch trees. To get to the maple trees, he usually takes his sleigh or a wagon if the road to the sugarbush is passable. It is too muddy today.

"This is a stupid idea," John says. "There's more mud than snow."

"I told you he'd say that," Charlotte says to the other women. They nod in agreement.

"He's right. The snow is too heavy. Let's turn back," says Cynthia Frost, one of the secretaries who work with Charlotte.

"I say we take a vote. Everybody who wants to turn back, raise your hand," John says. Everyone raises their hand except Charlotte.

"Then return to the house it is," John says. He pumps his fist in victory. Charlotte grabs a handful of slush and tosses it at his head.

"I've got lots of rum, whiskey, and gin and some beer I made myself. It's delicious," Arnold says. "Rum and good beer beat slogging through wet snow any day. I'll tap the trees next week."

. . .

Arnold's house has nine rooms. He lives alone. It was his parents' home before they died. His father fell off a ladder two summers ago and hit his head on the cement sidewalk. His mother died when he was six years old. He barely remembers her. He has been married and divorced twice and has a daughter who lives in Boston. She has a large family of eight children, and it is difficult and expensive for them to travel to Vermont. He is not interested in finding a new wife. He is forty-eight and has been single for fourteen years. He was lonely the first few months after the second divorce, but he has crafted a life without women and is very content alone. A companion now would just ruffle his routine.

The house is warm, almost too warm. Arnold instructs everyone to hang their coats in the hallway closet. He opens the living room window. Most of the furniture is worn and should be replaced. The wallpaper in the living room is faded, and the paint on all the doors and baseboards is chipped. "Who wants what?" he says and fills their orders.

"So, John, you need to tell us about yourself. That's why we're all here, in case you hadn't guessed," Cynthia says. "We're a very nosy bunch."

"I second that," Reina Delvechio says. She is the shortest adult John has ever seen.

"Not much to tell," John says.

"What do you mean 'Not much to tell'? You're filthy rich, but you're working as a low-paid, hardworking farmhand. You've been to Europe and India and who knows where else—none of us have ever been anywhere. You fell in love with an Indian girl and nearly lost your life. You read a lot, you're terribly handsome, and Charlotte is madly in love with you," Reina says.

"Reina!" Charlotte growls.

"Why do you think we're here today? To snowshoe in the mud? I don't think so," Reina says.

"What do you want to know?" John says.

"Everything."

"I'm twenty-seven years old, I was born in Hartford, Connecticut, and I'm a farmhand at the Doty Farm in East Providence, Vermont. It's Vermont's most successful farm, especially now that I am there." He chuckles and grins slightly. "I went to high school at St. George's School in Middletown, Rhode Island. Only rich kids go there. I went to college at Yale—just me and two thousand other rich boys. I have a BA in American literature. Despite that, I know next to nothing about anything that matters. I spent two years in India, and, yes, I did fall in love, but that was a lifetime ago, and I'm here now drinking rum with six beautiful women. End of the story."

"Do you have any sisters or brothers?" Beth Thompson asks. She is an eighth-grade teacher at Providence Elementary. All her students love her. She has a smile that says, "All is well."

"My sister died when I was eleven years old and she was eight. I think of her every day."

"I'm so sorry," Beth says.

"Don't be. The sadness is long gone, or at least most of the time. When I think of her now, I remember how she made me laugh. When she was four or five, she had a rag doll she called Margaret. She dragged that stupid doll everywhere she went. It was filthy. One time, when we were at the Bronx Zoo, a monkey reached through the bars and grabbed it from her and ran off with it, and hugged it like it was its own child. My sister wailed so loud that everyone near us froze. One of the zookeepers ran toward us. He thought the monkey had slashed her arm. When he learned what happened, he smiled and said, 'No problem, young lady,' and he rubbed the top of her head. The monkey didn't want to give the doll back, but he gave it back when a second zookeeper traded food for the doll. 'Next time, don't get so close to the cage,' the first zookeeper warned her and handed her a green lollipop. For the next several weeks, when she was in her room alone, she'd reenact the drama, but in her reenactments, it was our dad who saved the doll, not the zookeeper."

"You must miss her terribly," Beth says.

"I do. When she was very young—five, six at most—she had a game where I was the baby. She called me Brother Baby. I had to whine and cry and fuss. She'd hug me and rock me and put me to bed. 'Don't cry, Brother Baby,' she'd say. She'd cover my head with a blanket and then tend to her dolls. I couldn't leave the bed because I was her baby and I was sleeping. One time I snuck a book in with me because it got pretty boring laying under the covers listening to her scold her dolls. She must have seen the book through the blanket because she ripped the blanket off me, grabbed the book, and threw it against the wall. 'Babies don't read, John,' she said. She was so mad her temples were throbbing. It was several weeks before I had to be Brother Baby again."

Charlotte grabs his right hand and squeezes it. "Why didn't you tell me any of this before?"

"You never asked."

"More rum?" Arnold says.

"Absolutely," Charlotte says. She checks the clock on the kitchen wall. "John, we have to go in about fifteen minutes. One more shot for me and one more for John, one more for the road."

"Don't go. It's too early," Arnold says. "You haven't even tried my beer."

"I'd love to stay, but Mrs. Berlusconi has a special meal planned for us at six. She's so excited about it, she wouldn't tell me what it is."

"Are you guys getting engaged? You're not keeping secrets from us, are you?" Reina asks.

"No," John and Charlotte say together. They are each surprised by how quickly the other answered.

"Then why the special meal?"

"I don't know why. Sometimes I think she thinks I'm her daughter. Plus, she loves John."

"What are your intentions with Charlotte? You can't leave here until you tell us," Reina says to John. She speaks in a fake serious voice.

"I don't know, ask Charlotte," John says.

"I don't know either. We'll play it one day at a time."

John grabs her hand and squeezes it. "One day at a time sounds pretty good to me."

When they are outside the house, Charlotte grabs him, pulls him to her, and kisses him with a quick peck. The six people in the house watch them from the living room window.

"They're all watching us," John says.

"Yes, they are," Charlotte says.

"Kiss me again, longer this time," John says.

She does, a long passionate kiss.

The women watching from the house applaud them.

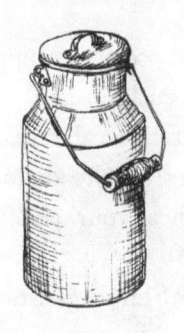

Chapter 22

May 1929
Doty Farm, East Providence, Vermont

"What are you doing here?" John says to Little John. It is two thirty in the morning. Little John is tickling John's nose and giggling. He had crawled from his room to John's room and used the sheets to pull himself upright, next to the bed. John grabs him and sits him on the pillow. "My goodness, you stink." A blob of green goop drips onto the pillowcase. John carries the baby to the changing table in Little John's room.

"What's going on?" Audrey says. She clears her throat and shakes her head. Sleep crust is stuck in the corners of her eyes. She scrapes the crust clean with her thumbs. "Damn, my head hurts." She shakes her head again. Her nightgown is milk-stained and clings to her body.

"The little man thought I should change him," John says.

She checks his work. "Not too bad for a novice. How'd he get out of his crib?"

"The crib gate was down. I think he just crawled out."

Audrey grabs the baby and carries him to the living room. "He must be hungry."

John turns toward his bedroom.

"Where are you going?"

"Back to bed."

"Sit here, next to me. I could use the company. It's lonely at three in the morning." She taps the couch cushion and positions Little John onto her breast. He sucks aggressively. "Tell me about you and Charlotte."

"Just a guess here—I suspect she's already told you everything."

"Pretty much, but I want to hear your take. Are you going to marry her?"

"What?"

"Are you going to marry her? Simple question."

"Maybe, I don't know. What did she say?"

"She's thinking about it. Are you?"

"Sometimes."

"Do you love her?"

"Yes, I do."

"Good. Don't string her along forever. She acts tough but she isn't."

"I won't."

"Do you love her?"

"You just asked me that."

"Yes, I did, but I'm asking you again. I want the truth this time. Do you really love her?"

"I do."

"I knew you would." She leans toward him and kisses his forehead. "She deserves to be happy, and so do you." Little John spits a stream of goo toward John. The warm gob lands on his face. "Sorry about that," Audrey says.

"Not a problem." He wipes the slimy wad with his undershirt and sniffs the shirt.

Little John falls asleep. John stands up and grabs him. "I'll take him to his room."

"Are you coming back here?"

"Do you want me to?"

"Yes."

"Then I will."

When John returns, Audrey is wearing a red flannel bathrobe and fuzzy slippers. She has combed her hair and washed the crud from her eyes. "I finished *Women in Love* yesterday."

"Did you like it?"

"I think so. I'm not sure. I found some of it confusing."

"You're not alone."

"What should I read next?"

"*An American Tragedy*. I think you'll like it."

"What's it about?"

"It's another love story that goes terribly wrong. A very exciting book."

"Are you trying to tell me something?"

"No, it's just a good book."

"You know I love Charles?"

"Of course you do."

She leans toward him and speaks in a low whisper, so low John can barely hear her. "I love Charles, but sometimes I wonder what my life would have been like if I hadn't gotten married at eighteen? I'm not complaining, just wondering."

"I didn't think you were."

"You can't tell anyone I said that."

"Who would I tell?"

"Charlotte? Please don't tell her."

"I won't."

"You must think I'm an evil woman."

"Why would you say that? Whatever we do, we always question what we didn't do. That's human nature. Sometimes I wonder what my life would have been like if I had married the girl from India or the Italian girl from college."

"The Italian girl? What Italian girl? I haven't heard about her. Were you in love with her too?"

"Not sure. She was beautiful . . . olive skin, long black hair, thin, muscular legs, and large, dark brown eyes with thick, black eyebrows. She'd make everybody laugh, even me, and I don't laugh easily."

"That's for sure. Was she a student?"

"No, she was a local. There were no girls at Yale—still aren't any. Her dad owned a small grocery store. I met her at the store. I was buying cigars for the dorm. We thought we were big shots smoking cigars, real men. We'd smoke cigars and drink bootlegged whiskey and complain about the world. We were a bunch of old farts, twenty going on forty. I'm younger than that now.

"When I bought the cigars, she, Gina Costa, said, 'Are you old enough for cigars, young man?' Then she smiled. My knees buckled. I thought I would faint. I couldn't stop thinking about her. I went back to the store every day for the next two weeks. I bought enough Italian bread to feed an army. I fed most of it to the pigeons on the college green. Finally, she said, 'I think you're here for something besides bread.'

"Her dad was watching us from behind the deli counter. He didn't say anything, but if looks could kill, I'd be a dead man. When she took me to her parents' apartment for the first time for dinner—they lived above the store—she was embarrassed because they barely spoke English. I think she was afraid I would think they were stupid. Halfway up the stairs to their apartment, she changed her mind and said we had to leave, but it was too late—her mother and father were standing on the porch watching us climb the steps. Gina knew I was a rich kid, and, for some reason, she thought I would think less of her because her family had no money and lived in a small apartment above the store. When we got to the top of the stairs, her mother hugged me and squeezed my cheek. 'Gina was right, you handsome boy,' she said. Gina rolled her eyes. I didn't know what to say.

"My mother hadn't hugged me since before my sister died. I don't know if I loved Gina or not. I think I loved her parents more than I loved her."

"You sure you weren't in love with her? You sound like you were."

"In lust for sure. In love? Maybe, maybe not. Sometimes I don't think I know what love is."

"Sometimes I don't either."

"What you and Charles have is pretty special. Most people would be lucky to have what you have. Charles respects you. My father doesn't respect my mother, not even close. He thinks she's stupid. Mom is very timid. She takes his insults as if it were normal for a husband to constantly ridicule his wife."

"You're right, I am very lucky. Charles is a decent man and a kind husband, and he works hard, and he is a great father. I couldn't ask for more."

"Then don't."

"It's not that simple. I went from being a child to a wife, nothing in between. I thought I was a woman, I thought I was ready to get married and have a family, but I wasn't. I was just a kid. I graduated from high school, June third, 1921, and was married three weeks and one day later. We took a two-day honeymoon to Burlington. I said to Charles, 'Let's go to New York City for a week.' I'd never been there. Still haven't. He said we couldn't go because his father wasn't well enough to milk the cows by himself for more than a couple of days. He had emphysema and had a hard time doing anything."

"You didn't miss much, New York isn't a big deal."

"Easy for you to say—you've been all over the world. I've never left Vermont."

"You and Charles should go to Boston for a weekend, or better yet, go to Montreal. I can run the farm for a few days."

"What about Little John?"

"I can handle him."

"Change one diaper and you're a parent?"

"Charlotte could help me. She'd love to help."

"Maybe, but even if she did, Charles would never leave the farm. Sometimes I think he's married to the cows, not to me."

"He left for a few days in January to help his brother build some shelves in his apartment."

"That was different. His brother is useless. He couldn't saw a board straight if you gave him a million dollars." She rises from the couch, walks to the living room window, and looks at the night sky. "I wonder what would have happened if I had met you first?"

"You would have hated me."

"Why?"

"Because I was an asshole."

"You still are." She smiles.

"True. But when I was eighteen, I was even worse, a total jerk. I took it for granted that I was entitled to a good life. I thought I knew everything about everything. I was a fool."

"You're still a fool," she jokes and sits back on the couch.

"Before I came here, I didn't know how to milk a cow. I didn't know a maple tree from an elm. I had never eaten a fresh egg or butchered a turkey, and I had never seen a bobcat except in a zoo."

Audrey grabs John's right arm. "Why are you here, John?"

"You asked me to stay up with you, remember? Just five minutes ago."

"Very funny. You know what I mean. Why are you here working as a farmhand at the Doty farm in East Nowhere, Vermont? In case you haven't guessed, this isn't the most successful farm in the world. We don't even own a truck."

"I told you and Charles months ago. I'm hiding from my father. I don't want to run his damn company. I hate his business. I hate what it's done to him. I hate what it's done to my mother. My parents have more money than God, but Dad always wants more. More, more, more. He's a sad, miserable man—the more money he gets, the more miserable he is. I don't want to be sad and miserable all my life. There's got to be more to life than just making money. I want my life to have meaning. I don't know exactly what yet. I'm still trying to figure that out."

"Okay, that makes sense, but why are you working as a farmhand in East Providence, Vermont? This is no life for you. Sixty hours a week—seven days most weeks. Up at four in the morning and not done until seven or eight at night. Twenty-five bucks a week."

"When I was seventeen, the summer between my junior and senior years in high school, I hiked for two weeks on the Long Trail."

"The what?"

"The Long Trail. It's a hiking trail along the spine of the Green Mountains."

"Never heard of it."

"It's new, or at least it was new then. Three buddies and I took the train from Hartford to Burlington. My father hired a hiking guide to pick us up at the train station. He was a crusty old geezer, probably sixty, maybe older. We figured we'd leave him in the dust on the hike, but we were wrong. He beat us up every mountain. We'd get to the top and he'd be there already, sitting against a tree, smoking a cigarette. "What took ya so long, boys?" he'd say every time, and laugh.

"We hiked from Camel's Hump to Mount Mansfield and back. One night, on top of Camel's Hump, the sunset over the Adirondack Mountains was so dramatic it took my breath away. The sky and clouds were blazed with red and gold. Lake Champlain glistened in the fading light. I told my buddies 'Someday I'm coming back here, that's a promise.' They started calling me Daniel Boone."

Audrey lightly taps his left shoulder. "You haven't hiked since you've been here. When we dragged the Christmas tree back to the house, you complained the whole time."

"That's different. That was work. Most of the time I've been here it's been winter. I have no interest in hiking in the snow. East Providence is the coldest place in the world."

"Colder than the Himalayas?"

"No, but I was in the Himalayas in the summer and only in the foothills."

"Are you going to hike this summer?"

"No. Farming is way harder than I ever imagined. On my days off, I'm so tired I just want to relax and read."

"Sometimes you write. I hear your typewriter. What are you writing?"

"I'm writing a novel about a young American man who falls in love with a girl in India."

"Based on anyone we know?" She smiles.

"Yes and no."

"Can I read it?"

"No. It's terrible."

"I bet it's wonderful."

"You'd lose that bet."

"I want to read it anyway."

"I could change my mind, but I doubt it. I write for myself, not for anyone else."

"Not even me?"

"Not yet. Maybe when I'm done."

"I will hold you to that."

"I said maybe. We'll see."

"You realize I will pester you until I read it."

"I'm sure you will." He stands up and walks toward his bedroom.

"Don't go yet, we've got more to talk about." She taps the couch cushion to beckon him back to the couch. "If farming is so hard, why not do something else?"

"Farming is hard, much harder than I ever imagined, but I love it. I love the cows—I love milking them, I love brushing them. At first, I thought they all looked alike, but I was wrong. They're all different. I love them all, even Cow Fifty. I love the early morning sunrise. I love the frigid morning air when Charles and I cross the yard from the house to the barn and my nostrils freeze. The daily routine is tiring, for sure, but satisfying. Every day I have a job to do, and I get it done, and I do it well, and I get to do it again next day. The only thing I don't like are the damn flies. I thought the cluster flies were bad, but the blackflies this month are way worse. I think they have teeth. You said I'd get used to them. You were wrong."

She smiles. "I lied. Where are you going to go next? I can't imagine you'll be here much longer."

"Are you trying to get rid of me?"

"No."

"I have no idea. If you and Charles will have me, I'd like to stay a while longer—another year, maybe two, who knows?"

"If it were up to me, you'd stay forever."

"I doubt Charles would agree."

"Probably not."

"Let's go outside and look at the moon. It's huge tonight," Audrey says. Moonlight has filled the room. She clutches his arm and guides him to the closet. She grabs jackets for both of them and covers her head with her flapper's hat. "Do you like my hat?"

"You know I do." He grabs his boots and pulls them on his bare feet.

She squeezes his hand and leads him to the porch. "What a beautiful moon."

"It is."

"What's that?" She points toward the barn. The silhouette of a bobcat is visible in the moonlight. The bobcat is trying to open the gate to the chicken coop with its nose. "Go get Charles's gun."

"I can't shoot him. I couldn't hit the side of the barn."

"Then I will."

John sprints to the gun cabinet and roughly opens the door. Two rifles crash to the floor. He fumbles with the ammo drawer. He pulls too hard, and bullets fly out of the drawer to the floor.

"What the hell is going on here?" Charles says. He's wearing boxer shorts and an undershirt that fit him fifteen pounds ago. John's fumbling has woken him up.

"The bobcat's back. He's trying to get into the barn."

Charles grabs a gun from the floor and loads it. "I'm gonna get that son of a bitch this time, that's for sure." He hustles toward the front door.

"It's cold out there," Audrey says.

He ignores her. He opens the door so hard, the pictures on the wall rattle. "Where is that son of a bitch?"

She points toward the chicken coop.

Charles steps off the porch, into the mud, and yells, "You're dead this time, you little bugger." He shoots and misses. The bobcat scampers into the woods. Charles walks toward the chicken coop, steps on a stone, and cuts his right big toe. "Dammit all to hell," he says.

"Come inside, your feet must be freezing," Audrey says from the porch. His feet and ankles are covered with mud. She grabs his arm and leads him to the kitchen. She fills a washbasin with warm water, places his feet in the bucket, and washes off the mud and blood with a soapy cloth. She checks the wound. She kisses his forehead. "Charles, I love you even when you're an idiot."

"What are you two doing up this early?" Charles says. He points to the kitchen clock.

"Little John woke John up. He crawled into John's room. Somebody left the crib rail down."

"It weren't me," Charles says.

"You put him to bed, remember?" Audrey says.

He slaps his forehead. "Right. Sorry about that."

"I'd go back to bed, but it's too late. It's already four o'clock," John says.

Charles checks the clock. "If we milk 'em early, we can finish early."

"Words to live by," John says.

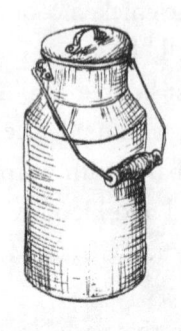

Chapter 23

May 1929
Doty Farm, East Providence, Vermont

"Charles, I'm going to town with you today," John says. He swats several blackflies away from his head.

"Why?"

"I just am." He claps his hands together, crushes a fly, and wipes the crushed fly on his pants.

"You must have a reason."

"Not really." He digs a fly out of his right ear and flicks it to the ground.

"You're a bad liar. And no, you don't got no time to see Charlotte, not even close. You'll just have to keep it in your pants today."

John swats more flies. "You didn't tell me about these damn blackflies."

"You wouldna stayed if I had."

"Probably not. They're vicious."

"Stop whining. They'll be gone in a month."

"Not sure if I'll have any blood left by then."

The wagon is packed with two dozen filled milk cans. The cows are in the grazing field for the first time since November. Audrey and the dog are standing on the porch. The dog is resting its head on her shoes. She's holding Little John, who is wrapped in a green wool blanket. He is asleep. She waves to Charles and beckons him to her. She hands him a grocery list, but he refuses to take it. "Don't have time, too damn busy," he says. She stuffs the paper into his shirt pocket. "Yes, you do," she says. She kisses his forehead. He grumbles, returns to the wagon, and hands the list to John. "Looks like you got sum shoppin' ta do today, Gauthier."

John reads the list. "We're getting more Indian food."

"Oh, please, no, my stomach can't take it. You gotta stop her. She won't listen to me. If you don't stop her, we'll both be dead," Charles says.

"I heard that," Audrey says from the porch.

John whispers, "My stomach can't take much more either. Last time I was on the john for half the day."

Both men smile.

"What ya gonna do in town today anyway?" Charles says.

"I'll tell you when we're down the road."

"Tell him what?" Audrey says. She strains to hear them.

"Nothing, none of your business," Charles says. "Stop being so damn nosy."

The dog sprints across the yard and jumps onto the wagon. "Stupid-assed dog," Charles says. He grabs the dog's collar and yanks it off the wagon. "Git," he says and points to the house. The dog runs to the house, its tail between its legs. "That dog'll never learn."

Audrey grabs the dog's head. "Good boy, Butch," she says, scratches its neck, and kisses its nose.

John waits until Audrey is back inside the house. "I'm going to buy Charlotte an engagement ring."

"No shit? I wondered about that."

"Yup. I'm going to ask her to marry me."

"When? Today?"

"No, not today, in July, when we go to Boston for July Fourth. You can't tell anybody."

"Not even Audrey?"

"Especially not her."

"Why not?"

"What if Charlotte says no?"

"She ain't gonna say no, dumbass. You're all she ever talks about. Gets pretty damn annoying."

"That may be so, but you never know."

"True. Women make no sense."

Charles taps his watch. "We better get our ass in gear, we're running late." Several of the cows didn't want to leave the barn and getting them to the field was a struggle. Cow Fifty led the rebellion.

Two miles later, John spots a wounded animal lying on the ground on the side of the road with half of its body in the road and half on the grass. "That looks like the bobcat," he says.

Charles pulls the horses to a stop, jumps off the wagon, and gingerly steps toward the animal. The bobcat's back legs are crushed. Tire tracks from a truck are etched in the dirt. The bobcat looks up at Charles and whimpers. "That's him alright." He lightly touches the bobcat's head with his fingertips. "Jesus Christ, bobcat, what the hell happened to you?" The bobcat lifts its head, looks at Charles, and sighs. Charles retrieves a shovel from the wagon. "I hate ta do this, good buddy, but I got no choice. I gotta put ya out of your misery." He bashes the bobcat's head with the shovel, grabs the body by the front legs, and drags it off the road to a flat spot on the grass. John grabs a second shovel and joins him. They dig a hole and bury the bobcat.

"I'm gonna miss you, you sorry son of a bitch." He pats the dirt with the shovel and returns to the wagon. "I got big news for you, Gauthier, bigger than your stupid engagement. Gonna get 'lectricity."

"I don't believe it. About time. Welcome to the twentieth century. Thought you'd never get here."

"Next week, 'lectricity in the house and in the barn. Maybe I'll buy a 'lectric refrigerator."

"Just don't make it a Christmas gift."

"Very funny. I could buy one of them milkin' machines. Put your sorry ass out of a job."

"Fine with me."

"Relax, just jokin'. Even if I get a milkin' machine, you still got a job."

"Good to know."

"If you marry Charlotte, where you gonna live? Can't live here. Two Andrews sisters in one house would be a nightmare. You and me, we'd end up sleeping in the barn half the time. I can see it now, the two of them teaming up against us. We'd lose for sure."

"If we end up sleeping in the barn, I get first dibs on the cot in the milk room," John says.

"Who's the boss here, Gauthier? I get first dibs. I get the cot—you can sleep in the hayloft." He grins.

"There's mice in the hay."

"Sleep with one of the barn cats."

"Are you serious? They scare me more than the mice." He jumps up to the wagon. "I'm thinking of buying the bookstore in Providence. I've talked to the owner, and he's ready to retire at the end of the year."

"So you're gonna leave me. Audrey said you might."

"Don't rent out my room just yet. Charlotte's got to say yes. No guarantees. Wouldn't be until after the wedding anyway and that won't be for another six months, at the earliest. You're stuck with me till fall, maybe longer."

"Could be worse."

"Thanks. You always know just what to say."

"I do."

. . .

Charles's wagon is third in line at Kennedy Brothers' dairy, behind two trucks. The first truck stalls. The driver jumps out of the cab and kicks the fender. "Goddamn, no good, goddamn piece of no good goddamn shit," he says to no one in particular. He punches his fist against the door. He raises the hood and fiddles with the carburettor. The plant foreman waves the second truck past the first. "See why I don't get a truck, Gauthier?" Charles says. "Total waste of money."

John points to the line of trucks behind them. "Look around, you're the only wagon left. You're a regular Luddite."

"A what?"

"A caveman."

"And proud of it." Charles hands John a five-dollar bill. "Put this toward the ring. Buy a good one, don't cheap out."

"Okay, Dad."

"Nice truck ya got there, Jenkins," Charles says to the angry truck driver when his wagon passes the stalled Ford.

"Fuck you, Doty." He smiles, walks to Charles, reaches up, and shakes his hand. "Ain't seen your sorry face since the fair last year."

"Your loss."

"You must be that rich kid from Connecticut," the driver says to John. John gives him a timid wave. The driver grabs John's hand and squeezes it hard. "Jeff Jenkins. I own the farm six miles up the road from Doty, just past the Catholic church, the big yellow barn with the slate roof that says 1878. Seen it?"

John nods.

"Of course, mine's a real farm, not that mess Doty calls a farm," Jenkins says

"Who got farmer of the year last year at the state fair? Weren't you," Charles says.

"You stuffed the ballot box, asshole," Jenkins says. He looks at John. "Doty and me been friends since we were little kids. He says you ain't too bad. High praise from him."

"I hear you had some trouble," Charles says.

"Waterline to the barn froze up. Had to haul water from the kitchen for nearly two weeks. Had to put down six cows—couldn't get 'em enough water."

"I can spare a couple cows. I sell 'em cheap. Come by Saturday. Bring your truck, if you can get that piece of shit goin'."

"You're just jealous."

"Sure, that's it."

The dairy foreman waves for Charles to pull his wagon to the loading dock. "Saturday, Jenkins, come for lunch. I'll have the wife fix you one of her Indian meals. That'll clear out your nostrils just good." Jenkins gives him a thumbs-up. Charles whispers to John, "I'll give him Cow Fifty—that'll teach him."

The jewelry store owner remembers them from before Christmas but forgets who was who. "So how'd your wife like the necklace?" he says to John.

"Loved it."

"She can't stop talkin' about it," Charles says. "Gauthier here, he owns the biggest farm in East Providence. I'm his hardworkin' farmhand. Works me to the bone, doesn't pay me shit. Should be a law 'gainst it."

The saleswoman remembers that Charles is the husband and whispers the truth into the store owner's ear. "So sorry about that, my mistake," he says.

"Nothin' to be sorry 'bout." Charles walks toward the door and points to the diner across the street. "I'll be gettin' lunch. Take your time but not too much time. We gotta get back and milk the cows."

"Don't worry, this won't take long."

At the newsstand, Charles grabs a *Providence Herald*. Charles Lindbergh has married Anne Morrow. "He's gonna be president someday, mark my words," he says to the newsstand vendor.

"He got my vote. Sure'd be better than that idiot, Hoover. Coolidge shoulda ran again," the vendor says.

"That's for damn sure," Charles says.

John shows the ring to Charles. "What do you think?"

"How much it cost?"

"What difference does that make? What do you think?"

"It ain't terrible. How much it cost?"

"Jesus, Charles, who cares what it cost? Thirty-seventy dollars."

"You're a liar—it cost ninety-seven dollars, I seen the price tag."

"Okay, so it cost ninety-seven dollars. Big deal. It's worth it."

"Not if she says no."

"Even if she says no."

"She's not gonna say no. Sometimes you're so stupid I can't figure you out. What they teach you at college anyway? It sure weren't seeing the obvious." He checks the clock on the wall. "We better get goin' or the girls will be real angry. They were in a bad enough mood this morning."

A beggar grabs Charles. "Gimme a quarter if I tell you where you got them shoes."

"I got them shoes on my feet." He hands the man a dime. "You asked for a dime last time."

"Inflation's a bitch," the panhandler says and laughs.

"You need to come up with a new line," Charles says.

"Not if you keep giving me money."

. . .

Audrey has guided the cows back to the barn. She is milking Cow Thirty-Seven. Little John is asleep in a basket near her feet. The dog is asleep next to the basket, its head resting on the basket rim. "Didn't think you two would ever get back. Figured you were out with some loose women." She smiles.

"Gauthier was, and I had to wait. Cost him ten bucks. Good thing he don't take him long." He smiles and looks to John for a reaction.

"Good thing," John says.

Charles walks to the sink, washes and dries his hands, returns to Audrey, and lifts her off the milking stool. John watches him milk the cow. "Gauthier, what the hell you doing? Grab a stool and start milkin'."

"I'd rather watch."

"Watch, my ass. Do some work for once."

"I got an Indian meal planned for tonight, whether you like it or not," Audrey says to Charles.

"Can't wait," Charles says.

Audrey carries Little John to the house. The dog walks through her feet and nearly trips her.

"I get first dibs on the toilet," John says.

"No, you don't. I do. I'm the boss, remember?" Charles says with a big grin.

Chapter 24

June 1929
Tent Revival, East Providence, Vermont

"You're comin' with me, Gauthier," Charles says. He secures the gate to the cow pasture and walks John toward the barn. His right hand is gripping John's left shoulder.

"Coming where? We don't deliver milk today."

"You'll see."

"I can't go. I've got a lot to do today."

"What you gonna do, read? Surprised you can see with all that readin' ya do. Ain't good for your eyes. You'll be blind by the time you're forty. I'm the boss, remember? You're coming with me." Charles hitches a horse to the buckboard. "Get your sorry ass up here."

"Where are you two going?" Audrey hollers from the porch. She is shading her eyes from the sun. Little John is standing at her feet, clutching her dress.

"None of your damn business," Charles says without looking at her. She smiles and waves them away.

Charles stops the buckboard at a large tent, nearly as large as a circus tent, pitched in a hayfield two miles from the farm. Twenty-five cars, possibly thirty, eight trucks, and six wagons are parked in the field next to the tent. The writing on the biggest truck, a large moving van, says "Pastor Jonathan Goddard, God's Voice in Troubled Times." A sign at the edge of the road reads "Revival Today, 11:00 A.M. Jesus is Our Salvation."

"You've got to be kidding me," John says.

"Nope. This is the real thing. None of that Catholic bullshit."

"I thought you weren't religious."

"I ain't, but I believe in Jesus." Charles waves to Jeff Jenkins, whose truck is parked three cars from his wagon. "I see you finally got that piece of shit goin'," Charles says.

"You're just jealous, asshole," Jenkins says. He walks to Charles and the two men shake hands with gusto.

"How them cows workin' out?" Charles asks.

"One cow's good, one's a pain-in-the-ass. Stubbornest cow I ever seen."

"That must be Cow Fifty."

"She's Cow Thirty-Seven now. Might just butcher that son of a bitch. More trouble than she's worth."

"Ain't that the truth." Charles chuckles.

Inside the tent, at the far end opposite the door, a tall, square-shouldered man with huge hands is standing on a low stage, one step from the ground, half reading a Bible. He is silently counting the people as they enter the tent. The air in the tent is hot and stale and smells like mud and rotted hay. There are about one hundred people inside, mostly adults, a few children, and two babies. One of the babies is crying. His frustrated mother is trying to quiet him with a bottle. Bibles are for sale at a table next to the entrance. John picks one up and opens the cover.

"That'll be fifty cents," says a short, fat woman with thinning gray hair. She opens a metal cash box.

"That's okay," he says. He puts the Bible back on the table. An usher points to the left and guides him and Charles to the last row of seats. The pastor wipes his forehead with a red handkerchief, sniffs hard, and checks his pocket watch. Two women and a man are standing in front of the stage, singing, "Old Rugged Cross." The man is playing a guitar and the women are keeping time with rhythm sticks.

The pastor's son, a skinny teenager with long blonde hair, whispers into his father's ear, "Time to get the show on the road, Dad."

Pastor Jonathan signals to the singers to stop. They finish the verse, walk to the entrance flap, and sit on chairs behind the Bible sales table. "Welcome, ladies and gentlemen, boys and girls, Christians, Vermonters, lovers of Jesus Christ, our savior." He pauses and slowly scans the crowd, making eye contact with as many people as he can. "Vermont . . . I love Vermont . . . God's country, farmer country," he says. Spittle sprays when he speaks.

"Yes, it is," yells someone from the crowd.

"I'm Pastor Jonathan Goddard of Westin, West Virginia. I am here today to share with you the joy and love of Jesus Christ." His voice booms as if he were commanding an army. "Turn to Galatians 5, verses nineteen to twenty-one." He waits a few seconds for everyone to find the page. "If you don't have a Bible, they're for sale at the table next to the entrance." He points to the table. The short woman waves to the crowd. Several people leave their seats to purchase one.

Jonathan adjusts his glasses, takes a deep breath, and reads: *"Now the works of the flesh are manifest, which are these, adultery, fornication, uncleanness, lasciviousness, idolatry, witchcraft, hatred, variance, emulations, wrath, strife, sedition, heresies, envying, murders, drunkenness."* He pauses, removes his glasses, closes the Bible, and pats dry his forehead.

"Amen," says a man with one leg. His wife rubs his shoulders.

"Jesus will forgive you, sinners. God is love, total love, infinite love. He loves everyone, rich man, poor man, sinner, and saint."

Several people in the audience mumble, "Amen."

One woman sprints to the stage, falls to her knees, and pleads, "I'm a sinner. I've sinned . . . I've fornicated with men for money. I've fornicated with women for money." The crowd gasps. "I don't deserve your love, Lord Jesus. Please forgive me." The man who had played the guitar lifts her off the ground and starts to guide her back to her seat. Pastor Johnathon leaps off the stage, grabs her shoulders, and shakes her. Her head bobs back and forth from the force of his shake.

"Forgive this woman, Jesus." He pokes her forehead. "You are forgiven." She collapses to the ground and trembles.

"Thank you, Pastor Jonathan," she says.

The pastor pulls her to her feet and hugs her. "Jesus loves you." He returns to the stage. The guitar man leads the saved woman to her seat.

Pastor Jonathan grabs a bottle of whiskey from a box at his feet, shows it to the crowd, removes the cap, and dumps the liquid onto the stage. "Whiskey, the sum of all villainies. It's worse than war and pestilence. It is the crime of crimes. It's the source of misery, crime, and poverty." He wipes his brow and glares at the audience.

"Tell it like it is, Pastor Jonathan," one man yells. He raises his arms above his head and shakes his body.

Pastor Jonathan wipes his brow. "The bootlegger is worse than a thief or a murderer. The thief steals your money, but the bootlegger steals your soul." He closes his eyes and tilts his head to the ceiling. "The saloon is the clearing house for damnation, and poverty, and insanity. If all you farmers were given a chance, you'd knock the whiskey business to hell."

"We would, Pastor Jonathan," says the man with one leg. He lifts one of his crutches and waves it several times above his head.

Several others shout, "Yes, we would."

"Whiskey ruined my life," says a woman in the front row. "My husband died a drunk, left me with nothing, left me to starve. Help me, Pastor Jonathan."

"Come here," he says, "come to me." She steps up next to him and kneels at his feet. "Do not kneel to me, kneel only to Jesus." She stands up, so close to him he can smell her breath. He cups her head in his hands. "Jesus will save you." When he lets go, she faints. The guitar man grabs her arms and lifts her to her feet. Pastor Jonathan grabs a second bottle of whiskey from the box and hands it to the woman, who is still shaken from her fall. "Dump this whiskey to the ground where it belongs." She pours the whiskey onto the dirt at the edge of the stage.

"Thank you, Pastor Jonathan," she says.

"Don't thank me, thank Jesus," he says. "Jesus died on the cross to save us from our sins." He closes his eyes and mouths a silent prayer. "Amen," he says.

He steps back behind the podium in the middle of the stage and looks directly at the crowd. "Like this poor woman's husband, I too was a sinner, a despicable sinner—a fornicator, an adulterer, a drunk, a miserable, worthless boozer, lower than a worm," he bellows. He opens his Bible. "God says in Proverbs, chapter 20, 'Wine is a mocker, strong drink is raging. Whosoever is deceived thereby is not wise.' I was not wise—I was a fool." He wipes the sweat from his brow and slowly paces across the stage.

The guitar player and the two women who were singing with him chant, "Amen, Brother Jonathan, amen," and raise their arms in exaltation. Several in the crowd lift their arms and sway their bodies.

Pastor Jonathan wipes his brow and glares at the crowd. "One night in New Orleans, just about fifteen years ago, I got into a fight with three bad men. I owed them money from gamblin'. The gamblin' halls and the saloons were my church . . . money was my salvation . . . sinnin' was my life. The men beat me and stabbed me and left me for dead. I laid there in a puddle of my own blood, looking up at the night sky, sure I was gonna die. I said to Jesus, 'Jesus, help me. I want to live.' 'I'll save you,' he said, 'but you must be a good man. No more sinnin', no more boozin'.'"

The three singers lead the crowd, chanting, "Praise the Lord, praise the Lord."

The sinner woman who had fainted jumps to the center aisle, drops to the ground, and slithers like a snake. "Thank you, Jesus. Thank you, Jesus."

"If you love Jesus, anything is possible. Believe in the Lord Jesus Christ and thou shalt be saved." He pauses and wipes sweat off his brow. "Are you ready to be saved?"

Someone from the crowd yells. "I am, Pastor Jonathan."

The guitar player and the two women sing "How Great Thou Art."

"Join in, brothers and sisters, join in this glorious song," the pastor says. Charles sings boldly and loudly. He elbows John, who is not singing. John mumbles the words.

Pastor Jonathan holds up several blank sheets of paper. "Sign this, and Jesus will burn your sins away." The three singers pass the papers and pencils from row to row and return the signed sheets to the pastor. Charles signs his name and John's name.

Pastor Jonathan holds one of the sheets to the crowd and lights it with a match. When the flame is too close to his hand, he drops the burning sheet to the stage floor, watches the paper burn to embers, and stomps the ashes with his feet. "Burn their sins away, Jesus, burn their sins away . . . forgive them with your love."

"Amen," the three helpers say.

The crowd roars, "Amen!"

The pastor wipes his brow and clutches his Bible to his chest. "Many of you are poor," he says. He pauses, scans the crowd, and shakes his head. "Do not be ashamed. Jesus loves you. God says in Proverbs 19, 'Better is a poor man who walks in his integrity than he that is perverse in his lips and is a fool.'"

"You're telling the truth, Pastor Jonathan," Charles bellows. John is surprised.

Pastor Jonathan steps off the stage and walks down the aisle to the entrance of the tent.

Sunshine is streaming through the edges of the tent's door. He pulls the canvas door open and points to the outside. The three singers are standing next to him, holding collection baskets. "Remember in Luke 6, chapter 38, God said, 'Give, and it will be given to you.'"

Charles drops a ten-dollar bill into one of the baskets.

"Are you crazy?" John says.

"Five from me, five from you. Next week's pay is twenty dollars."

John shakes his head. "I'm saved."

Jeff Jenkins hustles to Charles and taps his shoulder. "That were pretty damn powerful, wouldn't ya say?"

"It were," Charles says.

"You gonna dump your booze?" Jenkins asks.

"Maybe," Charles says.

"Maybe for me too. I sure do like beer."

Charles lightly swats the back of Jenkins's head. "You need more cows?"

"Naw, I'm alright. Gotta paint the barn before the wood rots. Just don't have the time. It's just me and the missus. Wilson left."

"Where'd he go?" Charles said.

"Beats me. Providence, I think. Not sure."

"He weren't much good anyway."

"Better than nobody."

"You gotta paint your barn, Jenkins. Ya got no choice."

"When? There ain't enough hours in the day."

"How 'bout tomorrow?"

"That ain't gonna happen."

Charles looks at John. "Looks like you're barn painting tomorrow, Gauthier."

"I can't take your charity," Jenkins says.

"It ain't charity, it's Gauthier."

Jenkins laughs.

"Very funny," John says.

Charles and John climb onto the wagon. Charles hands the reins to John. "You drive, I'm too tired." After a mile he says, "So what'd you think?"

"It was all right."

"You think Pastor Jonathan's a fake?"

"Yes."

"Could be. Who knows?"

"Then why did you give him ten bucks?"

"Want him to spread the word."

"He's a phony."

"You don't get it, Gauthier. It don't matter if he's a phony or not, it's the message that matters."

"What message—Demon Rum?"

"No, knucklehead—God loves you, Jesus loves you, Jesus is the way, the truth, through Him we're saved. How'd you miss that?" He looks at his watch. "Better speed up, the girls are waiting."

"They're always waiting," John says.

Chapter 25

December 1962
Sacred Heart Parish, Providence, Vermont

Monsignor Gauthier looks out the window of the church kitchen. It is five thirty in the morning. Three inches of new snow covers the ground. Twelve men and eight women are waiting outside the building, huddled in three circles, blowing hot air on their cold hands. Most are smoking cigarettes and chatting. One woman is having trouble standing. She has enormous legs. She had walked the seven blocks from the homeless shelter. Her legs are tired, and her knees are sore. She leaves her circle, waddles to the entrance steps of the church, and sits on the cold, wet granite. She gasps for air. "Damn, it's cold," she says.

Gauthier is cooking three dozen scrambled eggs and frying two pounds of bacon, a pound of breakfast sausages, and several pounds of hash brown potatoes on the kitchen grill. Father Cantone is filling a dozen saltshakers and Father Symanski is making coffee in a thirty-cup urn.

Last summer, Gauthier started the free breakfast program. Every Monday and Thursday morning he and the other two priests serve eggs, oatmeal, cold cereal, toast, coffee, juice, and donuts. He started the program after he saw two homeless men sifting through the dumpster behind Pratico's Italian restaurant in downtown Providence. The men were eating crust from a discarded pizza. He walks every morning from the church eight blocks to the downtown and back. He uses the time to pray and think.

In the beginning, the breakfast program was strongly supported by the parish council and most of the parishioners. Serving the poor was clearly part of the mission of the church. It is what Christ would have done, Gauthier said when he pitched the idea. For the first six months, there were more volunteers than work and more money and donated food than was needed. The *Providence Herald* ran a front-page story about the breakfast, with a quarter-page picture that showed senior warden Tim McCormick cooking scrambled eggs and giving a thumbs-up to the photographer. His apron said KISS THE COOK and he wore a chef's paper hat. But as the days wore on and the breakfast crowd grew to over sixty men, women, and children, support for the program waned.

"The need is clear, but the task is well beyond our capacity," McCormick told Gauthier. "We're not the Salvation Army." The parish council voted six to three to end the breakfasts.

"Good thing I get four votes. The vote is seven to six. The breakfasts will continue," Gauthier said with a nervous smile. None of the members of the council, even the three who had voted yes, smiled with him.

"We'll lose more members. We can't afford to continue," McCormick said.

"We can't afford not to," Gauthier said.

When the council approved the breakfasts, they didn't know it would get so big or that a dozen homeless men would hover outside the church every morning for an hour or more, smoking cigarettes, sometimes arguing loudly, as they waited for the church to open, and would stay on the church grounds long after the breakfast was done. Getting them to leave the church in bad weather often is a frustrating challenge for the three priests. On the coldest days, some of the breakfast crowd hide in one of the closets or lie quietly on one of the pews hoping no one will see them. The homeless shelter kicks them out at seven thirty every morning, even in the worst weather, and doesn't reopen until five o'clock. There have been several dozen fights at the breakfast, and three men have been arrested. One of the men arrested had a Bowie knife, and he had threatened to stab another man.

Even worse for many of the parishioners is that some of the homeless come filthy to church Sunday mornings and feast on the food available during the coffee hour after the eleven o'clock service. A dozen families have switched to the other two Catholic churches in town, and several more are threatening to leave.

Gauthier checks the wall clock. "It's time," he says to the other two priests. He unlocks the door. "Morning, Ralph, cold enough for you?" he says to one of the men. Ralph pushes a shopping cart through the door. The cart holds everything he owns: his clothes, a tent, a sleeping bag, two extra pairs of shoes, three jackets, and a garbage bag full of towels. Both of his children, his son Ralph Junior, who lives in Newport, Rhode Island, and his daughter Cindy, who lives in Manchester, New Hampshire, have tried to get him to live with them, but he prefers his tent.

"I need my coffee," says the woman with the sore legs. She walks to the coffee urn, fills half the cup with milk, and adds three tablespoons of sugar before she adds the coffee. She sniffs the cup and takes a sip. "Nectar of the gods. Best coffee in town," she says.

"Beth, you say that every day. Time for a new line," Ralph says.

"I say it cause it's true."

"Cold enough for ya?" Bob says to Gauthier as he walks through the door.

"Gonna get a lot worse, that's for sure," Beth says.

Bob lives in a two-room apartment above a laundromat on Center Street. Six weeks ago, the lint in one of the gas dryers caught fire, and he nearly suffocated in the smoke. One of the firemen found him unconscious in the hallway and dragged him to safety. Ever since then, the men at the breakfast have called him Smokey Bob.

There is a scuffle just outside the door. One man pushes another to the ground. "You took my pillow, you son of a bitch," says the man who is still standing.

"I didn't take your goddamn pillow," says the man on the ground. He gets up and brushes the wet snow off his pants.

"If you didn't, who did?"

"I don't know who took your stupid pillow. It wasn't me."

"What's the problem here, gentleman?" Gauthier says. He is standing between the two men.

"He stole my pillow."

"I didn't steal his goddamn pillow, I told him that."

Gauthier guides the man, called Starks, who has lost his pillow into the building.

"Happens every goddamn day, somebody steals something from me . . . a bunch of goddamn thieves . . . I'd be better off sleeping in a dumpster. Last week somebody stole my toothbrush, can you believe that? Stole my toothbrush. Who would do that?" Starks says.

"What do you care? You don't even brush your teeth," says Tom, the man Starks had pushed to the ground.

"At least I got teeth, asshole," Starks says.

Father Symanski hands Starks a cup of coffee. "Just the way you like it—two teaspoons of sugar and a squirt of half-and-half—not milk and not cream," Symanski says.

"Thanks, Father." He sniffs the steam from the cup.

"Jesus loves you," Symanski says to him.

"What?"

"Jesus loves you."

"Well, goody for him."

Gauthier taps a glass with a spoon to get everyone's attention. "We should say grace," he says.

"Grace," Ralph yells out.

"Talk about a new line. That joke's gettin' pretty old," Beth says.

Everyone bows their head. "Bless us, oh Lord, for this food and for all the gifts yet to come," Gauthier says.

Beth nods. "Amen."

"Anybody seen Concetta?" asks Gino.

He gets a chorus of *No*s from the crowd.

One man says, "Darn it all. No donuts." Concetta's apartment is on the second floor of the Grant building, just above Jones's bakery. The baker gives her a bag filled with two dozen donuts each day to take to the church breakfast.

Gino is a short man with a big nose, big ears, and thick, bushy eyebrows. He's been homeless for over twenty years since his wife and two daughters died in a car crash. He was the driver. He fell asleep at the wheel, and the car drifted off the road and down into a ditch and hit a tree. It was one thirty in the morning. They were on their way back from Florida. He was determined to make the trip in two days. At eleven on the night his family died, they were only one hundred and ten miles from Providence.

His wife, Martha, pleaded with him to stop. She was too tired to go on.

"You can sleep," he told her.

"You need sleep. It isn't safe," she said.

"I'm fine, stop pestering me. It's only three more hours to go." The next thing he knew, he was in the hospital, where the doctor told him his wife and daughters were dead. Two weeks after the funeral, he sold his house and quit his job. He lived in the Ho-Hum motel in East Providence for three years until his money ran out. He bought a tent, sleeping bag, and propane cooking stove with his last two hundred dollars and has been living in the Providence town forest ever since. He earns money by doing odd jobs no one else will do. When people want to hire him, they leave a note on the bulletin board at the corner market on East State Street. Last week the note said: *Gino, I need you to crawl under my porch and get three dead rats.* He was paid eight dollars.

Usually, Concetta is the first person at the breakfast and the last one to leave. Everyone is surprised she isn't here today. She hasn't missed a single day before today. She lives alone in her three-room apartment. She is sixty-eight. Her husband died twelve years ago, and they had no children. They had wanted to have a family, but it was never meant to be. Her best friend Josephine died two years ago from a heart attack. Concetta found Josephine's death harder to take than the death of her husband. She and Josephine had been friends since they were small children, before either of them could speak English. Concetta spends most of the three hours at the church breakfast telling funny stories about her life, stories the regulars have heard many times before. Every time she tells an old story she adds a new twist.

Her favorite story is about the time in 1941 when she and Josephine went to a Frank Sinatra concert at Madison Square Garden in New York City. They took a bus from Providence and packed two bottles of gin. When they got to New York they were solidly drunk.

The concert was sold out and they had to wait an hour in line in a cold drizzle before they got into the building. By the time they got inside, all of the best seats in the first two dozen rows were taken, except for two seats in the first row. She and Josephine sprinted down the aisle to the seats. Two other women sprinted with them. The four women got to the seats at the same time. One of the other women suggested they flip a coin to see who got the seats.

"Flip a coin, my ass," Concetta said. The women got into a brawl. All four of them were carried out of the hall by security guards.

"Concetta'll be here soon enough," Gauthier says.

"She's always the first person in the door," Gino says. "Something's up, something bad."

"Nothing's up," Gauthier says.

Officer Ted Wilson walks through the door. He's been coming to the breakfast every day since the near-knife fight. He pours himself a cup of coffee and sniffs the cup. "Perfect."

"Nectar of the gods," Beth says.

Wilson fills his plate with three pancakes and a heap of hash brown potatoes. "I think I'll have pancakes today . . . haven't had them in a couple of weeks," he says loudly to everyone.

"Might want to rethink that. If that belly gets any bigger, you're gonna need a new gun belt," says Richard Herbert, a man so skinny he has a hard time finding adult clothes.

Wilson sucks in his belly and hits it with his fist. "Hard as a rock."

"A Jell-O rock," Herbert says.

About a half dozen people at the tables laugh. Several of them punch their fat bellies. At nine, Gauthier says to the handful remaining, "Time to go, ladies and gentlemen."

"Concetta still isn't here," Gino says.

"I'll call her," Gauthier says. He walks down the hall to his office and makes the call.

"No answer. Maybe you should check on her," he says to Wilson when he returns to the kitchen. Wilson nods and tells him to join him.

Concetta arrives and taps on the window of the passenger door of the police cruiser. "Sorry I'm late, Father. Took a sleeping pill at three this morning. The neighbor's cat's in heat. She wouldn't shut up."

Gauthier thanks Wilson and exits the cruiser. Concetta hands him the bag of donuts. "Too late for these, I guess," she says.

"Never too late," says one of the men in a circle of others smoking cigarettes. He and eight others step to her and Gauthier. Gauthier hands the bag to the first man, who takes a donut and passes the bag to a second man. The donuts are still warm.

"Yummy," the first man says.

Gauthier tells Concetta to come inside the church with him. "You've come this far, might as well get breakfast," he says.

Father Cantone is washing the dishes, Father Symanski is sweeping the floor, and their housekeeper, Agnes LeSalle, is washing the tables with a wet sponge and a bottle of Windex.

"Good morning. We were worried about you," Symanski says to Concetta.

"No need to be," she says. She smiles and grabs a broom from the closet. "I'm not hungry. I'll help clean."

Gauthier joins Father Cantone in the kitchen, grabs a towel, and wipes the dishes dry.

"What did you think of Kennedy's speech last night?" Cantone asks Gauthier.

"I'm not sure it's a good idea to send troops to a foreign war."

"Got to stop communism," Symanski says from the dining room. "Got to nip it in the bud."

"Maybe. Probably won't end well. Didn't for the French," Gauthier says.

"We're not the French," Symanski says.

The five of them finish the cleaning. Gauthier invites Concetta to his apartment. "I have something to show you," he says. He pulls a heavy box from his living room closet and drags it to the coffee table in front of the couch. He empties the contents on the table and grabs a photo album. "I found this the other day when I was cleaning the cellar." He opens the album entitled *New Addition,* dated 1948. Some of the pictures are water damaged, and the albums in the box have a musty smell. There are a half dozen pictures of Concetta's husband, Graham. A much younger Bishop James—Father James, then—is in one of the pictures. Graham had volunteered to help with the construction of the new kitchen and meeting room.

"My goodness, I've never seen these before," she says. Her eyes fill with tears. "He died right there, right there in the dining room." She taps the picture. "He had a heart attack. He was carrying drywall from his truck. He told Monsignor Kelleher he could save the church a lot of money if he put up the Sheetrock and painted the rooms. He'd do it for free. When he was a younger man, he had been a carpenter. He gave it up when he was forty-five because his back hurt constantly. We bought a gift shop. Didn't make as much money but he could walk without pain. When he told me he was going to put up the Sheetrock, I told him he was too damn old. 'You haven't done that in ten years,' I said. He got really mad. 'I'm not too old,' he said. He was too old—I told him so, but he wouldn't listen to me."

"You must miss him?" Gauthier says.

"I do. I think of him every day."

"Are you lonely?"

"I was at first but not now. I'm alone, but I'm not lonely. That's different. I've got a good life. I've got lots of friends. Some days I help out at the bakery and meet lots of people. Clint says—he's the owner—he says, 'How about talking less and selling more,' and then he laughs because he knows most of the customers are there to hear my stories. And I love coming here. Best two mornings of the week. These breakfasts are wonderful. Everybody's great, even Smokey Bob."

"Even Smokey Bob," Gauthier says.

"How about you, Father? Being a priest must be lonely some days."

"Sometimes. But I've got you to talk to, twice a week."

"Were you ever in love?"

"Three times . . . three times was enough."

"What happened?"

"Some things aren't meant to be."

"That's for sure."

He hands her the pictures of her husband. "These are for you."

"Thank you. I do miss that old man. He made me laugh every day."

"I'll give you a ride home," Gauthier says.

"I'd rather walk."

"I've got to go there anyway. I need a donut. I didn't get one . . . I never get one."

"I'll save you one next time." She smiles, and he guides her to his car.

Chapter 26

June 1929
Bob Doty's Apartment, Burlington, Vermont

Charles stuffs his suitcase so full he asks Audrey to sit on the top so he can clasp the latch.

"Do you have enough underwear and socks?" she asks with an eye roll. She holds three pairs of underwear in her left hand and two pairs of socks, rolled into two balls, in her right hand.

Charles rips the underwear and socks from her and tosses them to the bed. "What do you think I am, six? Of course I got enough underwear. Now I got too many." He looks to John, who is standing in the doorway, for support. John waves his right hand to signal he has no comment.

Audrey rifles through his suitcase. "Eight pairs of underwear for two weeks and six pairs of socks. I don't think so." She retrieves another armload of underwear and socks. "A clean pair every day." She holds up a pair of underwear to make her point.

John grins and walks to the kitchen.

"I ain't got no room," Charles says.

She removes three sweaters. "You don't need five sweaters—it's June."

"What if it gets cold?"

"Two sweaters are more than enough." She shakes her head, returns the sweaters to the bedroom closet, walks to the bathroom and back, and hands Charles his shaving kit. "Forget something?" She hands it to him as if she were holding a dead mouse by its tail. Little John crawls between her legs and pulls on her dress to stand. She picks him up and holds him. He twirls her hair with his fingers and pokes her ear.

Charles and John walk to the barn. "Gauthier, you need to run the farm for two weeks. Can you do that? Audrey will help ya milk the cows."

John hitches the horses to the wagon and scrapes mud off his shoes. "Of course I can."

"Good. My brother Bob had an accident at work. His clothes caught fire and burned his body, bad. He needs me."

"Is he okay?"

"Would I go if he was?"

"What about your other brother, Harold? He lives in Burlington."

"He'll be there. Bob needs both of us."

The two men load the wagon with two dozen filled milk cans. Butch barks at them, jumps on the back of the wagon, and settles in between two cans. Charles considers shooing him back to the house but lets him stay.

"Bob's been snake bit ever since he were a little boy. Mom said he got no luck but bad luck. Never caught a break. When he were a baby, six months old, maybe seven, Dad picked him up, and he squirmed real bad and Dad dropped him. He got a concussion and broke his collarbone. Knocked him out cold. I thought he were dead. He was lucky he didn't break his frickin' neck. When he was thirteen, he fell off the hayloft and broke his left leg. Never did heal right . . . been walkin' with a limp ever since. When I wanted to piss him off, I'd call him Gimpy. He'd get so goddamn mad he'd want to punch me in the face, but I was too big. When he was fifteen, he were cutting brush and a twig slapped his eye. He didn't lose it, but he can barely see out of it. Good thing the twig didn't slap both eyes . . . he'd be on the street corner with a tin cup and a white cane."

Audrey and Little John are standing on the porch watching the men. One of the house cats is bumping its head into the baby's legs. Audrey is shading her eyes from the sun. Charles walks to her, hugs her, and kisses her forehead. He leans his head to her right ear and whispers, "See you in two weeks. I love you." John hears him and smiles.

"I love you too," she says.

Their wagon is first in line at the dairy. Jeff Jenkins's truck is behind them. He joins them and helps them lift their milk cans from the wagon. Butch jumps to the ground, greets Jenkins, whines, and pushes its head into Jenkins's legs to tell him to rub his head. "Good boy, Butch," Jenkins says. He scratches the dog's head. "Heard 'bout Bob. Sounds wicked awful."

"Is. Gonna see him today."

"Tell him I'm thinkin' about him. Good man, that Bob. Real good man. Funny as shit. When we were in third grade, he put a garter snake in the drawer of Miss Davis's desk. Remember her? Smelled like boiled cabbage. When she opened the drawer and saw the snake, she pissed her dress. Never laughed so hard in my life. She quit before the year was over." He laughs and hands the last milk can to the dairy foreman, spits a wad of mucus in the dirt, and wipes his lips with a handkerchief. "Whatever happen to Bob's wife, what's-her-name? She were ugly, that's for damn sure."

"She were. Left him for a cowboy from Utah. A big, burly bronco rider. Last I heard they were living on a dude ranch in Texas."

"Not surprised."

At the train station, Charles says, "You're early today, Gauthier. Got plenty of time to see Charlotte. Take her to lunch, or whatever." He winks to make sure John gets his meaning.

"Or whatever," John says and shakes his head. He grabs Butch's collar.

Charles gives him a thumbs-up and boards the train. "See you in two weeks. I trust you. Not sure why, but I do."

"Thanks. You always know just what to say."

"I do."

. . .

The train hits a cow in Panton and screeches to a stop. The jolt wakes Charles from a dead sleep. For a few seconds, he forgets he's on a train and panics that he hasn't milked the cows. He shakes his head and rubs his eyes with his palms. "What time is it?" he says to the man sitting next to him. His words are slurred with sleep. It is one thirty in the afternoon. One more hour to go. He walks to the dining car. The car is steaming hot and smells like moldy towels and coffee. He joins three other men in a game of Pitch. He wins two games in a row. One man with a fox-like face says, "What are you, a ringer or something?" He laughs.

Charles says, "Yup." His comment makes the other two men chuckle.

The hospital is a mile straight up a steep hill from the train station. By the time Charles gets to the top, he is panting hard, and his shirt is drenched with sweat. An elderly woman, standing next to the entrance door, asks him if he needs assistance. "That were a big frickin' hill," he says.

"It is," she says.

He catches his breath, lights a cigarette, and walks into the building. He doesn't know what to do or where to go. He mumbles, "Damn," and nearly kicks a chair.

A nurse taps his shoulder. "You look a bit lost." She guides him to the admissions desk.

. . .

"What the hell happened?" he asks Bob. Bob's arms, neck, and torso are covered with gauze bandages. He is lying on his hospital bed reading the *Burlington Free Press*. President Hoover says the economy is stronger than ever.

"Got careless, what can I say?" His voice is a whisper.

"At least you're alive."

"Barely. Last week the pain were so bad I wished I were dead. Not too bad now though. Doc says I can go back to work in about a month. Can't wait."

Charles rubs the top of Bob's head. "At least there are no burns on that ugly face of yours."

"Still handsome as ever." Bob mugs his chin and lips to prove it.

"Handsome as ever," Charles agrees.

The nurse shows Charles how to change the bandages and treat the wounds. She tells him he must clean Bob's skin twice a day and cover the burns with cream, and he must be very gentle. She softly pats Bob's arm with a cotton swab to show what must be done. "There's a risk of infection until the burns heal. Burns can be very painful for several days or longer," she says.

"Tell me sumthin' I don't know," Bob says. He is joking, but the nurse isn't sure.

. . .

Bob's apartment is much smaller than Charles thought it would be—basically one large room. The kitchen is at the front of the room near the entrance door, and a bed, two bureaus, a couch, and a chair are on the opposite side of the room. A four-seater table with two chairs is in the middle of the room on a threadbare brown rug. The sink is filled with dirty dishes. There is a pile of laundry next to the bed. The Sunday newspaper is crumbled in a ball on the couch. Bob shares a bathroom with three other men. The apartment is on the second floor above a shoe store and a small grocery store. On the left wall, there is a framed picture of the Doty farm and a picture of Charles and Bob with their sister Theresa and brother Harold. Charles, in the center of the picture, is wearing his high school graduation robe and cap.

"I remember that day. Dad took the picture. He were so drunk he could barely stand," Charles says. "My girlfriend . . ."

"Cecile," Bob says.

"Yes, Cecile. Dad made her so nervous she didn't know what to do. She told me he pinched her butt and grazed her breast with his elbow. I followed him into the barn and confronted him with my fists up. He denied it. 'She's a liar,' he said. 'What are you gonna do, beat me up? I'm twice the man you'll ever be.' Which was pretty funny cause by then he was already a weak, old man. Who was he kidding?"

"Dad did like women, for sure," Bob says. "I never told you 'bout the time I walked in on him and Arlene Butler on the cot in the milk room."

"No shit."

"Never told nobody. Dad didn't see me. They pounded away for about ten minutes. It was the year Mom was in the nuthouse in Brattleboro."

"I didn't know you knew 'bout the nut house. You were only eight. Who told you?"

"Nobody told me. Just knew. I heard Dad and Uncle Howard talkin' and figured it out. I remember everything 'bout that summer. Worst summer of my life, worst summer of your life, worst year ever."

"The year Mom killed herself—that were the worst year ever," Charles says.

"Suppose you're right—can't get much worse than your mom hanging herself. I saw her do it. Never told nobody, not until right now. I was in the hayloft playing with my army men. I saw Mom pull the chair to the wire. Our dog Rex had followed her into the barn, like he always did, right at her heels. She swatted his nose and said, 'Get,' and pointed toward the barn door. He walked out of the barn with his tail between his legs. I figured she were fixing the lantern. When she wrapped the wire around her neck and jumped off the chair, I didn't know what she was doing, I thought she were playing a game. I yelled, 'Mom, what are you doing?' Just when I were about to climb down to her, you and Rex came into the barn."

"Jesus, Bob, why didn't ya ever tell somebody?"

"I don't know why. Just didn't. When Dad cut her down and held her, he was crying so hard it froze me. I'd never seen him cry before."

"Me neither. He held her and he rocked her, and he whispered, 'God, why did you do this?' into her ear. And then he grabbed me and hugged me, and he cried and said he was sorry and told me it were his fault. His voice trembled. That was the last time he touched me."

"Remember when you and Mom went to Boston and went to a baseball game—the Red Sox and the Yankees? God, I wanted to go. Dad said I were too young, which made no sense. I was just two years younger than you. When you showed me the baseball you got, I was so damn jealous I could taste my blood."

"That were the only time I've ever left Vermont," Charles says.

"We got to get you and Audrey to Montreal."

"Can't leave the farm."

"You're here now. You got help. Let him do it. Audrey would love it."

"Maybe."

"No maybe about it. When I get better, I'm taking you and Audrey to Montreal. Two-hour train ride from here, that's all."

There is a knock at the door. "Who's that?" Charles says.

"No idea."

"I'm Rachael, Rachael Galfetti, your visiting nurse," the woman says when Charles opens the door. She has dark black hair, thick eyebrows, a large but attractive nose, and big brown eyes.

"Our what?" Charles says.

"Your visiting nurse. I'm here to show you how to help Bob."

"The nurse at the hospital showed me yesterday. I don't need another lesson."

"I need to watch you, just to be sure."

"I'm not an idiot. I don't need to be watched. I know what to do."

"Then prove it." She smiles. "Just kidding. There's a whole lot she didn't have time to tell you. That's why I'm here."

"Like what?" Charles says.

"Where do I start?" She hands Charles a box of bandages and several jars of ointment. "While the wounds are healing, bacteria can get in and cause an infection. You have to be especially careful. If your wounds aren't healing properly you need to call the agency."

"I don't have a phone," Bob says.

"Our office is just two blocks away," she says to Charles and hands him a list of warning signs. "If any of these happen, contact us immediately. Once the skin is healed, put this lotion on several times a day. This will help control itching and keep Bob's skin soft and moist." She leans toward Bob. "You can bathe, but don't soak in the bathtub—and make sure the water isn't hot. And you need to stretch—that's really important."

She watches Charles wrap the bandages. "Not bad. You're a natural."

"Ain't much different from wrapping an injured cow," Charles says.

"He's a farmer in case you ain't guessed," Bob says. "Best farmer in Vermont. Loves cows more than he does people."

"I do too," the nurse says. Both men laugh. "I'll see you tomorrow."

"We don't need you," Charles says.

"Maybe not, but I'm coming anyway." Her smile melts the two men.

"I think I'm in love," Charles says after the nurse leaves the apartment. "She were really beautiful."

"That's for sure," Bob says. "I'm in love too, and I'm not married."

Charles squeezes Bob's hands. "Need money?"

"No, I'm fine. How about you, you need money?"

"I'm okay. In debt up to my ass, but what else is new?"

"Know any farmers not in debt?"

"Nope."

"I never thanked you for taking charge after Mom died."

"I didn't do nothing."

"You saved us, Charles, all of us—me and Harold and Theresa. Not sure what we woulda done without you. You were only twelve years old when Mom died. You were more our parent than Dad was, even before Mom died.

Remember when they'd get in a fight, and Mom would hide in the cellar and Dad would hide in the hayloft? You'd feed us and make sure we were clean and get us to school, and then you'd milk the cows all by yourself. Took you all day."

"It were nothing."

"It was everything. And here you are, twenty years later, still caring for me."

"If you weren't such a clumsy son of a bitch I wouldn't be here."

"True. Glad you came. Next summer we're goin' to Montreal—you, me, and Audrey."

"Not gonna happen."

"You're a stubborn sucker. You're goin' to Montreal whether you want to or not—you, me, and Audrey, and I'll get Harold and Maddie to join us." He grabs Charles's hand and squeezes it. "You're the best. You've always been the best."

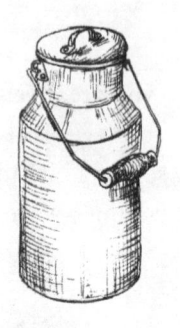

Chapter 27

June 1929
Doty Farm, East Providence, Vermont

Audrey is washing the dinner dishes, and John is drying them and putting them away in the cupboard. He lightly bumps her hip. She pretends not to notice. Little John is sitting in his high chair babbling, his face and hair covered with squash. Butch licks squash off the floor and wags his tail. Two of the cats are hissing at each other in the living room and *Amos 'n' Andy* is playing on the radio.

"If a stranger came to the door, he'd think we were married," Audrey says.

"Charles comes home tomorrow. Our marriage ends then. A two-week marriage—pretty short," John says.

"Yes, it is. It's been a good two weeks."

"It has."

"I like talking about books."

"I do too."

"There's jazz music on the radio tonight. Will you dance with me?"

"I don't know how."

"I don't know how to either. We'll make it up as we dance."

Audrey bathes Little John, feeds him, and puts him to bed. She checks the kitchen clock. "The music starts in twenty minutes. You need to get dressed."

"I am dressed."

"Overalls and wool socks aren't dancing clothes." She points to his room and tells him to wash and change. When he returns, she is wearing a tight, short black dress, her flapper's hat, and her jade necklace and earrings. The lights are off, and two candles are burning on the mantel above the fireplace.

"You look beautiful," he says.

"Thank you. You look pretty good yourself." John is wearing a gray jazz suit with a red tie and a white shirt with a high stiff collar.

"That goes without saying." He smiles.

She fills two shot glasses with whiskey and hands one of them to John. "Let's toast. To our last night alone." They clink their glasses together.

"To our last night."

On the radio, Louis Armstrong sings, "When You're Smiling." Audrey grabs John's right hand and leads him to the middle of the room.

"This is a slow dance. I can't slow dance," he says.

"Yes, you can." She pulls him close to her and guides him. His knees buckle. They shuffle across the floor with no apparent rhythm. She pulls him tight to her, rests her head on his shoulder, and squeezes his hands. "I haven't danced since my wedding."

"I haven't danced since sixth grade when I took dance classes."

"I thought you said you didn't know how to dance."

"I lied."

She punches his shoulder. "What else have you lied about?"

"Nothing."

"I doubt that."

They each drink another shot of whiskey. "Bottoms up," she says. They dance six dances—two slow and four fast. John is winded, and his hair is wet from sweat.

"I need a break," he says.

Audrey pours two more drinks. "Sit here." She taps the couch cushion. She drinks her shot in one gulp and rests her head on John's shoulder. "You're a good dancer. You told Charlotte you couldn't dance. You lied to her too."

"I did."

"Are you going to marry her?"

"Maybe, if she says yes."

"She will."

They dance five more dances—three slow dances, and two Charlestons. John shows her how to waltz. "It's easy. Just step to the music." Her hair tickles his nose and smells like roses.

She pours two more drinks. John rejects his glass. "Too much for me," he says.

She drinks both drinks. "Not for me. Just because you can't hold your liquor, I can. My legs are hollow." They dance some more. Her sweat clings her dress to her body. It is apparent that she has nothing on under the dress. She swallows two more shots of whiskey and then wobbles. "I think I'm gonna be sick."

She sprints to the bathroom and throws up in the toilet. Half of the vomit falls into the toilet bowl, and the rest lands in her hair, on her chin, on her dress, on the floor, and on the side of the toilet. John follows her to the bathroom. He kneels next to her, grabs her hair, and pulls it away from her neck when she pukes a second and third time. "I think I drank too much."

"What makes you think that?" He smiles. He wets a washcloth and washes the vomit off her chin and hair. He cleans the floor and the side of the toilet. He retrieves her hat from the floor, rinses it in the sink, and slowly removes her vomit-covered dress. His arms tremble when he pulls the dress over her shoulders. *She's so beautiful*, he thinks.

She nearly falls over from the struggle to get the wet dress off her sweaty body. He throws the dress and hat into a laundry basket in the bathroom and retrieves a bathrobe from her bedroom closet. He gently wipes the remaining vomit off her body, wipes her hair a second time with a clean, damp cloth, dries her skin with a bath towel, and helps her put on her robe. She shakily removes her earrings and hands them to John. Then she tries to unlatch her necklace but fails. John unhooks it and gently pulls it from her neck. The necklace is covered with vomit. He cleans it and places it on the dresser in her bedroom.

"I'm embarrassed," she says.

"Don't be. Christmas Eve, I was way worse."

"Yes, you were."

He guides her to the couch. Her legs are wobbly. "My head is spinning," she says.

"Not surprised."

"Are we evil?" she says.

"No, we've done nothing."

"I wanted to."

"I did too, but we didn't."

"You saw me naked."

"That's the second time. I walked in on you in your bedroom, remember?"

"I forgot. You turned so red you looked like a Christmas light."

"I did."

"Not red this time?"

"No, not this time."

"It's the third time, John, the third time you've seen me naked. Don't forget Little John's birth."

"That was different, way different. I'll never forget that night."

"I won't either."

She lies on the couch with her head on his lap. He caresses her hair. His fingers catch snarls with each stroke. She sends him to the bedroom to get a brush. He brushes her hair and removes all the snarls.

"That feels good," she says.

"What's next for us?" he asks.

"There is no next, John. This is it."

"Should I leave? Should I go back to Connecticut?"

"No, I want you to stay. Stay until you marry Charlotte."

"What if she says no?"

"She won't—she loves you. Do you love her?"

"I do, very much."

"Good. You'll marry Charlotte, and you and I will remain close friends. I'll love you as a friend, nothing more."

"I want more."

"There is no more, John. I wish there was, but there isn't. I was wrong. I shouldn't have danced with you."

"It takes two."

"We were both wrong."

"Should I go to my room?"

"No, stay here with me. Tomorrow's a new day. Let's have what we have here tonight, whatever it is, and tomorrow we'll forget what happened."

"I won't forget."

"I won't either."

He kisses her forehead. She is asleep. "I love Charlotte, but I love you too. I wish I didn't, but I do," he whispers into her ear.

. . .

Little John pulls on Audrey's robe. His diaper is full, and the whole room stinks. Audrey's head is on John's lap. John is asleep and snoring. His mouth is open, and his chin is covered with drool. She looks at the clock on the kitchen wall. It's six o'clock. She shakes John. "John, get up. You need to get up and milk the cows." She can hear them complaining from the barn.

He jogs his head. "What time is it?"

"Six o'clock. You're an hour late."

He walks to the kitchen sink, his legs unsteady, tilts his head under the faucet, and pours a stream of cold water on his hair. "How do you feel?"

"Like someone hit my head with a sledge hammer," Audrey says.

He goes to his room and changes into his work clothes.

"After I feed Little John and clean this mess, I'll help you milk the cows and get them into the field."

"You don't need to."

"I do. About last night, I'm sorry."

"Don't be—there's nothing to be sorry about."

"Don't tell Charlotte."

"Tell her what? There's really nothing to tell."

The cows are restless but cooperative. Audrey joins him after he's milked seven cows. She has a playpen in her left hand and is carrying Little John with her right arm. She opens the playpen and lowers Little John into it. He grabs a teddy bear and starts to suck on its fur.

"Did you know I lost a baby? Two, actually—one born, one miscarriage."

"Yes, Charles told me."

"It was awful, both times. The second time was the worst. My little girl was staring at me and smiling. The nurse said her smile was probably gas. She had blue eyes and almost no hair. Charles said, 'She looks like an Elizabeth. What do you think?' I said, 'I agree, Elizabeth Christine Doty, a beautiful name.' And then she stopped breathing. I don't know why, she just did. I screamed, and the nurse took her from me. My little girl never breathed again."

"I'm so sorry. I don't know what to say."

"There's nothing to say. It was as if someone had ripped my soul from my body. Father LeFebvre was chaplain at the hospital that day. He came to my room and held my hand. He didn't say anything. He just held my hand. I don't know for how long—an hour, maybe more. It's all a blur.

"I was walking dead for nearly a year. I couldn't think straight, I couldn't cook, I couldn't clean the house, I couldn't do anything. I blamed myself. I thought, *I am an evil woman, that's why my baby died*. I was sure I didn't deserve children. Father LeFebvre stopped by every day for months. He didn't have to . . . I wasn't a member of his church. At first, we said almost nothing. We talked about the weather and the cows and the Red Sox and the Yankees and Babe Ruth but never about Elizabeth. Eventually, we did talk about her death. He helped me understand her death wasn't my fault, that it was no one's fault, just part of life. 'Sometimes life is mean and nasty, but mostly it's joyful and wonderful,' he said. I didn't believe him, at least not at first. But now that I've got Little John, I do. He doesn't replace Elizabeth, but he's wonderful. Just wish he didn't poop so much." She picks up the baby and kisses his forehead and rubs her nose on his belly. "I love you, love you, love you," she says. Little John giggles.

John scratches his nose with the back of his hand. "I wish my mother could get where you are. It's been sixteen years since my sister died, and Mom's still terribly sad. Most days she lives in a fog. I wish I could help her, but I can't."

"How about you, John, do you ever think about your sister?"

"I do, every single day. Some nights I dream about her falling out the window. In my dream, she falls in slow motion. It seems to take forever. I always wake up just before she hits the ground."

Audrey squeezes his hands. "You're a good man, John Gauthier."

"Did you and Father LeFebvre talk about God?"

"Not really."

"Do you believe in God?" John says. He tosses his wiping cloth into a bucket and retrieves a clean towel.

"Most of the time . . . but sometimes I'm not sure. How about you?"

"Same as you—most of the time yes, sometimes no."

"You helped me too, John."

"How?"

"You're funny. You make me laugh."

"I'm not funny."

"Not on purpose, but you are funny. That day you came into the kitchen covered with cow shit from your shoulder to your feet, that was funny. First time I'd laughed in years. But not as funny as when you got sprayed by the skunk. I've never seen anyone who knows less about rural living than you. For future reference, a skunk is not a cat."

"Glad I can be a source of amusement for you."

She sniffs Little John's diaper. It is filled. "I just changed you twenty minutes ago, you little bugger." She grabs Little John and the teddy bear. "I'll be back," she says.

"Jesus, Gauthier, nine thirty and you ain't done yet?" Charles says. He is standing in the barn doorway. The sun is at his back. All John can see is Charles's silhouette against the bright sun.

"Got up late this morning, what can I say?"

"Got to get you an alarm clock. Looks like the pocket watch ain't enough."

Audrey runs to Charles with Little John in her hands, and hugs him. "I've missed you so much." She kisses him, a long, passionate kiss. "Didn't think you were coming home till this afternoon?"

"Changed my plans. Jenkins was supposed to tell you. He picked me up. I might get a truck—I just might do that. Took us just twenty-five minutes to get here, can you believe that?"

She kisses him again, even harder than the first kiss. "I missed you so much."

He tries to avoid her second kiss. "I get it, you missed me. Jeez, Audrey." He looks at John and rolls his eyes.

Chapter 28

July 1929
Parker House, Boston, Massachusetts

The train to Boston is running three hours late. John is restless. "Damn, damn, dammit," he says. He pounds his fists on the armrest with each damn.

The woman in the seat behind him sighs and pinches her husband's shirt. "Tell him to stop complaining," she whispers into his ear. He shakes his head. John has been bitching about the delays for the past hour.

"Give it a rest. We'll get there soon enough," Charlotte says. She squeezes his right knee.

"I wanted to take you to the Gardner Museum. There's a painting I want you to see, *El Jaleo*. It's wonderful. It will make your skin tingle. We won't get there on time."

"Relax, we'll go tomorrow."

"Tomorrow's July Fourth. The museum will be closed."

"Then we'll go Friday. We're here through the weekend. You're such a nervous little man. Sometimes it gets tiring." She grabs his hand, pulls him off his seat, and guides him to the dining car. "Let's have lunch."

"I should write a letter of complaint."

"No, you shouldn't. Calm down. We'll get there when we get there." She orders coffee for both of them and sandwiches. "He'll have roast beef, I'll have chicken," she tells the waiter.

"I don't want roast beef."

"Then what do you want, John?" She shakes her head, annoyed.

"I don't know."

"He'll have roast beef." The waiter hesitates, waiting for John to speak. "He'll have roast beef." She waves the waiter away with a flick of her right hand. "Tell me about that painting you want me to see, *El* something or other."

"*El Jaleo*. It's huge, ten feet wide, maybe more, and nearly as tall. I saw it three years ago just after I'd returned from India. I was sad. My dad brought me to Boston to cheer me up. He was sick of me being sad."

"Did it work?"

"Not really."

The waiter returns with the sandwiches. "I wanted chicken," John says.

"I'm so sorry, my mistake," the waiter says.

John grabs the sandwich plate from him. "Just kidding. This is perfect." He takes a bite. "Delicious." He takes a second bite and says, with his mouth full of food, "Where was I?"

"The painting is big."

"At the right side of the painting, a flamenco dancer is dancing across the stage. She is alive with energy. Her left arm is pointing off stage and her right arm is gripping her white dress. You can almost feel the fabric of the dress. Several musicians and fellow dancers are seated along the wall behind her. The musicians are totally focused on their guitars. One of the men looks like he's in a trance. Most of the painting is black and white and muted brown except for orange and red on the dancers seated on the far right, and there's a small dab of orange on the left. When you first see the painting, your eyes go right to the dancer and then to the musicians behind her and then to the blotches of red and orange, especially the red on the right side of the frame."

"Sounds wonderful."

"It is."

"What else are we going to do in Boston . . . I want to know. What. Else. Are. We. Going. To. Do. In. Boston?"

"You're making fun of me?"

"Yes, I am. I've never seen anyone more organized than you. I think you'll plan your own funeral."

"I will. No carnations—I hate carnations. And no crying—I hate crying."

"I'll cry. Audrey and me, we'll both cry."

"All right, you two can cry but nobody else."

"I bet you have a detailed list of things to do tomorrow."

"I do not."

"John?"

"Okay, I do. Actually, I have two lists, a good-weather list, and a bad-weather list."

"Why am I not surprised?"

"If it's good weather, we'll walk around Boston Common and take a ride on a swan boat. Then we'll walk through Faneuil Hall to the North End and go to an Italian restaurant, and then we'll go to Old North Church where Paul Revere started his ride."

"Listen, my children, and you shall hear, of the midnight ride of Paul Revere," Charlotte sings.

"You're making fun of me."

"You're an easy target." She leans over the table and kisses his forehead. "I don't have any say in what we do, do I?"

"Not really." He pulls the two lists from his pocket and reads the good-weather schedule for today. "*Get on the train at 7:00 A.M.* Did that. *Get to Boston at noon.* Not going to happen. *Eat lunch on the Boston Common at one.* We're having lunch on the train. *Visit the Isabella Stewart Gardner Museum at two thirty.* It's two thirty now and we're still on the damn train."

"Hand me the lists, both lists, I want to see what you've planned for tomorrow." She reads the good-weather list. "Sounds boring. This isn't a history tour. I don't care about the North Church or the South Church or any other damn church." She rips both lists apart and flutters the scraps onto the table. She leans close to him, her nose nearly touching his, and whispers, "What we're going to do today is we're going to the hotel, then we're going to have sex, and then we're going to dinner and dancing, and after that, we're going back to the hotel and have sex again. Can you do that?"

"Yes."

"Good. We'll figure out what to do tomorrow, tomorrow, and what to do Friday, on Friday. And I don't want to see the damn Liberty Bell, got it?" She kisses his nose.

"The Liberty Bell is in Philadelphia."

She shakes her head in fake dismay and kisses his cheek. "Sometimes you're insufferable."

"I am."

. . .

John and Charlotte are sitting in the Parker House restaurant. He is chipper. She is resting her head on the tabletop. He flips through the *Boston Globe*. "Some moron fell into a geyser at Yellowstone. What a boob." He looks for a reaction but gets none. "This is our last lunch in Boston. Did you have fun?"

"I did." Her eyes are red, and her voice sounds as if she has a handful of nails in her mouth. She lifts her head off the table and rubs her temples with her thumbs. "My head hurts."

"What did you like best?"

"I don't know, John, most everything was wonderful." She rubs her eyelids with her fists.

"What did you like best?"

"No talking. Please! No! Talking!" She shakes her head.

"We're at the Parker House and you haven't had Boston cream pie yet. Did you know the Parker House invented Boston cream pie?"

"Yes, you've told me already, twice at least." She rubs her temples again and squeezes her eyes shut.

"Sorry, Miss Grumpy, get up on the wrong side of the bed?"

"It's eleven thirty in the morning. We went to bed at three. I got four hours of sleep. Before we went to sleep I said, 'Let me sleep until noon.' But no, Mr. Early Morning gets me up at seven o'clock. 'Rise and shine, the early birds get the worms,' he says. I don't want any damn worms. I drank too much. My head hurts. My stomach hurts. I don't want to talk anymore. Please be quiet."

John orders eggs benedict, toast, coffee, and apple juice for both of them.

"I don't want eggs. I don't want anything. My head hurts, my stomach hurts, my feet hurt. Are you not listening?" she says.

"Okay, no eggs for you, but you must have a piece of Boston cream pie. You can't stay at the Parker House without eating a piece of Boston cream pie. It's the law."

"Yes, you can."

"No, you can't."

"If I say yes, will you shut the fuck up?"

"Yes." He grabs her left hand and kisses it. He eats both servings of eggs and all four pieces of toast. "That was delicious. I was starved."

"No talking—you promised." She rests her head on the table.

An elderly couple at the table next to them, who have been listening to their conversation, smile. "Must be newlyweds," the man whispers to his wife.

"I remember those days," the wife says.

The waiter brings the dessert. He smiles at John as if they were sharing a cherished secret. "Here you go, ma'am, you will absolutely love this dessert."

Charlotte pushes the plate away. "I really can't eat it. I'm not hungry."

"Just one bite," John says.

"I don't want it." She scowls at him.

"Just one bite, please."

"Only if you promise not to talk anymore."

"I promise."

She stabs the cake with her fork and hits something inside it. "What's in the cake, John?"

"Nothing." He and the waiter and the nosy couple all smile.

Audrey digs an engagement ring from the cake. She grabs it and examines the diamond. "This is a very beautiful ring." She slips it on her ring finger. It fits perfectly. "What's it for?"

"What do you think it's for?"

"Looks like an engagement ring."

"It is. Will you marry me?"

"No."

"What?" He is stunned.

"No, I will not marry you."

The nosy elderly couple looks away and pretends they weren't listening. The waiter retreats back to the kitchen.

"Why not? I love you, you love me, what else is there?"

"I do love you, John."

"Then say yes."

"I would have said yes Wednesday and Thursday and even Friday but not yesterday and definitely not today."

"What happened?"

"John, you talk in your sleep."

"What did I say?"

"You called out a name. It wasn't mine."

"Whose was it?"

"Who do you think?" She shakes her head and sighs.

"I don't know."

"Don't play me for a fool."

"Audrey?"

"Of course it was Audrey—who else?"

"It was just a dream. That doesn't mean anything."

"It wasn't just a dream, John, it's what you feel. I've been lying to myself for six months."

"I'm sorry."

"Don't be. At least the truth is out."

"The truth is I love you and I want to marry you."

"You probably do love me, John, but you love Audrey more. I love you, more than anyone I've ever loved before, but I don't want to be the consolation prize."

"You're not."

"Yes, I am." She kisses his forehead.

"But . . ."

"No talking." She rubs her temples with her thumbs and combs her hair with her hand.

. . .

When they reach Providence, John says, "Can I see you again?" There were no words between them from Boston to Providence, a six-hour trip. The other passengers assumed they were strangers.

"No, this is the end."

"I love you, Charlotte. I don't love Audrey more than you. I love you both the same."

"No, you don't, John." She grabs both of his hands and kisses them. "You need to leave the farm. The sooner the better."

"Better for who?"

"Better for everyone."

John grabs his suitcase and hers from the rack above their seats. "Can I walk you to your apartment?"

"No, I'd rather walk home alone."

"I love you. I want you to be my wife. I want to be your husband. Please give me a second chance."

"That's not going to happen, John." She grabs her suitcase from him. "I don't want to see you ever again."

"You're making a mistake. I love you—you love me. We should get married. We should have children together. We'll have a good life together."

"I'm not making a mistake, John. You're the one making a mistake. You're in love with my sister, a woman you can't have." She grabs her suitcase, walks down the aisle, and exits the train without turning back to look at him.

John walks toward the exit, stops, and sits on the seat closest to the door. "Damn, damn, damn," he says to himself. "I do love her. Can't she see that?" He rests his chin on his hands and weeps.

A train porter taps his shoulder. "Buddy, this is the end of the line. You got to get off. We got to clean the train."

"Sorry." John wipes his eyes dry, grabs his suitcase, exits the train, and walks toward the livery stable.

"Here, mister, give me a quarter if I tell you where you got them shoes," says the same man who had used that line with him and Charles just before Christmas.

"I got my shoes on my feet," John says. He steps to the man and hands him a twenty-dollar bill.

"Thank you, mister, you are so kind."

"I wish that were so." He opens his suitcase, removes the book *To The Lighthouse,* and hands the man his suitcase. "We look about the same size. You could use some new clothes."

Chapter 29

June 1963
Sacred Heart Parish, Providence, Vermont

"Testing, one, two, three," Monsignor Gauthier says. He taps the microphone three times. Standing at the back of the auditorium, Father Cantone gives him a thumbs-up. The banner at the back of the stage says "Congratulations, Eighth Graders." Thirty-seven graduates, dressed in dark blue gowns, are standing in two lines in the hallway, waiting for their cue to enter the auditorium. A blue balloon and a white balloon are tied to each chair for the graduates. Sister Bartholomew is counting heads and shushing the students.

She swats the back of Maurice Nolan's head.

"Gum?" she says. She points to a wastebasket inside one of the classrooms. He spits his wad into the can. Five other boys do the same.

Paul Fermonte pokes Patrick Colman's arm. "This is it, asshole, our last day together."

"No, it isn't."

"Yes, it is. You're goin' to Providence High, I'm goin' to Saint Francis."

"So?"

"So, this is the end."

"No, it isn't."

"It is, take my word for it." He pokes Patrick a second time. "My brother and Tim Connors were best friends forever, and then they weren't."

"That won't happen to us."

"Sure, and I'm Mickey Mantle."

The seventh grade band plays "Pomp and Circumstance." Several flutes and clarinets squeak off-key. One trumpeter's blasts are much louder than the others. One of the five drummers is a half beat behind. Sister Ryan is leading the band. Her forehead is sweaty. She is forcing a smile. The graduates enter the auditorium. Dozens of flashbulbs go off. Patrick Colman's mother, Tia, squeezes her husband's hands. "I think I'm going to cry," she says.

Tom grabs her shoulders and pulls her to him. "I think I'm going to cry too." He squeezes her hands back. "We must be old. We've got a boy graduating from eighth grade and a girl in high school," he says and grins.

"How did that happen?" Tia says.

"One year at a time," Tom says. He hugs her again.

"Ladies and gentlemen, parents, grandparents, friends, teachers, and graduates, welcome. We've come not to bury our students but to praise them," Monsignor Gauthier jokes. Several adults groan. He tells the parents they should be proud. He says he is proud. He warns the students that high school is hard, but tells them not to worry, they are prepared. He asks everyone to applaud the teachers. Several students win awards. Eileen Donner wins a five-dollar gift certificate for her essay "America Means Freedom," which was reprinted in the *Providence Herald*. Patrick Colman's essay, "My Dog Is Smarter than Me," didn't even rank in the top ten. Father Symanski said the essay should have been titled "My Dog Is Smarter than I Am."

Providence mayor Paul Hennessy tells the graduates today isn't the end but the beginning. He copies President Kennedy's inaugural speech. "Ask not what St. Francis High School can do for you—ask what you can do for St. Francis High."

Tom whispers, "What a boob," to Tia but loud enough so that several of the people sitting near him hear his words.

"He is a boob," says the man sitting directly behind Tia. He and Tom laugh.

Tia kicks Tom's leg. "Stop it," she says.

Elise Gallo, the best student in the class, says St. Francis High School better be ready because the class of 1967 is primed to take control. "Ready or not, here we come." She shakes her fists. The crowd roars with laughter.

Monsignor Gauthier regains the podium and signals to Sister Bartholomew that it is time to hand out the diplomas. He taps the microphone three times and starts to speak. Somebody's dog wanders into the auditorium and barks. The embarrassed owner grabs the dog by the collar and pulls it out of the room. "I guess even the dogs want me to shut up," Gauthier says. He chuckles but tells his story anyway. It is about the first day the graduates entered the school, nine years ago, when they were in kindergarten. Several of them were so scared they cried. "But look at you now, ready to take on high school. Let's stand up and give them a round of applause." All the adults stand and cheer.

At the end of the ceremony, the students shuffle to the gym. Maurice Nolan trips on his gown and falls to the floor. Sister Bartholomew holds up her hand in a swatting pose to make sure no one laughs. The parents, grandparents, and siblings follow them to the gym. The band plays, "Happy Days Are Here Again." The slow drummer is still a half beat behind, and the loud trumpeter is still too loud. Both basketball hoops are covered with blue and white crepe paper. Refreshments are available at the far end of the gym on a table under the scoreboard. There are three large punch bowls. One is filled with red punch, one with yellow, and one with bluish-green, and there are several bowls of potato chips. A dozen empty Hawaiian Punch cans and several empty Seven Up bottles that were used to make the punch are jammed in a box under the table.

Paul Fermonte squirts a stream of punch through his teeth toward Patrick. His father swats the back of his head. "Stop it."

Monsignor Gauthier is working the crowd, shaking hands, chatting, and offering to take family pictures. Tia hands him her camera. Tom is reluctant to pose but agrees. He pulls Patrick between him and Tia. Patrick's sisters Ginny and Marta stand at the two ends.

"I have something for you," Gauthier says to Patrick. "You're way too young for this book, so hold it for a few years." He hands him a well-worn paperback copy of *Catch-22*. "This may be the best book ever written. If it isn't, I don't know what is."

"Thank you, Father."

Father Symanski is standing twenty feet from them watching Gauthier hand the book to Patrick. He shakes his head and sighs.

Patrick opens the cover. There is a note inside: "Keep reading and writing." There is a list of one hundred books on the back of the note and another message: "Most of these books are too old for you, but keep this list. I've starred the books that you can read now." The book title at the top of the list is *Sister Carrie* and *Invisible Man* is at the bottom. Only two books are starred: *Where the Red Fern Grows* and *A Wrinkle in Time*. Gauthier watches Patrick read the list. "I hope you read them all," Gauthier says.

"I will. I promise, Father." Patrick says.

"And keep writing."

"I will."

Paul Fermonte sneaks up behind Colman. "Etslay ogay to the ideouthay," he whispers in Patrick's ear.

"Aren't you morons a little too old for a secret hideout?" Marta says with total disdain. "We all know where your stupid hideout is. Not much of a secret."

Tia grabs the book from Patrick, pulls the graduation gown off him, and waves him away. "Go. Just be home by nine thirty."

"You've got a good kid there," Gauthier says.

"We do," Tia says.

"He's a great writer," Gauthier says.

"He is?" Tia asks, surprised. "He got a C-plus in English."

"Don't let the C fool you. He's probably the best writer we've ever had at this school. His problem is he can't spell. He gets Cs on his papers because half the words are spelled wrong. I can't figure out how someone who reads so much and writes so well spells so poorly," Gauthier says.

"We can't either," Tia chortles.

"He couldn't spell 'cat' if you spotted him C.A.," Tom says. He looks for a laugh from Tia but she just shakes her head, annoyed. She has heard the joke a dozen times before.

Sister Bartholomew joins them. "We'll miss Patrick."

"Really? That surprises me," Tom says.

"We won't miss everything he does, but we will miss him."

"Like the time he and his four idiot friends got locked in the principal's office. What the hell were they doing in there?" Tom says.

"No, we won't miss that."

"Or the time he knocked over the altar candles and set the altar covers on fire and the Mass was canceled."

"No, we won't miss that either."

"What *will* you miss?" Tia asks.

"I'm not sure, but we will miss him, at least I think we will miss him." She smiles.

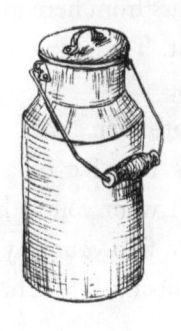

Chapter 30

*August 1929
Doty Farm, East Providence, Vermont*

"Gauthier, it's your last day. You don't need ta milk the cows today," Charles says.

"Yes, I do." John washes and lubricates his hands and grabs several towels, a stool, and a milk bucket.

"One year next week. Didn't think you'd last a month."

"I didn't either."

"You sure you gotta go?"

"I am. My dad's business is booming. He says there's no end in sight. Boom times, Charles, 1929, boom times."

"Not for dairy farmers."

"It's never boom time for dairy farmers."

"That's for sure."

They finish milking the cows and lead them to the grazing field. Charles guides the last cow past the gate and latches it.

John walks toward the barn and steps in a fresh pile of manure. "You'd think after a year, I'd watch where I was walking." He cleans his shoe on the grass.

"Guess that's the last time you're gonna step in shit," Charles says.

"I doubt that."

Charles taps John's right shoulder. "I gotta tell you somethin'. If you ever tell anyone I'll kick your sorry ass from here to kingdom come." He looks to the ground and clears his throat. "I'm gonna miss you. You weren't too bad."

"I weren't terrible," John says.

"No, you weren't terrible." Both men smile.

Charles retrieves a compass the size of a silver dollar from his front pocket and hands it to John. "I want you to have this. We're due north of Connecticut. You can use this to find your way back here."

"Thanks. I will." John turns his back to Charles and rubs the tears in his eyes with his thumbs.

"You ain't gonna cry, are ya?" Charles says.

"No, it's just the hay. The hay's bugging me."

"Sure it is."

"You're my best friend, Charles."

"I'm your only friend, dumbass, me and Audrey. It were me and Audrey and Charlotte but I guess the Charlotte friendship went up in smoke."

"That it did."

Charles grabs John's arm and pulls him to the porch. Audrey is waiting for them, holding a camera. She is straddling two brown suitcases. Little John pokes one of the cats with a stick. The cat hisses, leaps off the porch, and runs toward the barn.

"Gotta get your picture. You and me," Charles says. In the picture, he is resting his right hand on John's left shoulder. His shoulders are even with John's ears.

"Say cheese," Audrey says.

"How 'bout a picture of you and John?" Charles says to Audrey. He and Audrey trade places. "Say cheese."

Charles hitches a horse to the buckboard. "I'm gonna get me a truck, that's for damn sure. Soon as I get the money."

"When will that be? In my lifetime?" Audrey jokes.

"When hell freezes over. Could be next week."

John checks his pocket watch. "We gotta get going, Charles, I'll miss my train."

"Relax, you won't miss the train," Audrey says. She tosses her suitcase into the back of the wagon. "I'm taking you."

"Girls' weekend with her sister. Whatever the hell that means," Charles says.

"I don't want to be late. The next train isn't until ten tonight," John say.

Audrey climbs up to the seat. "What about your books?"

"You keep them."

"Then let's get on the road, farmhand." She nods toward the wagon.

Charles grabs John by both shoulders and hugs him. "You come up and see us, you hear?"

"I will."

Audrey grabs the reins. "Real men don't hug." Her eyes twinkle.

"I guess we ain't real men," Charles says.

"I guess not," John says.

John checks his pocket watch again and sighs. "We're not going to make it. It's already ten o'clock. The train leaves in two hours."

"John, stop fretting. It's nine thirty, not ten, and the train doesn't leave until one fifteen, not noon. It takes two hours and fifteen minutes to get there. We'll be there nearly an hour and a half early. We'll have time for lunch." She turns to Charles and gives him detailed instructions about how to care for Little John.

"I weren't born yesterday. I know what ta do." He grabs Butch by the collar to make sure the dog doesn't jump onto the wagon.

A quarter mile later Audrey hands the reins to John, rests her head on his shoulder, and clutches his arm. "Why are you leaving? I don't want you to go."

"I can't stay."

"Why not?"

"I just can't."

"I'm sorry Charlotte said no. She's a fool."

"I am sorry too."

"Do you love her?"

"I do."

"She said you love me more. Is that true?"

John doesn't respond.

"Is that true?"

"No, I love you both the same."

"I love you too. I wish I didn't, but I do."

"Sometimes love isn't enough."

"No, it isn't." She grabs the reins from him. "Tell me about your family. One year later, and all I really know is you like to read, you're rich, you fell in love once, your sister died, and your mom is still sad. There has to be more."

"Not much more to tell. I was a boring kid and now I'm a boring adult. What about you? I don't know much about you."

"Yes, you do."

"All I know is what Charlotte's told me. How do I know what she said is true?"

"What did she say?"

"She said you were a pain-in-the-ass little kid. You were stubborn and you had tantrums, lots of tantrums."

"I did—at least one a week. One time I was so mad at my parents I went into their room and pulled the dresser drawers to the floor and threw all their clothes out the window."

"Mean little bugger. Why were you so angry?"

"I had punched my sister. Can't remember why. To punish me my father took away my favorite doll and said I couldn't play with it for a week. That was bad enough, but what was worse was he held the doll up to my face and used a fake baby voice to pretend the doll was talking to me. 'Sorry Audrey, I can't play with you, you were bad today. I love Dad best,' the doll said. That drove me over the edge. I ran into my bedroom and cried, and then I ran into my parents' room and threw their clothes out the window.

"When I was a young teenager my mother and I fought constantly. I thought she was so stupid. Everything she did embarrassed me—the way she dressed, the way she talked, everything. One day she asked me to put a bottle of milk into the icebox. I said 'No, you can't make me.' That must have been the last straw because she grabbed the milk bottle, jammed it into my hand, and dragged me and the bottle across the kitchen floor to the icebox. Then she opened the icebox door, with me still holding the bottle, and forced me to place the bottle on the rack. By then the bottle was empty—the milk had spilled all over the floor. I was soaked, and Mom was soaked." She rests her head on his lap. "You can rub my head one last time. That would be nice."

"I'd love to."

….

John pulls the wagon into the Chevrolet dealer's lot. Stopping the wagon wakes Audrey. "What are you doing? This isn't the train station," she says in a sleeper's fog.

"I'm buying Charles a truck."

"Don't do that. He'll be furious."

"He'll get over it."

He selects a blue truck with blue wheels. "Get in."

She refuses.

"Get in."

Audrey climbs into the cab. "You've got too damn much money for your own good," she says.

"I do. It's a curse, and I mean that. I really do."

"Only a rich person would say that."

John hands the salesman a check.

"How much was it?"

"Does it matter?"

"Not really."

Audrey grabs John's hand and leads him to the wagon. He drives to a field behind the train station. "This is the end," he says.

"It is." Audrey grabs his shoulders and pulls him to her, so close their noses are nearly touching. She kisses him, not the kiss of a friend but the kiss of a lover, a long, deep kiss, so long and passionate they both lose their breath. "I love you, John Randolph Gauthier."

"Come with me."

"I can't. I have a son."

"Go get him. We can take the ten o'clock train tonight."

"I can't do that. My life is here. I'm a farmer's wife."

"You said you love me."

"I do, but I love Charles too."

"Who do you love more?"

"Love isn't a competition. I love Charles, and I love you. My life is here." She hugs him. "Some things just aren't meant to be."

"I'll write to you," John says.

"No, don't. It's best that I never hear from you again."

"You can't mean that?"

"I do. This really is the end. This past year was a wonderful dream that happened just once." She grabs his hand and slowly walks him to the train. They bump their hips with each step.

Charlotte is standing on the loading dock waiting for them. John hasn't seen her since the Boston trip. She grabs him and kisses him—a long, passionate kiss. He is surprised.

"I thought you hated me? I thought you said, 'I never want to see you again.'"

"I don't hate you. I love you. You're a lucky man, John Gauthier. You're loved by both Andrews sisters."

"Is that good luck or bad?"

"Both," Audrey says. She kisses him again and bites his lip. "I get the last kiss."

"I'll miss you two. My life will never be the same."

"We'll both miss you," Charlotte says. She grabs his shirt with both her hands. "Promise us you'll fall in love. You deserve that. You deserve to be with someone who loves you."

"What about you? You deserve to be in love too." He pulls the engagement ring from his pocket. "I still want to marry you. If you say yes, I won't leave."

"I can't say yes, John. Just promise me you'll find someone to love, and when you do you'll give her that ring."

"That won't happen. The two women I want are right here."

Charlotte kisses his right cheek; Audrey kisses his left.

"Do not forget us," Charlotte says.

"I won't. Don't forget me."

"How could we?" Audrey says.

The conductor yells, "All aboard."

John opens his suitcase, pulls out the manuscript for his novel about the hapless American man who falls in love with a young girl in India, and hands it to Audrey. "This is for you."

"What about me?" Charlotte says.

"It's for both of you. After you read it, burn it."

"Why would we do that?" Audrey says.

"Because I asked you to."

Audrey reads the first paragraph aloud.

"When John Carpenter went to India, he was seeking a grand

adventure; he'd hike the Himalayas, swim in the Ganges River, and walk through the Taj Mahal. He did all that, but he also fell in love. He hadn't planned on falling in love, but he did."

"Can't wait to read it," Charlotte says.

"Don't forget—burn it when you're done."

Audrey grabs John's left arm. "Have a good life, John Gauthier."

She and Charlotte both cry.

On the train, John pulls the compass from his pocket. The train is heading south. On the back of the compass, Charles had scratched the words, *Thanks—August 1929*. He sobs quietly in his seat.

"Hey, mister, you okay?" the man sitting behind him says.

"I'm fine."

"You don't sound fine."

"I'm fine. I just lost the two great loves of my life."

"So sorry for your loss."

"They're not dead. They're very much alive. They told me to go away and never see them again."

"That's harsh."

"It is, but I deserved it."

"Two might be one too many."

"It was."

Chapter 31

September 1934
Notre Dame Campus, Notre Dame, Indiana

John Gauthier looks up at the statue of Mary on top of the main building on the Notre Dame campus. The sky is dark blue with huge, white clouds. The golden dome is glistening in the sunlight. The trees' leaves are October red. "Mother Mary, if you're listening, please help me," he says out loud. He has lost a notebook he must find before anyone reads what's inside. He is a first-year student in the master's program in theology. Despite the cool morning air, he is sweating through his shirt.

"Damn, damn, damn," he says when he gets to the classroom and the notebook is not where he had left it.

"What's the problem, John?" asks Luke Demers, a fellow first-year student. Demers is ten years younger than Gauthier, as are most of the other students.

"I left my notebook right there." He points to a seat in the second row. "But it's not there now."

"Not a big deal. Father Costello probably has it."

"I hope not."

Father Costello enters the classroom. "Mr. Gauthier, is this your notebook?"

"Yes, it is, Father."

"We need to talk." He guides John down the hall to his office. The two men look so much alike, a stranger could easily mistake them for a father and son. "Have a seat." Costello points to the table and chairs at the far end of the room. John's heart is beating so hard he can feel it pounding against his ribs. "You wrote a novel."

"I did."

"Tell me about it."

"Have you read it?"

"Yes, I have. It's entertaining."

"Then you know what it's about."

"I do—a steamy love affair between a farmhand and the farmer's wife. I was a bit surprised by the details."

John blushes red.

"Very graphic. Probably a bit too explicit to get published," Costello says. He opens the notebook and reads the paragraph that describes the farmer's wife. "That description made my heart skip a beat." He closes the notebook and hands it to John. "I understand you were a farmhand in Vermont?"

"I was."

"Is this book about you?"

"No, it's fiction."

"It's a sin to lie." He chuckles, pulls a cigarette from a pack that is on the desk, and lights it. He takes a deep drag, tilts his head back, and exhales a cloud of smoke above his face. "Why are you here? Why do you want to be a priest?"

"I want to help people. I want to honor God."

"You don't need to be a priest to help people, and you definitely don't need to be a priest to honor God." He clears his throat and spits a wad of mucus into a handkerchief. "You love women, that's pretty obvious from your book."

"I've loved three women. I'm done."

"Are you sure?"

"Yes, absolutely."

"Why a Catholic priest? I read your file. You were an Episcopalian. You could be a priest and have a family."

"I'm a Catholic now. I have been one for the past six years."

"Why did you change?"

"I don't have a good answer. I wish I did, but I don't."

"You need a good answer. The priesthood is a very difficult life. It requires sacrifices most people think are crazy. Why would you give up the love of a woman, your own children, grandchildren? Why would you choose to be poor? That makes no sense."

"It made sense to you."

"You're not me, John. We're talking about you. Most men who study to become a Catholic priest don't make it. They find life without a woman, without a family, too hard. They get lonely and they leave. We lose about a third of our seminarians by the end of the first year. Are you going to be one of them? Wanting to do good isn't reason enough to become a priest."

"I don't have a simple answer. But what I do know is I can't continue to do what I've been doing. I need something more. My life is empty. I've worked for my dad since I left the farm. The stock market crashed two months after I left Vermont. I've spent most of the past five years firing people. Technically, I laid them off, but that assumes we'd rehire them. That's not going to happen, not anytime soon anyway. Week after week, month after month, I'd let someone go. One week I laid off thirty-eight men. I don't know how many I've laid off in all . . . six hundred men, seven hundred, maybe more. I have no idea.

"When I'd call the men into my office, most of them knew what was up. They'd just bow their heads and slink out the door as if they were beaten puppies. One man cried so hard I hugged him. He said his infant son was very sick, and if I laid him off he'd lose his home and his son would die. I didn't let him go, at least not that day, but my dad said, 'Take your heart off your sleeve. We don't have a choice. It's very sad his son is sick, but that's not our problem.' But if it wasn't our problem, whose problem was it?

"One day, about a year later, I saw the man in Central Park. He was homeless and alone. Everything he owned was jammed into two suitcases. He had slept on a cardboard box and used a tattered wool blanket for his bedcover. He had a scruffy beard, he was filthy, and he smelled terrible. He had pissed his pants and they were still damp. I was walking through some bushes when I spotted him. I hadn't seen him until I was nearly on top of him. I almost stepped on him. He was groggy and clearly hungover. I didn't recognize him, but he recognized me. 'John, John Gauthier,' he said, 'how the hell are you?' I was startled and started to hustle away from him. 'Don't run away from me, John, I'm not going to bite you. I'm not a monster,' he said.

"I sat with him on a park bench and we talked for several hours about his life and mine. He lost his apartment, six months after I sacked him. There were no jobs anywhere, he said. He and his wife and his three children moved to New Hampshire to stay with her parents. But that didn't work out for him. He and his father-in-law were constantly at each other's throats. 'I wasn't wanted, John. I was an intruder,' he said. He left three months later. I asked him if his son was still alive. He said as far as he knew he was. I asked him if he blamed me for his troubles. 'Wasn't your fault,' he said. He pulled a cross from his pocket, kissed it, and gave it to me. 'I want you to have this. You're sad, maybe this will help,' he said.

"Can you believe that? He had nothing, but he gave me his cross." John pulls the cross from under his shirt and shows it to Costello.

"He showed me a picture of his family. His father-in-law had taken the picture. They were all sitting at a picnic table. His frail son was sitting on his lap smiling and holding an ice-cream cone. The ice cream was melting and dripping on his hands. 'I'm not bitter. I have three wonderful children, and I had a role in that. I just hope they remember me,' he said. He cried, and I cried too. I bought him new clothes and new shoes and gave him all the money I had—seventeen dollars. The money made him weep. A week later I went back to that spot to give him more money, but he was gone.

"Nothing had changed for me and my family. When I got home that night my father was in the pool swimming. I told him about what had happened. He sensed I was upset. He got out of the pool, dripping wet, and hugged me, and said 'Life isn't fair. It's never been fair. Good people suffer. There is nothing we can do about it.'

"That night I lay in bed and stared at the ceiling. I couldn't sleep. At breakfast the next morning, I told my parents I was done. They weren't surprised. They'd been expecting me to quit since the first day I started. 'This work isn't for you. Never has been,' my mother said. Two months later I told them I had enrolled at Notre Dame to study to be a Catholic priest. 'We figured you were headed down that path. I won't lie, I'm not happy, not happy at all,' my father said. My mother sighed. 'If you want to be a priest, be an Episcopal priest. You can serve God and have a family. I want grandchildren.' I shook my head. 'I don't want a family, Mom.' 'Everybody wants a family,' she said. 'Not everybody . . . not me.' She grabbed me, hugged me hard, and we cried.

"So here I am, a middle-aged man trying to save the world, one soul at a time."

Costello crushes his cigarette butt into an ashtray on the table and clears his throat. "That still isn't enough. Do you believe in God?"

"Yes, I told you that a half hour ago."

"What about Christ—do you believe in Him?"

"I do. What I don't get is why people suffer. The Christian God supposedly is all-powerful, all-knowing, and all-loving. God could have made a perfect world, but he didn't. Why not?"

"God did make a perfect world, John. It was called Eden. But our sins cast us out to a land of mortal toil and trouble, and the wages of sin is death. The Bible says, 'He causes his sun to rise on the evil and the good, and sends rain on the righteous and the unrighteous.' Bad things happen to everyone—good and bad—and that is part of our faulty world."

"I've read that passage a thousand times, but I still don't understand why good people suffer. I've tried to make sense of it, but I just can't." John says.

Costello stands up from his chair, walks to the bookcase at the back of the room, finds *The Imitation of Christ*, and hands it to John. "Read this. It might guide you." He checks his watch and walks toward the door.

"Suffering is central to the human condition. It is now and always has been. We suffer through illness, loss of loved ones, loneliness, pain and injury, poverty, and war. Bad things happen to good people every day, especially now with the world in chaos. I've been a priest for thirty-four years and I will admit it—some days it seems life has no meaning. But most days I see joy and beauty and love. Have you ever watched a hummingbird hover for nectar? It's a magical sight. Only God could have created a hummingbird. Two weeks ago a young cafeteria worker had her baby right there on the floor in the kitchen. No one even knew she was pregnant. I watched the birth. I'd never seen a birth before. It left me speechless." He points out the door to let John know their conversation is coming to a close.

"Are you going to throw me out of school?" John asks.

"No. Whether you stay or leave is up to you. If you stay, do it for the right reasons. Stay because God is calling you, not because you want to end suffering or save souls. If you stay because you want to end suffering, you will be sadly disappointed." He looks at his watch. "We could go on for hours, but I have to go. I have to bless the football team and ask God to help us win. Every Saturday morning God says, 'Go, Fighting Irish, go, fight, win.' He's a big fan. Between you and me, God couldn't care less if we win or lose, and I don't care one way or the other. Of course, if you tell that to anyone, I will deny it three times." He laughs at his joke. "That's a priest joke, John, I've got dozens more."

"I've got hundreds of farm jokes," John says, smiling. "What do farmers talk about when they're milking cows?"

"I have no idea."

"Udder nonsense."

Costello smiles. "Remember, stay only for the right reasons."

"I will, I promise."

Chapter 32

September 1968
Sacred Heart Parish, Providence, Vermont

Agnes LeSalle scurries up the stairs to Monsignor Gauthier's apartment. At the top stair, she stops to catch her breath. She raps lightly on his door. "Monsignor, there's an elderly woman here to see you." He does not hear her. He is wearing earphones and following the rhythm of *Pavane* as if he were the orchestra's conductor, and reading *One Hundred Years of Solitude*. She opens the door, walks to him, pokes his left shoulder, and repeats what she just said. Her touch startles him. The book falls to the floor.

"Agnes, how many times have I told you? Call me John." He pulls the earphones off his head and places them on the floor next to his recliner. "Who is she, and what does she want?" He sighs.

"I don't know. She wouldn't give me her name. She said to tell you: 'Some things just aren't meant to be, farmhand.'"

"Oh my goodness." He is visibly shaken. "Tell her I'll be down in two minutes." He walks to the bathroom, brushes his hair, cleans his face, checks his shoulders for dandruff, and gargles a swig of mouthwash.

"Audrey! I never thought I'd see you again." He hugs her and guides her to his apartment.

"I never thought I'd see you again, either."

They both are surprised by the aged look of the other. "You look wonderful," he says.

"I'm an old woman, John." Her hair is thin and gray, and her face is wrinkled from the sun. She still has the same seductive smile she had forty years ago, and her eyes still gleam. Her body is slightly rounded but mostly strong and forceful.

"And I'm an old man." His arms and legs are as thin as they were when he was young, but his belly is pronounced. His hair and eyebrows are gray and his face has a few wrinkles but not many for a man his age. "What brings you here?"

"Charles is dying."

"I'm so sorry to hear that."

"Don't be, he's at peace with it. He wants to die. He's been sick for a very long time. He smoked too many cigarettes for far too long. He's been suffering for close to ten years."

"What can I do?"

"Come and see him. He wants you to give the sermon at his funeral, but he's too stubborn to ask."

"Why me? I haven't seen him in years."

"Why not you?"

"Your farm closed down?"

"It is. We've been selling pieces of it for the past twenty years. There are fifteen ranch houses on the grazing field, and the sugarbush is a Ford dealership. We sold all the cows eight years ago. None of the kids wanted to farm. Too much work for too little money."

"How many children do you have?"

"Five—three boys and two girls—and six grandchildren so far."

"Sounds like you've had a good life."

"I have." She opens her pocketbook and pulls out the picture of her and him that Charles had taken on his last day at the farm. "Do you remember when Charles took this picture?"

"I do. Have you ever wondered what our lives would have been like if you had come with me?"

"It wouldn't have worked, John. We were too different. We would have divorced. I wouldn't have fit in with your Connecticut friends."

"I didn't either—that's why I left."

"Did you ever fall in love again?"

"I was engaged but not in love. She was smart and clever and beautiful, a wonderful woman, and a great friend. She deserved better than me. She was a friend of the family. Her family was every bit as rich as we were. I'd known her since we were both five years old. When we were seven, we promised we'd marry each other. The promise almost came true. A month before the wedding, I pulled out. 'I can't do this, I wish I could but I can't,' I told her. She wasn't surprised. 'I still love you,' she said. 'You're my best friend, you always will be.' Mom wasn't surprised, either. 'This is the right decision for you,' she said. Dad was furious."

"Was it the right decision to become a priest?"

"Most of the time."

"Would you do it again?"

"Yes."

"Then it was the right decision." She hands him the picture. "I want you to have it."

He takes it from her and smiles. "We were a damn good-looking couple." In the picture, their hands are touching. He had forgotten about that.

"We were. How long have you been here in Providence?"

"Eighteen years."

"Why didn't you come and see us?"

"You told me not to, remember? 'This is the end,' you said."

"That was a lifetime ago. You should have come to the farm."

"You could have come here. You had to know I was here—East Providence isn't that far."

"You're avoiding my question, John. Why didn't you come to the farm?"

"I did. I drove by hundreds of times but never got up the nerve to knock on your door. One night, maybe fifteen years ago, I parked a mile from your house, walked to the grazing field, and watched you and Charles eat dinner."

"You did not!"

"I did. I saw how tender you two were with each other. You made the right decision." He fills a shot glass and drinks the rum with one gulp. "Why didn't you come here? The road runs both ways."

"We talked about it. Charles said, 'If he wants to see us, he'll come here. He knows where we live.' But you never came. He was very disappointed. He still is. I saw you a few times, mostly in the grocery store. You didn't recognize me, and I said nothing."

"Does Charles know you're here?"

"No, he thinks I'm having lunch with our daughter Anne."

"So you want me to come to the farm as if it were my idea."

"Yes, the former farm."

"I'll be there tomorrow."

"Tomorrow's too soon. Charles will know it was my idea. Come Saturday morning. I'll tell him you called me."

"What happened to Charlotte?"

"She married soon after you left. He was a widower, fifteen years older than her. He was her boss at the bank. He had three children, two teenage girls and a seven-year-old boy. I think he married her because he needed someone to care for his kids. Charlotte knew that, but she married him anyway. His oldest daughter, Darlene, was fifteen and a real troublemaker. She hated Charlotte, at least at first. 'You can't tell me what to do. You're not my mother,' she'd say just about every day for several years. Her husband, Matt, wasn't much help. Whenever there was a problem between Charlotte and Darlene, he'd hide in his office, too busy to get involved.

"Two years later he got transferred to Burlington. Charlotte didn't want to go but she didn't have much choice. Darlene thought the move was the end of the world. She was a junior in high school and had a boyfriend in Providence. She threatened to marry him. When the boy heard that, he bolted. I think he joined the army, but I'm not sure. Darlene blamed Charlotte, which was ridiculous, but try reasoning with a teenage girl. Now she and Charlotte are best friends. Life is strange, that's for sure."

"Is Charlotte still in Burlington?" John says.

"No, she lives alone in our parents' house in East Providence. Matt died six years ago. She moved back here a year after his death. She had no real friends in Burlington. Mom died eight years ago from cancer, and Dad died in a car accident in 1948. We're not sure, but we think he fell asleep at the wheel." She brushes her hair from her face. "How about you? How's your family?"

"My dad's still as rich and as ornery as ever. He'll be ninety-five in January. Mom died five years ago."

"Did she ever get over the sadness from your sister's death?"

"Yes and no. Her life got better, much better, but the sorrow never totally lifted from her heart. After I went into the seminary, she rejoined the Episcopal church. She called to tell me. She had considered joining the Catholic church, but she just couldn't do it. She thought I'd be disappointed. 'So you don't think the Pope is infallible?' I told her. She laughed."

Audrey steps close to John, grabs his face in her hands, lifts herself onto her tiptoes, and kisses his forehead. "See you Saturday."

. . .

Charles is sitting on a brown couch reading the newspaper, waiting for John to arrive. He checks his watch. "He shoulda been here fifteen minutes ago," he says to Audrey. She smiles. The room smells like rotten fruit and dirty laundry. There is a green oxygen tank behind the couch. Charles is breathing through a plastic hose attached to the tank. His arms and legs are withered. His chest has a barrel shape, the skin on his face is pale and drooping, and his chin is covered with gray stubble. There are several scabs on each arm, and his scalp is visible through his thin, gray hair. He wears a stained white undershirt, gray sweatpants, and slippers.

"So what's a monsignor? Are you a big shot or sumthin'?" he says when John enters the living room.

"I'm not a big shot, just a parish priest."

"That's not what I hear." He covers his legs with a wool blanket that was on the floor next to his chair. "Where the hell you been? Too damn important to see us?"

"No, not too important, just too stupid. I should have been here eighteen years ago."

"That's for damn sure."

The picture of Charles and John, taken on John's last day at the farm, is mounted in a dark walnut frame on the wall opposite the couch. The picture is so faded it's difficult to tell the men from the background.

"You got old and fat," Charles says.

"We all got old and fat," Audrey says.

Charles pulls the air hose from his nose. "Most nights I sleep right here in this chair . . . have for the past five years. Can't sleep lying down. Too much crap in my lungs." He points to a trash basket next to his chair that is filled with used tissues. "How long you been a priest?"

"Since 1940, and a parish priest in Providence since 1950."

"Why would anybody with half a brain become a Catholic priest? Can't marry nobody."

"I've asked myself that for the past twenty-eight years." He chuckles.

Charles slowly and with great effort rises from his chair and steps across the room. He hacks a wad of phlegm onto his right palm and wipes it on his pants, by his knee. He grabs a photo album from the bureau that holds the television, walks back to his chair, and sits down. He beckons John to sit next to him. Audrey is watching him from the hallway. "Aren't you going to Charlotte's for lunch?" he says to her.

"No."

"Pretty sure you are."

"I get the hint. I've got a lotta yard work to do." She leaves the room.

Charles opens the album. The first picture is of him and John standing next to a dead eight-point buck. The buck is hanging head down from a two-by-four nailed between two trees. The two hind legs are tied to the board, and the head and front legs just miss hitting the ground. "Remember that day?"

"I do."

"Couldn't get you to shoot it. Had to shoot it myself."

"Just couldn't do it."

"When I gutted it I thought you were gonna throw up."

"I did throw up."

Charles flips the page. The second picture is of John milking a cow, and Charles, holding a milk bucket and stool, is watching him. "I don't remember that picture," John says.

"Got it developed after you left."

The next picture is from Christmas 1928. Charles, Audrey, John, and Charlotte are standing on the porch. Audrey's father took the picture. Charlotte is holding a mistletoe above John's head. Audrey's right hand is touching John's side. "She were in love with you, that's for damn sure," Charles says.

"Maybe so, but she wouldn't marry me."

"Not Charlotte, knucklehead, Audrey. She were in love with you."

"You knew?"

"Of course I knew. How dumb do you think I am?"

"Why didn't you say something? Why didn't you beat the shit out of me?"

"Thought about it. But Audrey was happy, first time in years. You were such an idiot, you made both of us laugh. Remember the time the turkeys chased you across the yard pecking at your butt? I wish I'd had a movie camera. God, that were frickin' funny. Audrey and me, we told that story for years. What the hell did you do to piss them off?"

"I don't know. They hated me."

"They did." Charles places the photo album on the bureau, and shoves the oxygen hose back in his nose. He takes three deep breaths. "You left at the right time . . . don't think I coulda taken much more with you and Audrey."

"I'm sorry."

"Don't be. It were a long time ago." He takes several deep breaths. "So you're gonna give my funeral sermon?"

"If you want me to."

"I do."

"Why me?"

"Gauthier, you're the best man I ever knew, even if my wife were in love with you. You care about people . . . always did. I could tell that from day one. You never did nothing with Audrey, did ya?"

"No."

"That's what I figured. Course, you'd say no, no matter what." He grabs his wallet from his back pocket, removes a newspaper clipping, and hands it to John. The headline says, EAST PROVIDENCE'S LAST DAIRY FARM CLOSES. The article includes a picture of Charles and Audrey standing in front of the house and a picture of a cow being loaded onto a truck. "Worst day of my life."

"What do you want me to say at your funeral?"

"Tell a funny story."

"Which one?"

"I don't know . . . how 'bout the time when we got so goddamn lost in the woods we had ta sleep in a snow fort? I froze my ass off. We slept close to keep warm. Don't you put that in the story."

"I won't."

"I thought we were both gonna freeze to death."

"Me too."

Charles takes several deep breaths. His face is flushed. "I don't care what ya say. Just don't make me sound stupid."

"You're not stupid, Charles. You're one of the smartest men I've ever known. You're an electrician, a plumber, a carpenter, a roofer, a painter . . . anything needed doing on the farm you could do. I couldn't change a light bulb, still can't."

"That's for sure." Charles smiles. He sends John to his bedroom to get an envelope that is in his sock drawer. The envelope is faded yellow from age. "Open it," Charles says.

"What's in it?"

"Just open it, you'll see."

Inside there is a check for twenty-seven thousand dollars made out to John. The check is dated May 5, 1954.

"That's for the loan," Charles says.

"What loan?"

"The loan to pay off my brothers and sister for the farm. How could you forget?"

"I can't take it."

"Why not?"

"Banks don't cash checks after a year."

"I'll write you a new one." He takes several deep breaths, removes the oxygen hose and his blanket, walks to the kitchen, retrieves a checkbook from the junk drawer, writes a check for thirty thousand dollars, and hands it to John.

"Why thirty thousand?"

"I forgot about the truck. Sure did come in handy." With great effort, he walks back to his recliner, grabs the hose, and takes several deep breaths. "I expect you here every Saturday mornin' till I die. We got a lot to talk about."

"I'll be here." He folds the check and shoves it into his shirt pocket. "Next Saturday at ten."

Audrey greets him at his car. "Did he give you the check?"

"He did—a new one dated today . . . thirty thousand dollars."

"We don't have thirty thousand dollars."

"I didn't think you did."

She squeezes his hand. "When will we see you again?"

"Next Saturday. Every Saturday until Charles dies."

"Thanks. That will mean a lot."

"Next time you're in Providence, stop by the rectory. I'll take you to lunch. There's a new Indian restaurant in town."

"How about Italian?"

"Italian it is."

Chapter 33

December 1970
Sacred Heart Parish, Providence, Vermont

Monsignor Gauthier sits at his desk writing his Christmas sermon. Massenet's "Meditation" is playing on the stereo. The volume is low, almost too low to hear. A bottle of rum and a half empty shot glass with two ice cubes are on the desk. A dozen crumpled sheets of paper are scattered on the floor next to the wastebasket, and another two dozen sheets are in the basket. He wants the sermon to be just right, but so far, every attempt has failed. Three days ago, Pam O'Brien's son Sean died in Vietnam. He was twenty-one. He was shot in the chest. He died instantly. He had only eight weeks left in his tour of duty. He was engaged to Denise Ryan. Their wedding was set for St. Patrick's Day. Three hundred and fifty people were invited. It was going to be a glorious day.

There is a light tap, tap, tap at his door. "Go away," he says. Another tap, tap, tap. "Go away, I'm busy."

"It's me, Monsignor Gauthier, Patrick Colman."

"Oh dear." Gauthier rips the paper from the typewriter, crumples it into a ball, and tosses it toward the wastebasket. The paper ball bounces off the wall and drops into the basket. "The Celtics win again, the crowd goes wild," he mumbles. He jumps up and greets Patrick with a hug. "Great to see you young man. How long has it been?"

"Four years."

"Four years? Seems like just yesterday you were graduating from eighth grade."

"That was eight years ago."

"Have a seat. We need to catch up."

"I'm a senior at Middlebury. One semester to go."

"You got tall."

"You got short." He smiles.

"What's next?" Gauthier asks.

"I don't know. One of my professors wants me to go to Northwestern for grad school. She says I should get an MFA in writing."

"Are you going to go?"

"Probably not—I can't afford it. I'm in serious debt. I've been offered a job at the *Providence Herald*. I've worked there the past two summers. Got my first byline in August."

"I saw your story—something about a knitting circle who's been knitting together for thirty years."

"A real Pulitzer Prize winner." He unfolds a piece of paper and hands it to Gauthier.

"What's this?"

"Your list."

"What list?"

"The list you gave me at the eighth-grade graduation with the titles of a hundred books I should read. It took me eight years, but I've read them all."

"I totally forgot about that. Did you like them?"

"Most of them . . . some not so much."

"What didn't you like?"

Colman thinks for a minute. "I didn't like *Under the Volcano*. The protagonist— I can't remember his name . . ."

"Geoffrey Firmin."

"Geoffrey Firmin. He was too much of a drunk. I couldn't stand him."

"You don't have to like the main character for the book to be good."

"True, but I hated him."

"Anything else on your hate list?"

"I loved the story *Moby-Dick*, but I could have done without all the whale facts—probably half the book."

"True, but essential."

"Not for me. I skimmed most of those sections, barely paid attention."

"Tell me about the past four years."

"College has been okay. The teachers have been great and most of the courses are pretty interesting. Not a hell of a lot to do in Middlebury. I thought Providence was small—looks like a metropolis compared to Middlebury."

"More time to study."

"More time to drink."

"How's your dad? I see your mom every week, but your dad stopped coming to church just after you graduated from high school. She doesn't say much about him."

"He's okay . . . as stubborn as ever. Everything bugs him. Always has. I wrote a short story that was published in the college literary magazine about a gruff old man who chases the neighborhood boys from his lawn by spraying them with a garden hose. Dad was furious. 'That's me,' he said. 'You made me sound like an angry fool.' I told him the story was fiction . . . it wasn't about him, plus it was a comedy. The old man in the story was crusty but lovable. He wasn't appeased. He was really mad."

"Your father's a good man."

"He is. Grumpy but good. He sends me money every week—sometimes a five-dollar bill, sometimes ten. Some weeks he sends me twenty dollars. 'Don't tell your mother,' he writes every time—no other message. Most people who don't know him well think he's a mean son of a bitch because he complains so often and swears with every other word, but he's a softy."

"You are right. He is a softy. The day after my mother died, he followed me into the Grand Union, tapped my shoulder, and said, 'Monsignor Gauthier, sorry for your loss. You're sad today, but tomorrow you'll remember the good times. She'll be with you forever.' Then he turned and walked away. He said in three sentences what I've spent a lifetime trying to say."

"He does get right to the point."

"Have you written anything else?"

"Not really. We had to write a short novel for my writing class. My story was awful. Too corny and too preachy. My teacher said my writing was good, but I tried too hard to send a message. She was right."

"Writing a novel is like playing tennis—you don't get it on your first try. It takes practice. The first time I hit a tennis ball, I knocked it over the fence. Writing well is the same. It doesn't just happen. I suspect even Hemingway's first novel was terrible."

"His first novel was *The Sun Also Rises*—maybe his best."

"Okay, so Hemingway is a bad example. But writing is like anything else—you have to learn how to do it."

"Do you still write?"

"The only thing I write now is sermons. I'm trying to write one now for Christmas, but I'm stuck."

"Christmas sermon . . . how hard could it be—the season of hope and joy?"

"Tell that to Pam O'Brien. Her son was killed this week in Vietnam, apparently by friendly fire. Nothing friendly about a bullet to the chest."

"You could talk about him."

"I don't know what to say. I didn't know him very well. He went to Providence Junior High, not Sacred Heart."

"I didn't know him well either. I played rec basketball with him for five years. He was really good, and I was really bad. When I was open, he'd pass the ball to me even though he knew I'd probably miss the shot. He'd pass the ball to me, and I'd miss the shot, and then he'd pass me the ball again, and I'd miss the shot again. No matter how many times I missed, he'd still pass the ball to me when I was open, every single time. One time he said, 'Don't worry Colman, you'll get one eventually.' And then he slapped my back, not a hard slap but an encouraging slap. He wasn't making fun, he was serious."

"Can I use that story?"

"Yes, but don't use my name."

"I don't even know your name, Patrick something-or-other." He laughs.

"Don't even use Patrick."

"Okay, John Doe it is."

"I want to be a writer. I want to write a novel," Patrick says.

"Then do it."

"How?"

"There's no magic bullet. Just write," Gauthier says.

"I will. I think I'll start tomorrow. What if I can't get it published?"

"So what. Don't write because you want to get published. Write because you have a story to tell."

"Maybe I'll write about you," Patrick says.

"If you do that, you'll definitely not get published. I'm a pretty boring man. Nobody would read about my life."

"I would," Patrick says.

Chapter 34

August 1972
Sacred Heart Parish, Providence, Vermont

Monsignor Gauthier, Father Symanski, Father Cantone, and Bishop James are sitting in Gauthier's dining room. They have just finished eating. There is an empty bottle of rum in the middle of the table. Gauthier and James are smoking pipes. James is blowing smoke rings above his head. Symanski is nearly asleep.

"This is my last supper. Which one of you is Judas?" Gauthier asks. The three others chuckle. Agnes LeSalle removes the dirty dishes and brings them a cake. The wording on the top says "Congratulations on Your Retirement."

"I always figured I'd retire before you," Bishop James says. He shakes his head several times to focus.

"You're never going to retire. You'll die in office, just like the Pope," Gauthier says and smiles.

"You're probably right."

"What's next?" Symanski asks.

"I'm not sure. My father needs me. He'll be ninety-nine in January. I doubt he'll make it to one hundred."

Bishop James refills his shot glass and holds it up for a toast. "It's been a good run, John Gauthier—not a perfect one, but a good one."

"It has." The men click their shot glasses together.

Agnes leaves the room. "I'll be back in a few minutes." She walks out the door sobbing.

"You're getting out just at the right time. Everything's changing, but not for the better," James says.

"The Church is stronger now than ever," Father Symanski says.

"You're living in a dream world. Attendance is dropping every day. In thirty years, the pews will be empty," Bishop James says.

"Not if I have anything to say about it."

"Good luck to you," Gauthier says.

"The Church has been here for two thousand years and it will be here for two thousand more."

"Whatever you say," Bishop James says.

Gauthier cuts the cake into five huge pieces, places one piece each on five small dishes, and hands the plates to the other men. "Come join us," he calls out to Agnes.

She pokes her head into the room. "Thank you, but I'm too busy."

"Too much cake," Bishop James says. He taps his belly to prove his piece is too big.

"Not when you taste it," Gauthier says.

Agnes is listening from the living room. She blushes.

Bishop James eats his piece in six, mouth-stuffing bites. "Dee-licious." He taps his fork against his plate. "Agnes, I'm going to kidnap you and take you to Burlington," he says loudly. She blushes again. He pulls away from the table and brushes his chin with his napkin, a signal that it's time for Symanski and Cantone to leave. Both men get the hint and stand. "You get to do this again tomorrow with the whole parish."

"I do. It's going to be tough, very tough. They're my family. I don't want to leave them, but I can't stay forever."

"Leaving your family is never easy," Bishop James says.

Cantone hugs Gauthier. "It's been an honor working with you." He hands him a copy of *The Exorcist*. "You'll get a kick out of it. I've scheduled three exorcisms for next week."

Gauthier laughs.

Symanski gives him a signed copy of *The Religious Experience of Mankind*.

"Thank you. I'm impressed. I've been meaning to read it," Gauthier says.

"Sure you have," Bishop James says. He chuckles.

The two younger priests leave the apartment. Bishop James grabs a full bottle of rum and refills his shot glass and Gauthier glass. "One more toast," he says. "To us, two old fogies."

"Two old fogies," Gauthier says.

"Have you written your last sermon?"

"I have. Five months ago, I sat down and reread the scripture passages and general topics I would teach for the rest of my Sundays. I've had many thoughts about what I'll say at my last sermon, but in the end, I just want to thank the congregation for the privilege of allowing me to lead them."

"Good choice. I'll be here."

"Thank you."

James unbuttons his pants and exhales deeply. "I ate too much and drank too much. You're a bad influence on me, Monsignor John Gauthier. Always have been."

"I am."

"Any reason you've always had your parishioners call you Father and not Monsignor?"

"Not really. Father just seemed right, Monsignor, not so much."

"You've been a priest for thirty-plus years. Do you still believe in God?"

"I do . . . most of the time anyway. I don't see much of an alternative explanation."

"Atheists say the burden of proof lies with the believers, not with them."

"I agree. I'd argue Beethoven's Ninth Symphony is proof God exists. No human could have written that without help."

Bishop James nods in agreement. He picks up the rum bottle and holds it up to the light. "Should we empty it? Waiter, we need another drink," he jokes. "What about free will, does it exist?" His words slur, and his eyes are blurred.

"Where did that come from?" Gauthier says. His words are also slurred.

"From left field, where else?" James says.

"I don't know, ask the Calvinists." Gauthier pounds the table when he says Calvinist.

"Aren't they all dead?" Bishop James says.

Both men laugh. Gauthier pours each of them another shot.

"An omniscient God and free will seem contradictory. But at the same time life without free will makes no sense. I'd like to think I chose my life, but I'm not sure I did. When I was young, I fell in love with three women. I asked one to marry me and the other two to run away with me. I failed all three times. If any of them had said yes, my life would have been much different. I'd probably be spending my weekends playing with my grandchildren. 'Oh, Grandpa, you're so funny.' Never got that," Gauthier says.

"Me neither. Did the three women love you?"

"I thought so at the time. Forty years later, I'm not so sure. How about you—did you ever fall in love?"

"I never did. I wanted to, desperately wanted to, but I never did. Not sure why not. I think I was too much of an old fart, even when I was a little kid. It used to annoy me in school when the other students didn't behave. I wanted to yell out, 'Stop it, be quiet, behave.' Chaos bothered me. I decided to become a priest when I was just sixteen years old. Once I make up my mind, I never change it. We were preparing for confirmation and the bishop came to our school and talked to us about the missionaries in Quebec in the seventeenth century. His stories were mesmerizing. Those poor buggers kept getting their thumbs and ears cut off. Didn't matter to them—they fought on, fingerless, earless superheroes, like Superman or Batman, bringing Christ to the heathens. I wanted to be like them. I wanted to be a superhero for Christ. I knew Canada wasn't an option anymore, so I figured I'd go to Africa or to a Pacific Island where the half-clothed men had bones in their noses and ran around with spears. I'd convert them to civilized, Christian men; save their souls so they could go to heaven. I spent three years in Lagos, Nigeria. I thought I'd find straw huts and noble savages, but what I found was a modern city with modern city problems. What a fool I was."

"Same for me in India. I wasn't a priest yet, but I was a fool."

James holds up his empty shot glass. "To two fools."

Gauthier offers to refill the two shot glasses but Bishop James declines with a hand wave. "Don't take this wrong, John, but I always thought you'd quit. Why did you stay?"

"This church is my home. The people here are my family. I've spent every Christmas since the first year here with the O'Briens. I baptized their children, Amy and John and Chris. One Christmas I was very sick and I couldn't go to their house, so they came to me. Amy had a guitar and stood outside my window with the whole family, and about two dozen others from the church, and they sang Christmas hymns to me. It was ten below zero, but they stood there in the cold for eight songs. When I close my eyes, I can still see them and hear them.

"I've shared with my parishioners their highest joys and their deepest sadness. I've married probably three hundred couples and baptized two times that many babies. I've presided over hundreds of funerals. You never get over the death of a child. I've helped battered women and lonely men. I've heard stories in confession that made me blush and stories that made me cry and stories that filled me with joy. Would I do this again? Absolutely."

"You get to thank them tomorrow."

"I do. It will be the hardest speech I've ever given. I hope I can hold it together."

"You can."

"I'm not sure. I'm leaving my family. It's never easy to leave your family, especially when you know you're never coming back."

"You can come back and visit, fill in on an occasional Sunday."

"It wouldn't be the same."

. . .

Gauthier packs his car with everything he owns except his novels and records.

"What about your books?" Agnes LeSalle asks.

"I'll leave them for the next guy. Most of the records are too scratched to listen to. Time for me to move to tape cassettes anyway."

"Do you think the next monsignor will be Father Symanski?"

"No."

"Good."

Gauthier's lips show a sly smile.

Agnes grabs him and hugs him hard and long. "You saved me."

"You're wrong, you saved me. Being a priest is a very lonely life. You're my best friend."

She smiles. "I've cherished our time together. You're my best friend too."

He hugs her just as hard and long as she had hugged him. He walks through the church one last time. Agnes follows him. On the ceiling above the altar, there is a painting of Mary ascending to heaven. Gauthier paid for the painting during his second year at the church. Several parishioners complained Mary's skin was too dark.

"That painting didn't win you any friends," Agnes says.

"No, it did not."

They walk to the car. "Goodbye, my good friend," Gauthier says.

"Be well."

"I will."

They hug and smile. She stands in the driveway and watches him leave. Father Symanski and Father Cantone join her and wave to the disappearing car. Symanski hugs Agnes. "We'll all miss him," he says.

"We will," Cantone says. He is crying.

. . .

John drives to the Doty farm. Audrey is sitting on the edge of the porch, shucking corn and tossing the husks into a pile next to the stairs. "My goodness, look what the cat dragged in," she says. She steps off the porch, trots to him, and hugs him. She points to his car. "Looks like you're going somewhere."

"I am. I've retired."

"I didn't think priests retired."

"We do."

"Where are you going?"

"Not sure. Depends. I'll probably go back to Connecticut. My dad's house is still there."

"Depends on what?"

"I thought I might stay here with you."

"Live with me?"

"Yes." He pulls a picture of the two from his shirt pocket. "Look at this young couple. They obviously were in love."

"They were."

"Are they still?"

"I don't know . . . it's been a long time, John, a lifetime ago. We're different people now than we were then—way different."

"We are, but I would like to find out if the love is still there."

"I don't know if that's such a good idea. What would Charles think? He was the love of my life, not you."

"He told me to do it."

"He did not."

"He did, really."

She smiles, grabs his arm, and leads him to the living room. "Wait right here. I have something for you." She returns five minutes later with the manuscript of his novel that he had given her and Charlotte at the train station the day he left Providence. The pages have yellowed, and the typed words are barely visible.

"It is a wonderful novel. Charlotte and I read it together. We took turns on who would read. It made me cry. It made both of us cry."

"My goodness, I'd forgotten all about it." He takes the manuscript from her and reads the first paragraph aloud.

"You read those lines to me at the train station," Audrey says.

"I did."

She steps to the stereo at the back wall next to the couch and pulls a record from a stack of albums on a shelf. "I bought this two weeks after you left the farm." She holds up a Louis Armstrong record. "Actually this is the seventh copy. The other six wore out." She places the album on the stereo and moves the needle to "When You're Smiling."

"Will you dance with me?"

"I will."

She pinches his arm and leads him to the center of the room. "I don't know if this is the right thing to do or not. One month trial, that's it. If it doesn't work, you're out."

"Who decides?"

"I do."

"I have no say?"

"None."

He nods and grabs her arms. They dance slowly across the living room floor.

I never stopped loving her, he thinks, but he says nothing.

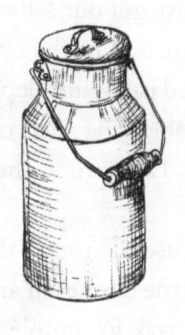

Epilogue

August 1982
Doty Farm, East Providence, Vermont

Audrey died four days ago. The funeral was yesterday. She was picking blueberries when she had a heart attack. She hadn't been sick one day since I moved in. I found her under the bushes. She looked like she was asleep. Our border collie was sleeping with her, his head resting on her legs. Even at seventy-eight, she was the most beautiful woman I'd ever seen.

We had ten years together, ten more than I deserved. Her three great-grandchildren call me Papa. I like that. They tire me out terribly. Elise never shuts up. She talks from the minute she enters the house until she leaves. "What do you think, Papa, what do you think?" she says a hundred times an hour. I love her, but she gives me a headache.

When I moved in with Audrey, her children were pretty upset with us, but they got used to me. Her oldest daughter, Betty, kept asking us if Audrey and I had had an affair when we were young. No matter how many times I said no, she didn't believe me. The phantom affair was more exciting than the truth. She wanted Audrey and me to get married, but we never did.

The first few months were very awkward. We both had settled ways that irritated each other. I liked spending my evenings reading and listening to music. After a few weeks she said, "If you're not going to talk to me, why did you move in here?" Eventually, we got our schedules more in sync. I'd read in the mornings, before she got up, and in the evenings after she had gone to bed. Fortunately, she went to bed early and slept fairly late. Most nights we'd watch television and play Scrabble. She was very good. I thought she'd be a humble winner, but she wasn't. Every time she'd win, she'd say, "Take that, college man."

My inability to do anything useful around the house drove her nuts. Not cleaning or cooking or washing the clothes or any other household chores—I did those. What I couldn't do was fix simple things that needed fixing or make basic repairs to the house. I can't saw a board straight and whenever I measure, I screw up and cut the board the wrong length. I can't fix the ballcock on the toilet or repair a malfunctioning wall switch or fix a leaking faucet—simple tasks for most husbands. I've never changed a tire, and I don't even know where to put the window washer fluid in the car. I've never fixed a chimney, and I can't level a porch or fix a roof. "You're totally incompetent," she'd tell me every time we had to hire a repairman, and then she'd laugh and remind me that Charles was an expert handyman.

She drove me nuts too. Her showers were so long, she'd use up all the hot water. And she fretted too much. Thanksgiving was the worst week of the year. She'd insist the dinner be at our house even though both of her daughters said it was time for her to pass the burden to them. But she wouldn't give it up. One year I offered to do all the deep cleaning for the Thanksgiving dinner. I washed the windows and floors, cleaned the walls, removed the dust above the door sills, scrubbed the bathrooms clean, and organized all the plates and silverware. She redid everything I had done as if I had done nothing. I was so angry my arms shook. I'll miss every annoying minute with her. I already do.

Charlotte ate with us two to three days a week or more until last May when she moved to a nursing home in Providence. Her eyesight and hearing have failed her. When she was well, she and Audrey spent nearly as much time together as Audrey and I did, maybe more.

"You can change your husband, but your sister is always your sister. We've got history. We've got history even before Charles," she said to me once when I complained.

One day Charlotte whispered in my ear, "Thank you for loving Audrey." Then she squeezed my hand and said, "I should have married you." I said nothing. I didn't know what to say.

Little John lost the name Little the day after I left. Good thing, because he grew up to be a mountain of a man, a six-foot-six behemoth. He's as gentle as he is big. The first time he saw me he said, "So you're the man I'm named after, well, son of a bitch." Then he picked me up over his head like I was a small child. He runs a house construction company in Manchester, New Hampshire. He's every bit as skilled at everything as his dad was.

Father Cantone gave the eulogy at Audrey's funeral. It was a beautiful sermon. He read, "Death Be Not Proud" by John Donne. His death sermons are always beautiful. He knows just what to say. Mine were never as good as his. He's Monsignor Cantone now. He heads the Church of the Immaculate Heart in Providence. He's a good man and a good priest.

Father Symanski was transferred two years after I left, to a tiny town in upper Maine, a town so remote there are more moose than people. He and the new rector at Sacred Heart never got along, not from day one.

As I predicted, my good friend Bishop James died in office, two years ago on Holy Thursday. He had lung cancer. He never did step down, not even when he knew he should. I visited him a month before he died. He was in a good mood. He said he was going to buy two mopeds, one for me and one for him, so we could ride to New York City. "You must come with me. Audrey can live without you for a few weeks." He wanted to see the inside of the Episcopal cathedral, St. John the Divine. He had been to New York several times but had never gone into that church. "Something I deeply regret," he said. I said I would go with him.

Father LeFebvre died seven years ago while serving Mass. It was the first Sunday of Lent. Audrey and I were there. There were only twenty-two other people in the church. Bishop James had considered closing the church but had agreed with my plea to keep it open until after Father LeFebvre retired. "He deserves that honor," I said.

Father LeFebvre died while walking toward the altar rail to give us communion. He stopped halfway between the altar and the altar rail and said, "I'm not well." He looked frightened. He returned to the altar, placed the chalice on the top of it, and crumpled to the ground like a slowly deflating balloon. I rushed to him. "This is the end for me. God wants me home," he said. He died before the ambulance got to the church. No one left even after the ambulance had gone. Audrey and I started to clean the altar.

Mike Fisk, the only parishioner under fifty, said, "Why don't you finish the Mass, John?" I had filled in several times when Dan was ill or out of town. The first time he asked me to fill in for him, I said, "What will the congregation think? I'm living with Audrey." He told me not to worry. He was right. No one cared. I finished the Mass and served at his funeral two days later. Over three hundred people showed up for the funeral. Four generations of parishioners. I hooked up a loudspeaker so those outside the church could follow the Mass.

A year after I moved in with Audrey, I got a mysterious package from Patrick Colman. I hadn't thought about him since the day he returned my list of one hundred novels he should read. The letter attached said: "To my teacher, mentor, and friend." The package was a reader's copy of his first novel, *The Five Musketeers*. The book is dedicated to me. The opening scene is of five boys on the top of a hill in winter with their sleds. They speak in what they think is pig Latin, and they dare each other to slide as close as possible to the tree at the bottom of the hill without hitting it. The protagonist, John Gauthier, hits the tree and is knocked out. When I read my name, I cried.

"What are you crying about?" Audrey said. I showed her my name in the book.

Colman has written five books since then, each one a bestseller. One morning he was on *The Today Show*. Jane Pauley asked him if a teacher had inspired him. He said he was inspired by his parish priest. "You're not going to cry again, are you?" Audrey said and swatted the back of my head as if I were a ten-year-old.

Four years ago, Patrick and I went canoeing on Kent's Pond. He was in Vermont for his father's funeral. His father died too young—of stomach cancer—at only fifty-nine years old. I thought Patrick would ask me for guidance, ask me why God took his father so young, but he didn't. I had prepared a ten-minute conversation that would be both thoughtful and compassionate. I was disappointed when he didn't ask me for my help. When we got back to the shore, I was too stiff and too old to get out of the boat by myself. He steadied the boat and pulled me free.

He told me about the other four Musketeers. Paul Fermonte is a staff sergeant in the army. He has been married and divorced three times. Their friendship ended after eighth grade. They hung together that summer, all five of them, but drifted apart soon after summer ended. "Paul was right. He said our friendship would end after eighth grade, and it did," Patrick said.

The O'Riley twins run a used car dealership in South Pomfret. I'm familiar with their radio ad: "We don't sell cars, we sell fun." Apparently, it's the biggest used car dealership in the state.

Maurice Nolan dropped out of sight for ten years and resurfaced two years ago in West Providence. He has a young wife and three stepchildren. They love him as if he was their father.

Agnes LeSalle died peacefully in her sleep two years ago. She and I had dinner together every Wednesday starting six weeks after I left the church. We didn't miss a Wednesday in eight years. We always went to Pratico's Italian restaurant, never any other restaurant. She'd study the menu from top to bottom as if it changed from one week to the next, which it never did.

"I wonder what I'll get," she'd say, and then she'd order spaghetti and meatballs, week after week—spaghetti and meatballs, a house salad with ranch dressing, and a glass of white wine. For dessert, she always had vanilla ice cream and a brownie. "I really shouldn't do this, I don't need the calories," she'd say every week, and then she'd order the ice cream and brownie anyway. When I turned seventy-five, she gave me an expensive wristwatch. "For all the good times we've spent together," she said.

Audrey would tease me and say, "I think she's your second wife."

"We're not married," I'd say.

"Maybe not in God's eyes, but I'm your wife, don't forget that."

I'm not sure what I am going to do next. I still have plenty of family money. I'd give it all away, but my father's will says I can't do that until after I'm dead. My will divides half the money among Audrey's children and grandchildren, and the rest goes to the shelter for the homeless in Providence. I haven't told them yet, either the shelter or Audrey's family. Let them be surprised.

I suppose I could go anywhere and do anything an eighty-year-old man can do. Maybe I'll take a cruise around the world. I wouldn't mind going back to India for a visit, but I think I'm too old and too frail for that. I'd rather stay right here anyway, on this former farm. It is my home now; it has been for ten years. On the wall above the fireplace, I've mounted the pocket watch and the compass Charles gave me. It took me forty-one years to find my way back here to this farm, directly north of Connecticut and east of Providence. But I made it back—the best decision in my life.

Even if I wanted to leave, I couldn't. Elise has a lot more stories to tell me, and I want to hear them, all of them. If I'm lucky, I'll watch her graduate from high school. I'll be ninety-two.

The End

Author's Note

Most Vermont farms got electricity in 1936 or later. The Doty Farm in this book was wired for electricity in 1929. This is not a great stretch, as some farms got electricity earlier than 1936. The joke told by Bishop James about the bad eggs was a joke told by Roman Catholic bishop Fulton Sheen in the 1950s. Much of the sermon in the tent revival chapter was borrowed from a sermon given by the famous evangelist Billy Sunday.

Acknowledgments

I need to thank my early readers—my wife Cindy, and my late sister Anne Balk. Both proofread and edited the text. Other readers I need to thank are my daughter Colleen LeFebvre, my granddaughter Alice Hammond, my friend Warren Hebert, and my niece Kathrine Pearce. And thanks to my daughter Leslie Hammond, who keeps me online, a task well beyond my abilities. Another thanks to Randy Pratt.

Tremendous thanks also to my two technical advisors, Kate Couture and the Rev. Earl Kooperkamp. Kate and her family ran the Andrews dairy farm in Richmond, Vermont, for many years. She proofread the farm sections and made many corrections. Any technical errors remaining are mine, not hers. Earl reviewed the religious sections in the book. Like Monsignor Gauthier in this novel, Earl had a calling to do what he does, and he does it well.

Finally, I want to thank Rootstock Publishing for working with me for my second novel.

About the Author

J. Peter Cobb was the executive director for thirty-three years of VNAs of Vermont, the professional association for Vermont's visiting nurse associations. He has been a reporter, grant writer, soccer coach, and mental health worker. He lives in Barre Town, Vermont, with his wife, Cindy. *Some Things Aren't Meant to Be* is his second novel. His first novel, *To Alice*, about home care/hospice workers, debuted in 2022.

Also by J. Peter Cobb:

To Alice: A Novel ($15.99, TouchPoint Press, 2022)

Alice Hammond is a troubled soul. She dropped out of medical school when one of her professors made it too stressful for her to stay. Now she works as a home health and hospice aide in Providence, Vermont. She is a wonderful aide, the quality of her work is high, and her patients love her. But Alice tends to become too involved with them. She has made their lives her life—a problem both for them and herself.

Praise for *To Alice*:

"*To Alice* is a compelling, compassionate, humorous and oh-so-human story of the amazing caregivers that work in our towns every day. The author's detailed knowledge and respect of those in need of care and those doing the care through home health services creates a cast of characters true to life. Most of us will end up in these professional hands and we can be grateful for this eloquent and complex story of the burdens and blessings of caring so well."

—Virginia Lynn Fry, author of *Part of Me Died Too—Stories of Creative Survival among Bereaved Children and Teenagers*

"The novel switches effectively from Alice's perspective—in her shabby apartment and at work—with portraits of the homebound clients she visits. We read about her life, her struggles to make a living, and to balance her private and professional worlds. There is beauty amid the grittiness in Cobb's novel. The subtitle of *To Alice* asks, 'Is caring too much a bad thing?' There is no clear-cut answer, a mark of a realistic novel. Cobb pays tribute to those who provide home health care in sometimes difficult circumstances, and, through a main character who rings true in every chapter, explores the complicated but rewarding relationships of caretakers in our communities."

—*The Montpelier Bridge*

"At what point does a caregiver cross the boundary between providing professional, compassionate care to getting too involved with her patients' lives? That question is at the heart of the new novel. This book sends a powerful message about giving care."

—*The Rutland Herald*

More Fiction from Rootstock Publishing:

A Reason to Run: A Novel by Mike Magluilo

All Men Glad and Wise: A Mystery by Laura C. Stevenson

An Intent to Commit: A Novel by Bernie Lambek

Augusta: A Novel by Celia Ryker

Blue Desert: A Novel by Celia Jeffries

Granite Kingdom: A Novel by Eric Pope

Hawai'i Calls: A Novel by Marjorie Nelson Matthews

Horodno Burning: A Novel by Michael Freed-Thall

Junkyard at No Town: A Novel by J.C. Myers

The Funny Moon: A Novel by Chris Lincoln

The Hospice Singer: A Novel by Larry Duberstein

The Red Wheelbarrow: A Novel by Marjorie Nelson Matthews

The Inland Sea: A Mystery by Sam Clark

Uncivil Liberties: A Novel by Bernie Lambek

Venice Beach: A Novel by William Mark Habeeb

Whole Worlds Could Pass Away: Collected Stories by Rickey Gard Diamond

To learn about our titles in nonfiction, poetry, and children's literature, visit our website www.rootstockpublishing.com.